D0474155

Chapter 1

What the hell am I doing here?

Simon Byrne knew exactly. Postponing what he ought to be doing. And ogling the woman he'd avoided for over two years. She didn't notice him at the Technical Support Lab door because whatever gizmo she was fiddling with had her mesmerized.

Janna Harris wore a nondescript pantsuit, the type she'd adopted after her marriage. No more short skirts or cropped tops that bared skin. Professional, she'd insisted.

Boring, he'd said. He still thought so, but he hadn't called it nun wear out loud. He'd kept his trap shut to avoid friction with her new husband. No chance of that now since the man was dead.

Oblivious to Simon's presence amid the din of computers and techs speaking geek to one another, she carried the ciga-rette-pack-sized gizmo past metal cabinets, cubicles and other technicians to an empty worktable.

At least this outfit had a short jacket that didn't hide all the good stuff. A man could watch the sway of her hips, the stride of her model-length legs as sleek as a thoroughbred's. And the suit was nearly the same gray as her eyes. Eyes he could never forget, witchy eyes that invited a man to drown in them. Happily.

After gathering some small metal tools, she settled on a stool at a worktable. She plied a screwdriver to the gizmo and, after a moment, pressed a button. A light flashed. She smiled.

The sexy curve of her lips warmed Simon in inconvenient places. Damn! Time hadn't dulled her effect on him—one major reason he'd stayed away. He gritted his teeth.

She was the wrong woman for him. Why didn't his body listen to him?

Keeping her eyes on her work, she spared not even a sideways glance toward the doorway.

He might as well have been invisible.

Damn straight. As far as Janna was concerned, he preferred invisibility. For over a year, he'd checked on her, watched over her. Guilt had kept him at a distance.

The Anti-Terrorism Security Agency had other ideas. *You're on, turkey.* He strode over to her table.

"How you doin', Q?" He stretched his lips into a wide grin. "I got a good one for you. How many software engineers does it take to change a lightbulb?"

A couple of other techs glanced up briefly before returning to computer screens and mysterious devices.

Janna slipped on dark-rimmed glasses before she faced him. She pushed them firmly on the bridge of her nose and peered down at him from her perch on the high stool.

When did she start wearing those things? He'd never seen her in glasses before.

Hard as granite behind the unexpected lenses, her narrowed eyes pinned him like a bug on flypaper. "If you think you can prance in here after all this time and pick up where you left off with the geek jokes, Simon, you're sadly mistaken."

He deserved that. And worse for what he was going to do over the next few days.

"I don't prance" was all he could muster.

Color bloomed high on her cheeks. *"Simon."*

He swallowed his emotion and another quip. He shoved fingers through his hair in a futile effort at control. "Look, I screwed up. After…after…"

"After Gabe's death," she prompted.

"After that, kidding around with you didn't seem right. He was under my command. I could've prevented his death."

Janna's gray eyes widened as she seemed to grasp that truth for the first time. She shook her head, her layered hair swaying like silk. "Simon, you're not responsible for Gabe's death. He was called Hero Harris for a reason. Even if you'd been there, you couldn't have stopped his reckless heroics."

He didn't buy it, but her forgiveness winked on a tiny light in the dark space inside him. "Thanks, but protecting my people was part of being the control officer."

"So that's the reason you deserted me."

He winced at hearing the truth aloud. He had deserted her, deserted their friendship. "Partly. As time passed, going back was weird…awkward." But no more awkward than this conversation. "Hell, I'm sorry."

He crossed mental fingers that she would let his apology go at that. In fact, he'd eased away from her even before Gabriel Harris. In her eyes, in her body language, he'd seen that she wanted more than friendship. Her come-on at Vanessa Wade's reception had rung wedding bells in her head and warning bells in his.

Impossible, but he hadn't wanted to hurt her.

If she pushed, what excuse could he give? That she deserved the home-and-family kind of guy, not a one-night-stand kind of guy like him? That was what he told himself when Gabe asked him to introduce them in the cafeteria. Regret had cinched his gut, even though envy made no sense and didn't change who he was. Or wasn't.

Or the more concrete excuse that, after Gabe had begun seeing her, he'd warned Simon off? Once Mr. Perfect had given her the rush, she had no time for Simon anyway.

"I understand. Really. Let's forget it." She offered no smile of encouragement, and wariness lurked in her eyes.

He'd take what he could get. "Sweet." He held out a hand. "A new beginning?"

After a moment's hesitation, she shook his hand. He wanted to hold on and savor her impossibly soft skin, but she pulled back and gripped her gizmo like an anchor.

"What've you got there?" He nodded toward the toy.

"An SC cam." She held the thing up proudly. "A self-contained video system. Watch." She slid the slim canister into a slot in a thick hardcover book. The camera's spy eye blended in with the lettering on the book's spine. "This baby's a one-fourth-inch CCD imager with 420 lines of resolution and a high-power 2.45-gigahertz transmitter. The self-charging battery has a run time of eight hours."

Janna began working for ATSA a few years ago here at its Washington, D.C., headquarters where he was a field officer. She'd been so green then she'd used the agency's letters instead of the usual acronym, *At-suh.* But green or not, he'd seen her create, modify and repair any low or high-tech equipment an operative could dream up.

"Way cool," he said. "I know a little about bugs, but the only words you said that sounded like English were *camera* and *battery.*" He grinned, a little more at ease. "So what's with the glasses? It'd be a hell of a shame if working with microscopic bugs is ruining those beautiful eyes."

Lines formed between her brows. Setting down the book camera, she hesitated, then shook her head. "Simon, what are you doing in the lab? What do you want?" The corners of her mouth twitched toward a smile he could feel in his chest. "And don't call me Q."

Hot damn, he'd managed to dent her shield a little. She usually didn't mind the teasing, but he'd drop it. For now. If James Bond had ever had this beautiful tech genius instead of the old man, he'd never have left the lab.

When she smoothed her hair, he admired the effect. Around her head, light-toffee-and-cream layers curved, controlled like the woman. Her hair used to swing behind her like the shining mane of the buckskin horse he had exercised when he was a kid in Baltimore. But after her husband's death, she'd cut it short. He didn't expect to like the new look, but the sleek cap invited touching.

He gripped his portfolio to avoid reaching out to her. "I'm here officially. Raines assigned us to work together for a few days." He paused to let that sink in.

She pursed her lips, as though having to work with Simon left a bad taste. It might, given his other, covert job.

"The assistant director mentioned he was giving me a field assignment as a tech advisor and translator, but that's as far as his explanation went."

Simon shrugged, relieved she knew that much already. He'd followed her advancement to tech officer. Observed her on the shooting range and in martial arts classes. He hadn't expected to work with her, but the gig was only for three days.

"Secrecy is Raines's middle name. Goes with the territory. He's the control officer for this mission. That says how high priority it is. I'll fill you in. Where can we talk?"

Mouth prim and taut, she led him into an empty office.

He stared at the portfolio. The report inside had triggered the assignment—at least, the official part.

The other part of the assignment was bad news. Raines had hinted at evidence, had called it checking on Officer Harris's loyalty. Simon called it spying on Janna. Bunch of crap, but what could he do? He knew her integrity was rock solid. True to his secretive nature, the AD had disclosed nothing more.

Simon didn't know what Janna was suspected of—only that ATSA's suspicions somehow tied her to this assignment. Did it have something to do with her dead husband? With some past assignment of Gabe's?

He didn't know much about their marriage except for Gabe's bragging about how happy they were. They'd moved into a fancy house in Virginia, away from her D.C. friends. Come to think of it, Simon hadn't seen them at parties or dinners except for those hosted by the director. Could Gabe have dragged her into something dirty?

The speculation was driving him crazy.

"We're to go to New York," she prompted as she closed the door. She leaned against a desk stacked with files.

Nodding, he handed her a copy of his summary. "After a two-year undercover operation, the ATSA office in Manhattan has Leo Wharton in custody. Picked him up on his yacht in the Virgin Islands."

Simon noted Janna's blank stare. She didn't know who Wharton was. Good sign.

He continued. "Wharton is a former U.S. Special Forces colonel. He was booted from the military for having illicit side interests. Went mercenary for a while, then turned to buying arms for terrorist groups. We've wanted to nail him for a long time."

She glanced at the summary. "It says here that Wharton is suspected of buying weapons from an international arms broker named Viktor Roszca." She turned her penetrating gaze on Simon. "Why is that name familiar?"

"Intelligence reports from the NCTC conclude that Roszca was the big supplier to the New Dawn Warriors." The National Counterterrorism Center was the agency created to coordinate analysis and operations among all intelligence services.

She paled and a small gasp escaped her lips. "The terrorist group that set up the assassination where—"

"Yes, where Gabe was killed."

Pain flickered across her face before she could school her expression.

Dammit. She still loved her husband, was still mourning him, and Simon was supposed to find out if she was dirty. He was the one who felt dirty.

Her gaze dropped to the report. "Go on."

He cleared his throat. "We want this guy. *I* want this guy. Bad. Roszca's weapons and explosives have injured or killed countless people, including ATSA officers. If we can get evidence that he armed avowed enemies of the U.S., we can convict the bastard in a U.S. federal court." Simon's white-hot hatred had been tempered and forged into steely determination.

"I see. Go on," Janna said, her expression thoughtful.

"Part of New York's undercover investigation involved surveillance tapes." He slid out a picture taken from one of the videotapes and passed it to her. "A couple of the tapes show Wharton in meetings with Roszca and other arms buyers—one from August over a year ago and one from last month."

Janna let her gaze lift to Simon as she listened to his explanation.

His diamond earring winked at her, teased her like Simon used to. Never under control, his thatch of brown hair had been styled with something like a Weedwhacker trimmer. His perpetual two-day beard looked scruffy but soft and touchable.

Ever the rebel, he wore snug, faded jeans and a T-shirt emblazoned with the words Spies Do It Undercover. Not that every man in ATSA wore a tie, but at headquarters, most wore dress shirts and slacks. Higher-ups like the AD tolerated Simon's in-your-face attitude because of his sharp intellect and street savvy.

She and Simon were such opposites. How had they ever managed to be friends?

Once upon a time. No more.

When Raines announced her first field assignment, anticipation had tingled through her. But why did her partner have
to be Simon? Why not someone dull? Married? Safe?

Simon was describing the arms broker's history. "Viktor
Roszca comes from what is now the independent Republic of
Cleatia. Even before the breakup of the Soviet Union, Roszca
used his base there to build an arms-dealing empire. Since the
Cleatian government exiled him, he's promoted himself as a re-
spectable international entrepreneur.

"He moved from small-arms theft from the Soviets and later
the Russians to American weaponry, including Stinger shoulder-fired antiaircraft missiles. Word is, he armed former Iraqi-
regime loyalists."

"I speak Cleatian fluently. Is that the translating part of it?"
She needed the security of knowing her role in the op.

"After we view the tapes. The last meeting Wharton had with
Roszca took place in a New York hotel. Soon after that meeting, Roszca vanished and hasn't surfaced. Also present were
some bottom feeders in Eastern bloc organized crime, guys
who've played both sides before. There's a chance they know
where Roszca is. We'll go talk to Wharton and view the tapes.
Then I'll need you to translate for the two goons. I'll want you
to record it." A beat passed. "Standard procedure."

Janna wondered why he'd said that almost apologetically.
Her stomach tightened as she began to grasp another implication. "Just the two of us, then? Not a team?"

"We're just talking to people, Q, uh, Janna. If we hit trouble, New York can provide backup. You okay with this arrange-
ment? Us working together?"

Her heart did an anxious flip. How could she work so closely
with this man who used to be her friend?

He'd begun putting the brakes on their friendship around the
time she met Gabe. His assuming responsibility for Gabe's

death explained why he'd continued to ignore her. The analytical part of her said her stung feelings weren't rational. The emotional part of her regretted the loss of her friendship with Simon.

But that was in the past. She'd moved on. So had he. She'd have to remain professional to keep her dignity.

There was a part of her—a dark part deep inside—that she could never reveal to him. Or to anyone. She would keep her private pain just that—private.

She squared her shoulders, ready to do her job.

"New York. The Big Apple." Janna forced her voice to an even tone. "Yes, Simon. I can't wait."

The tension between Simon and his tech-officer-turned-ice-princess rendered the short shuttle ride from D.C. to La-Guardia into sheer torture. At least for him. She spent most of the time ignoring him and organizing report forms on her laptop.

Twice, he'd started to kid her about being too rule conscious. Man, she followed regs before they had regs to follow or anything to report. Twice, he'd bitten his tongue.

The cab ride into the city was no different.

He watched her stare out the passenger window at city traffic, yellow cabs and gas-guzzling SUVs that no city dweller needed except for status.

Janna had avoided conversation the entire time. She'd refused his offer of help with her suitcase with a vigorous headshake. When his hand brushed her arm, she'd jumped as if he'd zapped her with a stun gun. And, worst of all, she was hiding her beautiful, smoky-gray eyes behind those glasses.

Hiding from him.

Apologizing hadn't rewound time to their easy friendship. Maybe friendship was impossible, especially with a sexy woman. A woman in mourning. He knew all too well the pain and hollowness of losing someone you loved. But talking to her about it wasn't his deal.

Dammit, he was no good at relationships.

The cab crossed the East River into Manhattan's maze of streets and headed across town. As they turned left on Broadway, traffic snarled around a parked truck unloading at a Starbucks café. A traffic sign on the corner warned No Horns.

Horns blared from all sides.

The noise and confusion sent Simon back a year and a half in time.

Gabe Harris had been part of an operation that Simon had headed to nail an extremist leader. While Simon and one unit lay in wait miles away at Arlington National Cemetery, the extremists planned to assassinate dignitaries at a ceremony on the Washington Mall. Alerted to the deception, Simon sent Harris and his unit ahead. Harris fought with one of the terrorists. He prevented the man from igniting a blast that could've killed a hundred and leveled a museum.

It wasn't the first time Gabe Harris had been a hero, but it would be the last.

In the struggle, the terrorist stabbed him in the heart. Harris died within seconds.

Simon should've been there instead of en route.

Having to tell Janna that her husband had died a hero had made Simon feel as hollow as a tolling church bell.

Hero that time merely meant the man she loved was dead. The gold ring on the third finger of her left hand more than a year later meant she still loved the man.

Short term was all Simon had to offer. One bad marriage was enough for him. She'd left.

People always left.

Each loss ripped away pieces of him. And gouged an aching void that never healed. His ex-wife hadn't been the first to leave, but he promised himself she would be the last to have the chance. Brief no-strings liaisons suited him better.

Work and building his mountain cabin in western Maryland were all he needed. He wouldn't set himself up again to be knocked on his ass and have his heart stomped on.

But he missed chatting and kidding around with Janna. He missed their long conversations and her laughter.

The cab passed Washington Square. Greenwich Village. They'd be at the ATSA offices in a few more blocks.

More cars crowded the street. The cabbie edged into the left lane, squeezing out another cab by a half inch of fender. The other driver yelled and waved a fist, but theirs merely shrugged as he turned onto the cross street. Just another day in New York traffic.

He'd nearly forgotten that Janna had spent her childhood with her diplomat parents in various Eastern European countries. She spoke several languages—not just Russian and the more-obscure Cleatian. A multitalented woman.

But working together meant communicating with more than long silences. The silent treatment could hinder the op. He had to figure out a way to thaw the cold war—and soon.

Janna peered upward at the tower that housed the New York branch of the Anti-Terrorism Security Agency. ATSA occupied the sixteenth through thirty-fifth floors of a steel-and-glass office building two blocks from the FBI in Lower Manhattan.

"They have the same drill as in D.C.," she said as they approached ATSA's private side entrance.

She slipped her leather ID bifold from her purse and opened it. On one side, the gold ATSA insignia glinted at her. From the other side, she extracted a plastic card.

Beside her, Simon chuckled, a sensual sound that rippled through her senses. She'd missed it.

"Of course they have the same drill. But I bet you researched the security process, didn't you, Marian?"

She couldn't help smiling at him calling her Marian, like the librarian in *The Music Man*. Simon teased without cruelty or humiliation. Simon's kidding never hurt.

"I checked. I admit it. Why not?" She missed their easy camaraderie, but it wasn't safe to open herself up too much.

With tension between them thick enough to soundproof a room, his teasing fell flat. He didn't try again, but merely waited for her to complete the security sequence. Silently but not patiently. Annoyance radiated from him.

Being with Simon jangled Janna's nerves more than this assignment. Her stomach buzzed as though she'd swallowed one of her bug detectors.

She slid her plastic ID into the designated slot, then placed her right palm on the glowing green screen above it. When the door clicked open, she entered the building. Once inside, she retrieved her card from the machine's other end. The guard handed her a visitor's badge to clip on her collar.

Via video monitor, she watched Simon go through the same process. His attire was only marginally less disreputable today. At least the T-shirt beneath his leather jacket had no logo, subversive or otherwise. A few inches taller than her gawky five-foot-eight frame, his was a compact build.

When he glowered at the handprint detector, she realized that his resentment of red tape, not her, was the cause of his mood—part of it anyway.

Growing up on the streets and then at Pimlico Race Course had honed the mutinous aspect of his personality. He rebelled against authority even when he was part of the authority. He'd probably prefer to sneak in and let them find him with his feet on the polished desk of the assistant director in charge.

Relax, rebel without a clue. She suppressed an affectionate grin. Simon swung into the reception area with his typical economy of movement.

Affection? No, I can't afford even that. At that insight, the warmth of pleasure dissipated, leaving behind only cold fear. She was still attracted to Simon, but she wouldn't go there with anyone again—especially not with Simon.

They submitted their briefcases for a search by the guard on duty. He barely glanced at her new bug detector: a miniature unit in ballpoint-pen form she'd designed herself. Her other toys were tucked away in her rolling overnight bag. She scrupulously followed agency regs, but this outing was a field trial for the mini-detector. So far, it passed.

The dour guard gave a disapproving sniff at Simon's scuffed-leather courier bag, more like a saddlebag than a professional briefcase. But it, too, passed inspection.

The guard then called upstairs to announce their arrival. They left their suitcases with him and entered the elevator.

Janna stood stiffly beside Simon as the car rose with a barely perceptible hum. She stared at the steel door as he stared at his feet. His clean male scent drifted to her on the conditioned air—soap and pure Simon, no designer cologne or aftershave—a door to familiar feelings and memories.

She should slam the door, not allow his nearness to tempt her. She had to work with the man. That was all. She had good reason for her rule against anything but professional ties.

She cleared her throat. "I hope we get to see Vanessa Wade. Didn't she transfer here?"

Simon shifted his feet, but didn't look at her. "She's out of the country with her husband. Hong Kong. I asked."

"Oh, too bad." Janna had looked forward to seeing her friend. The kind ATSA officer had gone out of her way to comfort her when Gabe died.

Vanessa's wedding had been the end of Janna's closeness with Simon. She had a champagne-hazed memory of catching the bouquet and slobbering all over Simon on the dance floor. No wonder he ran like one of his precious horses. She nearly groaned aloud.

She was searching for a new topic of conversation when the elevator whispered to a stop and the doors slid open.

Simon and Janna stepped out of the express elevator onto the twentieth floor.

A balding officer with a bulldog face greeted them and introduced himself as Tony Mascolo. Simon's New York contact, he'd arranged for them to view the surveillance videos.

"Harris." Mascolo chewed on the name. Janna's stomach clenched at what she knew was coming. When would the attention go away? "You related to Gabriel Harris?"

She squared her shoulders. "He was my husband."

The officer nodded solemnly. "My sympathies, then. A brave man and a credit to the country."

"I'm very proud of what he did that day." Front pages and TV stations had broadcast Gabe's heroism. Internal ATSA memos had reinforced the news. Facing reminders constantly, she'd developed a stock reply. Truthful as far as it went.

"I'll want to interview Leo Wharton after we see the videos," Simon said, and Janna was grateful that he directed the conversation back to business.

"We got Wharton stashed in a safe house instead of the Metropolitan Correctional Center," Mascolo said as they wove through a maze of cubicles. "Figured it was easier to keep his arrest under wraps that way. Only us and his attorney know his location. I'll have him brought in. Tomorrow morning okay?"

With a glance at Janna for confirmation, Simon agreed. The fact that he considered her opinion pleased her more than it should. Normal for operatives working together as partners, but she'd learned the hard way not to take consideration for granted.

Mascolo showed them into an office with a large-screen television, folding chairs and a kitchenette. He picked up two videotapes from a table. "These are the two that show Roszca. I'll start the recent one, from last month. Make yourselves comfortable. Soda is in the mini-fridge over there." He took a seat in the back and opened a folder he'd brought with him.

Janna headed to the fridge. "Simon?"

"Anything's fine." He was already studying the footage beginning to roll in vivid color.

"Technical quality's good," Janna said, handing Simon a cola. "One of the new smart cameras." Light sensors allowed the camera to switch from color to black and white as the light dimmed. She'd hooked up more than a few of those babies.

She popped open her diet orange and sat beside Simon.

"This tape shows the local talent," Mascolo said, looking up from his work. "Our guy installed a camera and a mike on the bookshelf. Here's Wharton on the fancy gilt sofa. You probably know his mug anyway. Roszca's at the door."

Wharton's bodyguard went to the door. After a moment, long enough to frisk the visitors, Wharton greeted his guest. Roszca strode across the ankle-deep carpet. The two men shook hands, and Roszca took the armchair beside his host.

Before the trip Janna had studied Roszca's news footage as well as his file. The flamboyant arms broker frequented film premieres and charity galas. Insisting on the legitimacy of his businesses, he'd given newsmaker interviews on European television.

In suits that cost as much as the camera recording them, both men looked slick, well fed and respectable enough for Wall Street. Except for the bulked-up, armed bodyguards at their sides.

"Here come your guys," Mascolo said. "NYPD knows them. Petro Kravka and Dmitri Tarlev are knee breakers for the Russian mob. Enforcers. Local bosses farm them out as bodyguards to visiting muck-a-mucks."

The two men, who'd been out of camera range, sidled closer behind Roszca. Kravka was a bear of a man with long, greasy hair. He stood at attention behind the arms broker. Tarlev, shorter but no less muscular, with short, red hair, lumbered across the room to stand at the settee's end. After desultory pleasantries, a discussion ensued about arms sales.

"That's the entire segment with Roszca," Mascolo said a few moments later as he changed tapes. "Here's the tape from twenty months ago. This one's a dinner in an Eastern European café on Second Avenue. Private room. You'll see Roszca's goons and some other arms buyers."

Janna watched the taped gathering, but her awareness focused on the man beside her. Curiosity, she told herself.

This serious, intense side of Simon was new to her. Until his visit that fatal day, she'd seen only his fun-loving side. She hadn't seen his intuitive mind focused on his work. His mocking brown eyes were solemn, and his sensual mouth, so often in a wry smirk, thinned to a taut line.

Simon's shoulders stiffened at something on the screen.

Janna slid her gaze back to the videotape and received the shock of her life.

The tall, dark-haired man shaking hands with Roszca looked all too familiar. A man who usually had sandy-blond hair.

The man she'd buried only a few months after this scene took place.

Gabriel Harris.

Chapter 2

Simon's pulse took off like a thoroughbred out of the starting gate. His mind raced on its heels with more questions than he could handle. He was watching Wharton and Roszca and the same bodyguards from the first tape when who should waltz in but the all-American golden boy—and with dyed hair.

What the hell was Gabe Harris doing in the same room with these scumbag arms brokers? Simon had figured maybe leaks to other agencies or an ally, maybe a little moonlighting, but illegal arms dealing? Mr. Perfect? No way.

This tape was why the AD hadn't given him details about what Janna might have done. He wanted Janna's reaction for sure, but he wanted Simon's shock to be genuine. It sure as hell was genuine.

Was the agency's favorite hero a traitor as bad as Wharton? No. Worse. Had he dragged his wife into his dirty business? The notion churned bile in his belly.

Janna's sharp intake of breath told him the moment she, too, saw her deceased husband on the tape.

She gripped his arm. "Simon, no," she mouthed, her expression pleading. Her gaze flicked to the rear of the room, to the New York officer.

Simon knew what her frightened gray eyes were asking.

She wanted him to keep the secret. But did she want him to protect the memory of the dead husband she loved? The reputation of a dead hero?

Or did she want him to cover up treason?

The acrid taste of nausea backed up in his throat. He couldn't swallow any more cola. A stiff shot of something stronger would go down easier.

He glanced at Mascolo. The man was reading his file, hadn't even looked up at them or at the screen. He'd probably seen all the tapes a dozen times. Either the New York office didn't recognize the agency's hero, or Mascolo had orders to keep mum and observe what Janna did.

Simon swallowed the bitter taste and his better judgment. She couldn't be involved. He couldn't believe it. But he had to follow her lead to prove it to ATSA.

His gut knotted with nerves, he nodded and gave Janna's trembling hand a pat. He felt the iciness of her soft skin before she pulled away.

Her eyelids fluttered in recognition of his agreement to her plea. Shock had blanched her creamy complexion to chalk. Simon longed to reassure her, but nothing he could say or do would erase the horrible reality before them.

Hell, *his* mug was probably just as pale.

Both forced their gazes back to the television.

A drink in his hand—bourbon straight up, from the looks of it—Harris conversed cordially with Roszca after Wharton strolled away.

The gist of their chat was to arrange an appointment to negotiate for automatic weapons and rocket-propelled grenades for a Middle Eastern militia group. Roszca agreed to meet the next afternoon.

When the dinner ended, the screen went black. Mascolo strode to the VCR and ejected the tape.

Raines had for damn sure already seen it. He'd set up Simon—and Janna—but Simon needed time to analyze the footage. "I'd like a copy of those to take back to D.C."

"These *are* copies," Mascolo said. "They're yours. The AD approved their release."

From the man's zeal, Simon got the impression that New York wanted this complicated part of the operation out of their hair. Rolling up Wharton was clean and simple: possession of illegal weapons and treason for arming enemies of the country.

But nothing involving Roszca was clean. Or simple.

Especially this time.

Janna snatched the videotapes from Mascolo's hand before Simon could move. She tucked them in her slim leather case. "You have all the people's names?" she asked.

Mascolo didn't seem to notice her nervousness, but he didn't know her like Simon did. Her jerky movements and trapped look reminded him of a frightened filly—a filly he couldn't draw into his arms to protect.

"Some." He shrugged. "I'll give you what I got. You can take it from there."

Take it from there, yeah, Simon thought, his pulse bounding again. What he'd do with the volatile information was up for grabs. The bile in his belly congealed into a hard knot of dread.

By tacit agreement, neither spoke as the elevator descended to the reception area.

Janna didn't dare use her new bug detector in here, but she figured every square foot of the building was wired for sound and video surveillance—likely for motion and heat sensors also.

Her nerves screamed with anxiety over the names in the envelope that Mascolo had handed over. Simon had tucked it in his bag without a glance. If only she had the necessary technical marvel—X-ray vision—to read the list through the scarred leather of his bag.

The New York ATSA investigation must not have identified Gabe as a fellow officer. That much was certain. Otherwise Raines wouldn't have included her in this op. But who did New York think he was?

If they knew the man buying arms from Roszca was the agency's poster boy, they'd choke on their ID badges. Everyone sang her hero husband's praises to her, forcing her to guard her secret shame. She'd accepted his medals, smiled at the accolades and dabbed at tears.

He'd win no prizes as a husband, but she believed his dedication to the agency and his country had been beyond reproach. That was one reason she'd kept her scars private.

Or maybe he'd been undercover for Raines without anyone's knowledge. Did the AD send her here on purpose, for some obscure security reason she couldn't fathom?

Nothing made sense.

Did she want Gabe to be innocent? Did she want him to be guilty? Shock and fear and anger tumbled around in her heart like stones in a riverbed. Of course she wanted him to be innocent.

But emotion clogged her throat at the reason. If Gabe was guilty of selling arms or treason or God knew what else, that made her even more of a fool than she was already.

She had to know what he had been up to.

A scandal involving ATSA's hero would rock the agency to the core. The resulting investigation would surely open up her pain and shame to scrutiny. And pity.

She'd face exposure if she *had* to—the pity spotlight, the shame, the scandal, her parents' shock. They thought the sun rose and set on Gabe.

Though Simon had been her friend, he wouldn't understand. No one could understand. Her stomach rolled at the prospect.

She couldn't let it happen. Not now. Not yet. She needed time. Her heart pounded at how many agency rules she would trash, but she had no choice.

She had to convince Simon to help her.

Once out on the sidewalk, she extracted the mini-detector and extended its antenna. The electronic eyes in the facade's decor were obvious to her and probably to Simon, but hidden mikes were another story.

At first, Simon peered at the device with surprise, but he caught on fast. "Well?"

The unit blinked its red-light warning. ATSA protected the building's exterior, too. No surprise.

Turning her back on the building, she mouthed, "No."

Yellow cabs crowded the street. Mid-afternoon and you'd think it was rush hour. The first three cabs Simon tried to flag down had passengers. The next raised his Off Duty sign as soon as Simon stepped into the street. Ten minutes and eight cabs later, an empty taxi pulled over to the curb.

"The hotel will have surveillance," Simon said.

That had occurred to her, too. They needed to talk. Now.

Janna consulted her Manhattan map. "There's a park across the street. It looks like a little green square."

Several minutes later, the cab let them out at the Delancey Hotel between the East Village and the Lower East Side. The U.S. government owned the small hotel and used it as a secure residence for transient personnel from various government entities. A brass plate below the hotel's name on the door read Private.

The unassuming brick structure stood in a residential block on a cross street off Delancey Street. Along with other buildings—apartments judging from the windows with plants and curtains—it ringed the green square that Janna had pointed out on the map. He wondered if little old ladies peeking through lace curtains had puzzled out the function of their mysterious neighbor.

Simon surveyed the area as he waited for the cab to disappear around the corner. Good placement for security. The hotel had a clear view of all buildings and anyone arriving. Nobody on the street. Nobody in the park. He glimpsed movement behind a second-floor hotel window.

Let 'em wait and wonder. If he had to endure another damn security check, they could sure as hell hold their horses.

He hoisted his duffel bag onto his free shoulder. The envelope containing the list of names in his other bag weighed heavily on the other shoulder. Turning their backs on the hotel, they crossed to the handkerchief park—nothing more than dusty grass, a stone bench and a couple of skinny trees behind wire cages. April's new green leaves fanned out on the branches.

He didn't have to say a thing. Janna pulled out her magic pen and extended its slim antenna. "Park's clear," she said. "Hotel side of the street has ears. Keep your voice low."

They sat facing away from the hotel.

He withdrew the manila envelope from his bag and pried open its clips. "It's not a list. He gave us prints from the video with names handwritten on the back."

Janna leaned so close he could inhale the almond fragrance of her hair, feel the warmth of her arm pressed against his. He wished... *Aw, hell.*

"Look through them, quick." Anxiety roughened her voice.

He shuffled the prints one by one. Roszca. Wharton. Roszca's two Cleatian muscle. A couple of other arms buyers, no names on the back. And Gabriel Harris, with smug satisfaction on his pretty-boy profile.

"Nothing written on the back."

Janna exhaled. "His picture was everywhere. Why didn't they recognize him?"

Her naive question had to mean she was innocent. The knot

of dread eased a fraction. "The dark hair and the camera angle. The New Yorkers don't know him personally."

. "Thank God," she said in a breathy voice. "In disguise. Dyed hair. Why?"

Simon hated to, but he had to ask—for himself as well as for the agency. "Do *you* know anything about this? Why Gabe was at that dinner?"

She shook her head, layers of curls in strands of toffee and gold swinging with the movement. "Are you sure he wasn't part of ATSA's undercover op to roll up Wharton? Or Roszca?"

Simon scrubbed his knuckles over his chin. "If he was undercover for New York, Mascolo would've known him. Roszca's *our* quarry. As far as I know, Raines sent nobody undercover."

Janna slipped off her eyeglasses and rubbed the bridge of her nose. Eyes the color of a summer rain cloud looked to him for help. Big and wide, long-lashed and slightly tipped up at the outer corners. Eyes of feminine mystery. Eyes a man could get lost in.

Fear and grief swirled in their depths, and Simon felt helpless to comfort her. Hell, he shouldn't even touch her. She didn't want his hands on her. She'd made that obvious.

Every instinct told him she knew nothing of whatever Gabe had done, but if she suspected Simon was checking on her, she wouldn't want him within a mile of her. Either way, she sure as hell wouldn't want his sympathy.

So he sat in silence.

"Simon, if Gabe wasn't there on ATSA orders…" She swallowed, apparently unable to continue.

The sentence didn't need finishing. Both knew the implications.

"Try to think back to when that transaction was taped," Simon said. "August, over a year ago. What was Harris, um, Gabe doing then? Was he away much?"

Janna slid the glasses back on. Shield in place, she pressed fingers to both temples and massaged them. "He made several trips that summer. I'd have to look in my planner to know when."

"What were the trips?"

She shook her head. "Agency business. He never told me more than that. He couldn't talk about his assignments. You know that."

Naturally, Mr. Perfect followed agency regs while he was off screwing the system. Simon wished the man was alive so he could deck him.

"I went along with keeping quiet earlier." How the hell should he word this? "But we have to alert Raines."

Janna gripped his arm as hard as she had when they'd seen Harris on the tape with Roszca. Her eyes were stark with anxiety. "No, Simon, please. I beg you not to tell anyone."

If the whole thing wasn't a setup, it would be a hell of a twist—she wanted to break the rules, and he had to follow them. His orders said to play out the scenario, to see where she would lead.

He covered her hand tentatively. Patted. Before he could savor her soft skin and relax his fingers over hers, she slid away and scooted to the far end of the stone bench.

"Look, I know you loved the guy. This must be painful as hell. But his meeting with Roszca is bound to come out. New York could find out and call Raines. Or the director. Maybe—"

"I know it will come out eventually, but not yet."

He shoved the envelope into her hands and stood. "You're not seeing the ramifications. If we don't level with the agency from the start, our careers will be on the line. Concealing damaging information like this definitely violates agency regs—due diligence, failure to disclose, among others."

He was under orders, but hell, *she* could face criminal charges of conspiracy and obstruction of justice. That the object of the concealment was dead would make no difference to ATSA, even if Janna hadn't participated in whatever Gabe did.

Hands tight around the incriminating picture of her dead husband, Janna said, "I know. I understand the risks. But the mere rumor that Gabe might have been selling arms would destroy his memory and disillusion everyone. Gabe is a national hero. I have his medals as proof. I'm asking you to help me find out the truth before we tell anyone."

He paced in front of the small bench. "Ah, Janna, you don't know what you're asking."

"But I do, Simon. I'm willing to risk my career, and I'm asking you to risk yours. If we learn that Gabe was dirty, I'll be the first to tell Raines. But would you want to destroy a hero's memory if there's some other reason he's on that tape? What if there's a legitimate reason?"

Finding a legitimate reason had as much chance as Simon bringing in Roszca single-handedly. He gazed into her pleading eyes. If she wanted Simon to help cover up Gabe's crimes to protect herself, she was a damn good actress.

Hell, the real reason she wanted to protect Harris's memory was that she still loved him. That knowledge hurt. It was a good bet that Raines knew all about the tapes and that Gabe was guilty.

Simon's only consolation was his hope that if Janna was innocent, investigating along with her would prove that. He owed her that much for old times' sake. For his negligence in Gabe's death.

"I'll agree to secrecy for now," he said, watching her features soften as his words sank in. "I'll see what I can find out while we're here. Maybe Wharton or the two local Cleatian muscle know something."

"Thank you, Simon. You're doing the right thing. I'm sure of it." She sprang to her feet. If he expected her to give him a thank-you hug, he was a damn fool. She hoisted her laptop case and grasped the handle of her rolling bag.

He shouldered his bags and turned toward the hotel. "Two or three days of interviews. After that, we'll see. That's as far as I'll go."

She beamed a heart-stumbling smile at him. "Agreed. Now let's go register at the hotel. I need a shower."

He almost groaned at the image that triggered. The sooner he made it to a room alone, the calmer he'd be. He needed a shower, too. A cold one.

After undergoing a security check, they entered the lobby of the Delancey Hotel. The exterior was plain brick, but the interior exploded with intense green-and-yellow carpeting and draperies with geometric designs. Simon wished he'd brought sunglasses.

"Oh, it's so New York," Janna said, gazing at an abstract wall sconce. "Art deco, like Radio City Music Hall."

Simon mumbled in agreement. Maybe he should've paid more attention in art appreciation. All he could think was that the hotel had turned loose a Picasso wanna-be to decorate it.

The bored-looking clerk at the reception desk signed them in with brisk efficiency. "Here you are. Room 1215. Two key cards." He extended an envelope to Simon.

"But that's only one room," Janna said.

"Reservations were for separate rooms." Simon slapped the envelope back on the desk. The day had gone to hell enough without a room snafu.

The clerk recoiled at the ferocity in Simon's voice. He tapped at some computer keys and studied the screen. He smiled apologetically. "I'm sorry, sir, ma'am. The reservation is for a suite."

Janna explored the room as she listened to Simon's phone conversation with the agency's travel desk in Washington. She could tell a woman was on the other end of the line because Simon was kidding and cajoling in spite of his anger.

"If anybody can fix this, Jennifer, honey, it's you," he said. "It's too long after April Fools' Day for a joke."

Janna knew they were stuck with the suite before they came upstairs. There was no room at the inn. Both the clerk and the manager had informed them that the hotel was full. The manager had apologized three times during a ramble about extra bookings because of Earth Day demonstrations at the United Nations.

She stowed her faux pen in her pocket. The tiny detector had picked up no bugs in the shared bathroom, the sitting room or the bedroom. Apparently, once they passed security checks, government officers were allowed privacy.

The suite itself cheered her up a bit. The muted blues and greens on the walls and on the spreads covering the two double beds toned down the art deco.

Two beds, she assured herself. And a couch. She wouldn't trust her future to another person again, but she'd trust Simon in this situation. He'd be a gentleman.

Of course, she'd trust him not to jump her bones. He'd made his feelings about her clear enough—he had none.

Her feelings—and secrets—were the problem. Sharing a suite might mean détente. Resuming friendship would lower barriers she needed to protect herself.

Maybe Jennifer-honey could twist some arms here at the Delancey to find another room. But Janna doubted it. She sat on the edge of the couch and waited.

Simon slammed down the receiver. "No luck." He shoved a shock of unruly hair off his forehead. It fell back down.

She thought better of mentioning that she'd expected no results. "Why did headquarters reserve a suite?"

He tore off his leather jacket. He tossed it and his duffel bag on the other bed. "Raines's aide had the travel desk reserve a suite. Cheaper than two rooms. He figured we'd work it out, be professional." He threw up his hands.

"I see. Well, we can manage for a couple of days." And nights. But she wouldn't think about that. "We have two beds. No one has to sleep on the couch. I can be as professional as the next person."

From the scowl on Simon's face, she saw that he didn't like the situation any more than she did.

Janna carried her suitcase into the bedroom, tossed it on one bed and unzipped it. She lifted her folded peach silk nightie and underwear from on top of her toiletries. "Do you want to shower first or shall I?"

Simon gaped at her from the doorway between the bedroom and the sitting room. His Adam's apple rose and fell faster than an express elevator. He snatched up his jacket and strode to the door. "You go ahead. I'll be in the bar. Come down when you're ready to go out to dinner."

He closed the door behind him before Janna could open her mouth to speak.

Now he wasn't merely ignoring her. He was angry. Angry about Gabe. Angry about the suite. Angry at her.

He was so different, so much the rebel. Before she met Gabe, she'd resisted acting on her attraction to Simon. Until that wedding reception anyway. An affair with him would've been a walk on the wild side.

Renewing their friendship was impossible, but so was hostility if they had to work together. She had to loosen up without treading into sensitive areas.

She carried her cosmetic kit and a clean blouse into the black-and-white-tiled bathroom. After covering her hair with the hotel's shower cap, she stepped into the shower. Maybe the steamy water would infuse her with the strength she needed.

Gabe hadn't wanted her to further her career beyond the tech lab, but after his death, she'd jumped at the chance. Here was her first assignment as a tech officer, and she felt more like a track runner facing ever-higher hurdles. Interpreting and doing security sweeps rolled out an easy path. But Raines had paired her with her first hurdle, Simon. Working with Simon revived tender feelings that violated her personal rule against men.

Seeing Gabe on that videotape had raised the bar. Searching for the truth meant working together with a shared secret. Everyone, including Simon, believed she practically kept a shrine to Saint Gabriel.

She and Simon had to communicate enough to work together, and that was all she ought to want. Closeness might set her up for more pain. Closeness would complicate feelings she'd buried long ago. Closeness might lead to confidences.

And sharing a hotel room had raised the bar to another, insurmountable height. Intimacy to an extent she never would've imagined. Toothbrushes on the same sink. The sound of a shower sluicing down a naked body. Beds side by side. Soft good-nights in the darkened room.

As if to eradicate the enticing images, she scrubbed her body until the skin turned as pink as a sunburn.

She couldn't slip or let down her guard even a micrometer, or Simon might see through her defenses. Maintaining a professional tone was her only recourse.

Simon was the last person she wanted to know that marrying Gabe Harris was the biggest mistake she'd ever made.

Chapter 3

The glowing red numerals on the nightstand clock read three o'clock.

Simon sighed his sleepless frustration into the darkness and rolled onto his back. His sweatpants were giving him a wedgie. He usually slept in the buff and hadn't planned on a damn roommate. Seeing Janna bop around in that flimsy nightie made matters worse. An icy shower had temporarily doused the fire down below, but hadn't washed away his problems.

Any of them.

Problem number one slept like a baby in the other bed. Too close for comfort. Did her soft, even breathing mean her conscience was clear? Or was she simply exhausted?

The day's stresses and strains should've exhausted him, too. Instead, his brain wouldn't shut down.

When she came downstairs earlier, he'd looked up from his beer to see her all freshly scrubbed and looking too damned appetizing in a silky blouse that clung in all the right places. The worry and strain in her incredible eyes slammed him in the belly. But she'd remained cool and professional, armed with a list of neighborhood eateries.

A few blocks south had taken them into Little Italy, where they found Mama Maria's Trattoria. He'd wolfed down pasta and meatballs while she'd picked at spinach ravioli. Had she become a vegetarian? He hadn't dared to ask. Personal questions were a bad idea. And now the meatballs and garlic churned in his stomach while the widow Harris lay temptingly within reach.

He stacked the two thick pillows beneath his head and stared at the blinking smoke-detector light on the ceiling. What in hell had Gabriel Harris intended by meeting with Viktor Roszca? Harris had been with the Bureau of Alcohol, Tobacco and Firearms before joining ATSA. Did the ATF link mean anything? Had a case led him to Roszca? Janna might know, whether the bastard had involved her or not.

Insisting they keep the tape evidence secret sure as hell made her look involved. Simon didn't believe she'd committed any crime—even sampling at the supermarket salad bar— but his gut said she was keeping something from him.

If not guilt, then what?

Following his orders from the AD bound him to Janna. Hadn't he hoped for open communication? He'd gotten his wish, but it was a hell of an icebreaker.

Some space from her would go a long way toward restoring his equilibrium. Toward quelling his libido. Toward clearing his head so he could sort this puzzle out.

He didn't need her to translate or scan security when he interrogated Wharton. Yeah, that was it. He'd go to the ATSA office alone to see Wharton in the morning.

Satisfied that he'd made a decision, Simon turned over and buried himself in the covers.

When Janna detected her roommate's light snoring, she

opened her eyes. Out of necessity, she'd learned to feign sleep.
The old habit died hard. Simon wasn't Gabe, she told herself
as she let her eyelids drift. That small comfort should've relaxed
her, but she and a good night's sleep hadn't found each other
in months.

Janna couldn't imagine a starker setting than the ATSA interrogation room. Painted battleship-gray, the walls had no
decorations of any kind, not even a calendar. The ceiling and
floor were gray. Even the one-way glass that separated her
from Simon and Wharton had a steely cast. An ex-Navy painter
nostalgic for his ship must've designed the space.

She rose early and got dressed before Simon had awoken.
From his grumpy attitude at breakfast, she figured he meant to
skip out on her and do this interview solo. No way. If he found
out anything about Gabe, she wanted to hear it firsthand. No
sugar coating. No hedging on the truth.

She already knew the worst. Didn't she?

"Would you like some coffee, Harris?" Mascolo asked.

Caffeine, yes. The stronger the better. "Yes, please." In the
past, she'd have asked a fellow operative to call her by her first
name. But strictly professional and formal was her new rule.
The reason for her glasses. And last names only.

"Regular java," the bulldog-faced ATSA operative said with
a half grin. "None of that flavored crap."

She pushed the glasses firmly on her nose and nodded.
"Fine. Black, please. No sugar."

"Be right back."

With his official presence gone, Janna turned her attention
to the interrogation on the other side of the glass.

The two men facing each other were a study in contrasts.
Simon slouched in the metal folding chair at a battered wooden
table. His hair defied taming, like its owner. Seen in profile, his
look—scuffed leather jacket, faded jeans and curled upper

lip—projected street tough. Anyone who didn't know better would label Simon the suspect and the other man the official.

Except for the metal cuffs locked on Wharton's wrists.

Leo Wharton looked every inch the college football star and Army colonel he'd been. About six foot three and in his midforties, he wore his salt-and-pepper hair in a military cut. His biceps stretched the pressed cotton of his white monogrammed dress shirt. He sat at attention and glared at Simon with dark eyes like black coals.

Simon had introduced himself when Wharton entered. The two men had been waging a silent staring duel for the past ten minutes.

"Here you go." The operative handed her a steaming brew in a foam cup.

She thanked him and sipped the coffee—bitter and strong enough to power the space shuttle—as she waited for something to happen. At this rate, they'd be here all day.

Wharton frowned and leaned forward slightly. "Either get to your questions or send me back to the safe house. At least there, I don't have to look at your ugly face."

Ah, finally. Simon had gotten the reaction he wanted. His opponent caved first. Janna smiled as she studied Wharton.

Simon straightened his shoulders. "I understand your pal Viktor Roszca has a special consignment for sale. You know anything about a shipment from Cleatia?"

Wharton matched Simon's lip curl with his own. "Roszca doesn't confide in me." He cocked his head. "What kind of shipment?"

Janna knew the smuggled nuclear material hadn't come up in Wharton's last meeting with the arms broker. Maybe he didn't know. But how would this line of questioning lead them to Roszca's hideout?

Her chest tightened with anxiety about the other line of inquiry. When would Simon ask about Gabe?

"I don't buy your ignorance act, Wharton." Simon shrugged.

"You might not be Roszca's confidant, but you're on the grape-vine. Or you *were*."

Wharton said nothing.

Janna wondered if the man's fear of Roszca's reprisal kept him silent.

Simon continued evenly, "Anything you tell me won't be used in your case. That's the main reason your lawyer okayed this interview."

Still mute, Wharton stared at the scuffed tabletop.

"Too bad your clients'll miss out on this chance. You could've made enough to retire. Oh, sorry. You *are* retired." Simon grinned.

"You should do stand-up on The Comedy Channel," Wharton said, his face impassive. "You won't get anything out of me."

Simon slid a single sheet of paper across the table. "Roszca might not think so when he sees this press release that the New York ATSA office'll send out after I leave here."

As the former colonel read the three paragraphs, beads of sweat broke out on his forehead. So the possibility that Roszca might think he blabbed did strike fear in his heart. Janna knew the press release was a bluff, but Wharton didn't. Encouraged, she stepped closer to the glass.

"Not too close, Harris," Mascolo said. "He can see your shadow on his side."

She curtailed her anxious impulse and backed up a step.

"If you help me out," Simon continued, "I'll tear this up. No word of our discussion will reach the media."

Hatred burned in Wharton's black eyes. His shoulders bulged as he curled his big hands into fists. "How do I know I can trust you to keep your word?"

Simon shrugged. "You don't."

After a few minutes of a new staring session, Wharton sagged, apparently conceding defeat. "I don't know much. The shipment's about five kilos of weapons-grade uranium."

Elbows on the table, Simon leaned forward into Wharton's

space. "If it's going to the highest bidder, how's he running the sale?"

Wharton wiped sweat from his upper lip with his manacled hands. "He's arranged a summit for the big players. A private auction."

"Where's this summit to take place?"

The arms dealer shook his head. "I don't know. Roszca has a hideaway somewhere. And I don't know when." Once again, he sat at attention, smirking. "You feds picked me up too soon for me to get any farther."

Simon ignored the jibe. "Where is this hideaway?"

Wharton shifted in his chair. "We're done here. I've told you all I know. Now tear up that press release."

"One more thing." Simon fanned out the set of still pictures from the tapes.

Janna held her breath when she saw Gabe's picture in front of the other man. Her chest tightened so much she thought it might crush her lungs.

"I need names for some of these guys." Simon tapped a finger on Gabe's forehead. "This one, for instance."

Wharton's mouth turned down at the corners. He shook his head. "Roszca likes to entertain. He invites lots of people to his dinners. I saw this man a few times. Don't know his name or his game."

Janna's heart sank. What had she expected? That Wharton would finger Gabe as an undercover fed? All his recognition of Gabe had accomplished was to verify what they already knew.

Except that Wharton had seen Gabe more than once. What did that mean?s

In the afternoon, Simon and Janna toured coffeehouses in the Eastern European sector of the East Village, where Mascolo indicated the two Cleatians worked.

Simon doubted the two low-level goons knew anything helpful. He wanted to get the interviews out of the way fast so they could fly back to Washington. Then he could dump the thorny internal mess in Raines's lap. What he couldn't dump was his creeping grime of guilt about Janna.

A quick return to D.C. would also mean avoiding a second night of her female scent and soft sighs.

Finally, at the last coffeehouse on Second Avenue, they found one of the thugs. Dmitri Tarlev was wiping down a stained oak bar in the back, where they served liquor as well as coffee and pastries.

Janna spoke to the red-haired man in his native language. To Simon's untutored ear, Cleatian sounded sort of like Russian. He didn't understand a word, but knew from her reaction that Tarlev agreed to meet with them. He supposed he ought to be suspicious of her translating.

Damn, Raines had to be wrong about her.

After they left the bar, Janna said, "The other man, Kravka, didn't show up for work today, but Tarlev will bring him to meet us at a bar he told me about."

That was the good news. The bad news was the time—after midnight.

One more night at the Delancey Hotel. With Janna.

After midnight also meant backup from local ATSA. No venturing into Russian Mafia territory that late at night without support. They could lose more than the envelope of cash he had in his pocket.

He searched for a way to leave Janna at the hotel in safety, but she couldn't teach him enough Cleatian or Russian in eight hours. Damn, his protective instincts would only get him in deeper trouble with her than he already was for trying to duck out on her that morning. Condescending, patronizing, she'd say. She was a fully trained tech officer. She carried a weapon like he did and didn't need a protector.

Right.

But the mere thought of those two gorillas anywhere near her made his stomach muscles seize up.

At midnight, the Astor Place subway stop bustled with New Yorkers headed to and from bars and restaurants in the East Village.

"The Danube Bar and Restaurant is on the corner of Jaffe and Stanislaus, a block past Saint Mark's Place," Janna said as they exited at street level. "Tarlev said it's beside this deli that's in my guidebook. This is *such* a quaint district."

Simon glanced at the page where Janna was pointing.

Of course she carried a city guidebook. When she bought the book and map, he'd thought it was a good ploy, camouflaging themselves as tourists. Then he realized she probably bought it for research as much as for cover. She was the most curious woman—correction, person, male or female—that he'd ever met.

And the most enigmatic. What the hell was she wearing those black-rimmed glasses for? He'd looked through them when she left them on the nightstand. Clear glass. She was hiding behind them. But why?

Her scent made him want to rip the glasses off, bury his fingers in her hair and pull her into his arms, but he kept his hands to himself. She'd made it clear that she didn't want him touching her, that she still mourned her damn hero.

Once the truth came out, Harris wouldn't be anybody's hero. What would that do to Janna? Something he shouldn't concern himself with. They weren't really friends again. And nothing else was possible. No relationship for him.

Less pain when everything inevitably went to hell.

They walked briskly past closed shops and vendors' locked carts. On the long blocks that formed Saint Mark's Place, a few shops and sidewalk vendors stayed open for business, catering to the late bar crowd.

Good. The more people around, the safer he felt. The ATSA

backups—a man and woman on foot—picked them up when he and Janna left the subway. Another in a car would drive them away once the meeting ended.

Shops and vendors lined the street. He bet that counterculture funk like vintage clothing, 1960s memorabilia and piercing shops fronted for drug sales. Or maybe his old DEA habits had made him too suspicious.

Janna wasn't paying attention to the funky shops. He watched her gaze with longing at embroidered peasant blouses and silver jewelry from the Ukraine and its neighbors.

"You lived in the Ukraine with your parents once, didn't you?" He immediately wished he'd stifled the personal stuff. Jamming his hands in his jeans pockets, he picked up the pace.

A wistful smile curved her lips. "I was very small, but I especially remember the decorated Easter eggs called *pysanky*. They make something similar out of wood in Cleatia. So intricate and beautiful. But I don't see any of them here."

"We have some time. You can look around if you want." Cut the woman some slack, he thought. He didn't need to be such a hard-ass all the time.

Janna paused to look at a table of carved wooden bowls and leather purses. "The bowls definitely have Ukrainian designs, but not the bags," she said, picking up a red tote.

"These guys buy designer knockoffs," Simon said. Street vendors all over the city sold fake designer watches, bags and sunglasses. He'd forked over a ten for shades that afternoon.

The vendor—a tall, thin man with bags under his eyes big enough to rival his wares—ambled closer to Janna. "You like?" he said. And in a quieter voice, "Ve haf de labels."

Janna's brow pleated in confusion. "What do you mean?"

"De labels." He extracted a plastic box from beneath a cloth and opened it. "Ve haf de labels. You vant DKNY, Hermès, Prada. Ve haf. Stick on bag."

Sure enough, inside the box were faux brass tags with those

logos and more. Chanel, Coach, Gucci. To be matched to whatever bag the customer wanted with a hot-glue gun, also in the
box. Simon sucked in his cheeks to hold back the laughter that
bubbled up in his throat.

Color flared in Janna's cheeks. She stuck her chin in the air
and glared at the vendor. Witchy gray eyes glinting with steely
purpose behind her lenses, she shoved the tote into his arms.
"But that's ill—"

"Sorry, man. We gotta go now." Simon gripped her hand and
dragged her toward their destination. "Chill, Sergeant Friday.
We don't want an international incident. And we don't want to
draw attention."

If there'd been a cop around, she'd have hauled the uniform
over to the vendor. Simon winced at the possibility.

Behind them, the vendor shrugged and replaced the red bag
on his table. The two ATSA minders, expressions bland and un-
fazed, passed him.

"But…but," she sputtered, "that man had fake labels for
cheap bags. Piracy. It's against the law." She wrenched from
his grasp but continued to walk with him.

"Ah, who's he gonna hurt? No woman buying from a street
hawker thinks she's getting a real designer purse. A Gucci label
makes a woman without very much money feel good, and the
guy makes a living."

"But Simon, rip-offs like that are illegal because they cheat
the real designers."

"Big deal. So the big boys lose a few pennies."

"But we have to have laws and rules." She shook her guidebook at him in indignation.

"Yes, Ms. Strictly-by-the-Rules. And rules—"

"Are made to be broken. Or challenged." She finished his
usual line for him.

"Like old times," he said, enjoying her rare smile. "Our old
argument. Feels good to be friends again."

What a crock. As if they *could* be friends with him probing her. Ms. Strictly-by-the-Rules guilty of anything but loving her husband? Not a chance. Simon ached to ditch Raines's dirty suspicions.

What else he ached to do was hold her and inhale her subtle fragrance. Almond and woman. He wanted to press his lips to the soft skin of her temple.

But reality and orders he hated brought him up short.

He spotted the Danube on the next corner. They halted in front of the next-door deli, which was closing. The sandwich board being dragged inside by a stout waiter touted a stuffed-cabbage special. Aromas of cabbage and sauerkraut wafted out the open door.

"I'm ready to go talk to these guys," she said, coolly professional again. Then she bit her lower lip as if to bite back nerves. "Wharton said Gabe met with Roszca more than once. Maybe they can tell us more. And about Roszca's plans, of course."

"Look, I know Gabe was a great guy and all." The false words almost gagged him, but he had to start gently. "He was real competitive. Maybe he got into arms dealing for the money. There may have been a side to him you didn't know. You two had the fairy-tale marriage, but you gotta be prepared for—"

"Don't you worry about me." Her anger at the shady vendor was nothing compared to the fire she unleashed on him. Her eyes shot mercury darts at him. "Whatever Gabe was doing with Roszca, I can handle it. Now let's go inside and talk to the Cleatians, shall we?"

He raised his hands in defeat. She was tougher than she looked. He remembered the dignity and grace that had sustained her through Gabe's funeral. "I'm cool with that if you are. Activate the recorder whenever you're ready."

Recording the interview was meant to keep her honest, but for her sake, verifying her integrity was his plan.

Cheeks still pink with temper, she opened her purse to reach for the button on the mini-recorder, then stopped. "One more thing, Simon. Leave my marriage out of it. You have no idea what my marriage was like."

She jabbed the button and stormed past him into the dark-ened cavern of the Danube.

Janna couldn't believe she'd yelled at Simon that way. She immediately regretted blurting out that defensive line about her marriage. She didn't want to pique his curiosity. She inhaled deeply to clear her head.

New York had banned smoking in restaurants and bars, but other odors assaulted her in the murky atmosphere. Beer, vodka, tomatoes, a mélange of spices and more cabbage.

The Danube Bar had tables in the front and a bar in the dingy back. She anticipated a sleazy tavern, but the reality was more an Old World-style pub, the social hub of the neighborhood. Couples and families were socializing in groups. The singing usually started after midnight.

The press of her compact Sig Sauer P239 semiautomatic be-neath her arm reminded her that they weren't here to soak up the atmosphere. Her heart rate kicked as adrenaline pumped. She'd forgotten to be nervous about her first field assignment. All the anxiety about Gabe and working with Simon had con-sumed her. She needed to be focused and sharp, not distracted.

They wove through trestle tables with people laughing and talking across tables. Patrons drank coffee, beer and wine and ate cheese blintzes and apple cakes.

She noticed Simon peering at the sweets. They'd had din-ner, but his sweet tooth could always go for a pastry. She used to bring him cookies when she made them. She shunted aside the pang of regret and told herself to be happy that they'd agreed on a truce. Now maybe they could work in peace.

Their truce raised another hurdle for her—a challenge to maintain her barriers. She couldn't risk letting Simon see her troubles. He wouldn't understand, and she couldn't tolerate his revulsion.

She blinked away her worry and looked farther into the gloom. The bar area was dim, with dark woods and a small number of even darker looking clientele drooping over what looked like shots of vodka. The lone drinkers were here, after all.

Behind her, Simon said, "There's Tarlev in the corner."

She turned toward where he indicated. In a back booth, the hulking enforcer was a rooted tree trunk with a crown of red leaves. He sat with his back to the wall, like an old Western gunfighter or the modern gangster he was. He listened with a furrowed brow to the man across from him.

"Who's that with him? It's not Kravka." She remembered the man's long, greasy hair. This man was older and bald.

"Let's find out." Simon nudged her forward.

Tarlev looked up as the two of them approached. The bald man stood up and slipped away without giving them a glance.

"Dorka," Janna said, greeting Tarlev in his native Cleatian. "We appreciate you meeting with us tonight. Will your, um, colleague join us soon?"

Before she and Simon could take seats, Tarlev leaped to his feet faster than such a big man should be able to move.

"Nich, nich," he said, shaking his head emphatically. "Kravka is not coming. I can't stay. I have nothing to tell you. I must leave now."

On the videotape, the gangster had been expressionless, a mask of watchful protection. Now, anxiety pinched his forehead. Sweat trickled down his ruddy face. Fear radiated from him.

"What's he saying?" Simon turned to her in alarm.

She gave him a succinct summary, then asked Tarlev in Cleatian, "But why? This afternoon you promised you would answer some questions. We'll pay you."

"Nich! I cannot." He lowered his voice and added, "Talking to you is not worth my life."

Before she could press the hulking bodyguard further, he lumbered off through the maze of tables and people.

"Don't let him get away." Simon said, starting after him.

Janna stopped the recorder and jammed the guidebook in her purse as she raced after Simon.

A waiter bearing a tray of dirty crockery on his shoulder stopped to stare, but the vodka drinkers continued their bibulous meditation. A woman holding a tankard barked a rebuke in Ukrainian at Janna.

Outside, she found Simon looking for their quarry. Barhopping citizens blocked the sidewalk and the view.

Inside the bar, a strong tenor voice began a folk song in Cleatian.

Across the street, beside a vendor cart, the two ATSA backups threw down their cigarettes and pointed to the left. Simon nodded.

All four of them took off running.

Halfway down the block, Janna heard the loud report of a gunshot.

Chapter 4

At the tap, tap, tap from across the room, Simon opened one eye. He stretched. Yawned.

He'd gotten half his wish. He was still spending the night in the same room with Janna. But with a major change in plans. He was catching z's on a waiting-room sofa in the ICU, and she was hunched over her laptop. Fully clothed, dammit.

He rolled to a sitting position and scrubbed a hand over his stubbly chin. A bed of stable hay was more comfortable than this sofa that'd been used by Ali as a punching bag. "What time is it?"

"4:23." She didn't look up as her fingers flew over the keyboard.

Simon had dozed off after the thug named Tarlev had been wheeled from surgery into intensive care. The ATSA officers had found the man bleeding in an alley down the street from the Danube. Whoever'd shot him in the neck had vanished over a back fence. Either the shooter'd intended the wound as a warning, or he'd fired in a hurry when he heard feet beating toward him. Sooner than Simon had expected, the NYPD and an ambulance had arrived in a chorus of sirens.

The red-haired gangster had spilled a lot of blood, but it looked like he'd make it. Everything had happened so fast that Simon wasn't sure what hospital the ambulance had led them to. Bellevue, maybe. The room had plenty of industrial-grade upholstered chairs, two sofas, a bookcase stocked with children's games, Bibles and *Reader's Digest* magazines—things to keep worried families busy during anxious hours.

For the moment, only Simon and Janna were waiting for the wounded man to regain consciousness. Mascolo had promised to check in, but so far was a no-show.

He levered to his feet and found a restroom. A few minutes later, washed and refreshed, he returned to find Janna scowling at the blinking cursor. She'd hooked into an Internet port at a desk set in a wall niche.

Even Janna couldn't spend *this* much time on red tape. And how did she manage to look so great after a sleepless night? She'd pushed the phony glasses up on her head, giving her a rumpled look, like she'd just gotten out of bed. He'd watched her sleep. He knew. Damn.

Working with her without putting his hands—and more—on her was giving him the terminal hots.

Stifling his heated reaction, he said, "What we have to report won't fill three paragraphs. What the hell are you doing?" He flopped down on the chair beside her. Her unique scent barely penetrated the hospital miasma of antiseptic and medicinal odors, but he scooted closer anyway.

"Wasting my time." With a disgusted snort, she shut down the laptop and clicked the lid shut. Before she raised her gaze to Simon, she slid the glasses in place.

Wasting time? He'd never known her to fritter away a nanosecond. "Playing Battleship? Hearts?" When she gave him a disgusted look, he said, "Care to let me in on it?"

Janna leaned closer and whispered, "I was hacking into ATSA's personnel records."

A string of obscenities sprang to his tongue, but he swallowed them. "Going for Gabe's files? You're certifiably nuts! Don't you know—" But of course she did. This woman would give him an ulcer.

She shrugged, but her mouth was a taut line. "If I have a record of his assignments and travel, I can see if they match when Roszca was known to be in the U.S. Or if he had legitimate assignments."

"So why the long face?"

"I couldn't get past ATSA security. Don't worry. I didn't leave a calling card." She unplugged her computer and slipped it into the case.

He slumped back in his chair. Relief swept over him. Hacking into ATSA files could mean big trouble, even if she'd done nothing else. "I hope you're keeping track of all the rules we break."

The woeful look in her big gray eyes twisted a knife into his heart. "I just want the truth."

But her hacking hadn't worked. He straightened. "Wait a minute. The ultimate geek couldn't penetrate a firewall? With all those geek degrees, you were hobbled?"

"A BS in electrical engineering, a master's in computer engineering and nada."

"Hoo boy, Q, if *you* can't get in, ATSA's secrets are safe from the bad guys."

"What a relief." Sarcasm colored her words, but amusement danced in her eyes for the first time Simon had noticed in a long time. "But how will I find that information on Gabe without going through official channels and blowing secrecy?"

"No sweat. I'll share a Snickers bar with Sherry in Personnel." Worming a printout from her might take more than candy, but Janna didn't need that much information. The idea of hitting on Sherry didn't grab him as much as it should. Damned weird. He must be getting old.

"But won't she wonder why you're asking about Gabe?"

"I'll tell her it's for a memorial. I'll be cool."

"I know. They all do whatever Simon says. You charm—"

"Okay, kids, you're on." Officer Mascolo rushed into the room and stopped behind Janna. He placed his hands on her shoulders. "Tarlev's awake and asking for 'agent voman.'"

Janna leaped to her feet, neatly ducking away from the New York operative's light grasp. Her eyes widened with fear and her cheeks paled.

Did she think Mascolo might've heard their conversation?

Her lashes fluttered. She bent to pick up her laptop case as she collected her composure. "Oh, that's great. So he can talk okay?" The breathy pitch of her voice betrayed emotion.

Mascolo had the look of a man who'd been shot down. Simon ran his tongue around his teeth to hide a grin. She'd ducked away from somebody besides him. Electric zings of pleasure darted through him.

The other man slugged his hands in the pockets of his dress slacks. "Uh, yeah, he can talk, but it ain't English. And he sounds like a rusty chainsaw."

Simon and Janna followed Mascolo into the ICU hub. A nurse station with banks of electronics dominated the center of the room. Small single-patient alcoves ringed the hub, equipped with monitoring devices connected to the central station. High tech, thought Simon. Janna'd probably like a look at that stuff.

Mascolo led them to a room on the other side of the hub.

Blinking and beeping monitors surrounded Tarlev's bed. IVs dripped medication and blood into his left arm. White bandages swathed his neck and shoulders in unfinished mummy wrappings.

Janna flicked on the tiny recorder and spoke to Tarlev in Cleatian.

His answer was part whisper, part creaky gate. The doctor said his vocal cords suffered no real damage, but were swollen from trauma to the throat.

Simon saw sympathy soften Janna's eyes, heard comfort in words he couldn't understand. Seeing this man immobilized and pale with pain evidently tugged at her maternal instincts.

He was a gangster, a tough pug who took money to beat up people on a regular basis—or eliminate them. He'd probably killed his bosses' enemies. No sympathy plucked at Simon's heartstrings, but the soothing ripple of Janna's voice made his whole body clench.

He knew the tape would be translated afterward. Raines had insisted, as a backup. Simon trusted Janna, but he wanted answers. Now. After the wounded man replied, he could wait no longer. "What's he saying?"

She turned to him. "He says he doesn't know much. I think he's still afraid."

Simon sighed. "Dammit. Offer him protection. Anything. Roszca's pals would've killed him whether he talked to us or not. They'll try again."

She explained to Tarlev in Cleatian.

Watery blue eyes flickered from her to Simon and back. *"Dak,"* he agreed, apparently satisfied with the offer. Simon understood that much.

Janna listened intently to the rest of his raspy speech. Then she put up a hand to stop him and translated. "He says he owes them nothing after what they did. But he wants us to find Kravka because they'll kill him, too."

"We can try. No guarantees. Mascolo?"

The New York operative shrugged. "I can check a few places. Talk to the NYPD or the Feebs."

Simon turned back to Janna. "Our guy looks like he's fading. Find out what you can before he passes out." He handed her the surveillance photos.

He watched as she showed the photos to the gangster, whose eyes lowered to half mast. Her hand trembled when she came to her husband's picture. Simon understood little, but caught the only other Cleatian word he knew—*nich,* no. Tarlev didn't know Gabe. He had few words to say about any of them.

After more questions and halting answers in Cleatian, they left the man drifting into sleep and returned to the waiting room.

"What'd you get?" Simon hated to sound impatient, but he was beat and they needed a break in this mess.

Janna chewed her lip and frowned. Her smoky eyes were bleak as a winter sky when she raised them. "He didn't know names for any of the men in the pictures—except for Roszca and Wharton, of course."

He knew she'd hoped for something more about Gabe—anything. There was no comforting her about that, whether or not Mascolo was looking on curiously. "Anything else?"

"The name of Roszca's hideout, but not where it is."

"Yeah?"

"A place called Isla Alta."

The next afternoon, Janna slotted her Prius hatchback in its space and cut the engine. She sagged with tiredness; her head buzzed with questions and her insides quivered with anxiety.

She'd accustomed herself to people's casual touches to the point where she could breathe normally and her chest didn't tighten. But being with Simon and discovering Gabe on that tape had revived all the turmoil she'd fought to calm during the past several months. When the New York operative put his hands on her, she'd gone into fight-or-flight mode, as though a bear had attacked her. She had to defeat her fear of being trapped so she could feel normal again.

Thank goodness it was Sunday. She could stitch herself together before reporting to the AD. She lifted her weekend suitcase and briefcase from the hatchback, locked up and traipsed from the garage building, across the commons to her townhouse condominium.

She'd driven to the airport, but usually the car sat right where it was, and she took the subway to work downtown from the Takoma Metro stop only a block away from the condo complex.

Gabe had insisted they drive to and from Virginia every day. Subways were for the peons and the tourists, he'd said. She'd commuted by subway before her marriage and liked being part of the city's dynamic life, not isolated in a luxury sedan and a sterile, gated community.

As soon as she sold the pseudo mansion suburban house Gabe had chosen, she moved into this older section of the city. The condo complex was new, but designed to blend in. And all around her spread the comfort of a real neighborhood with tree-lined streets and old brick houses, each one different. She loved Takoma Park, with its parks, eclectic shops, restaurants and farmer's market.

"Hi, Janna! Glad you finally did something other than work. Have a nice weekend?" Deena Blair jogged up to join her. The energetic woman lived a few doors down from Janna and worked at the National Institutes of Health.

Janna couldn't disclose that she'd been working and didn't want to disappoint her friend. "I did. Good to get away. How were things here?"

Six feet tall and the color of coffee ice cream but warm as caramel, Deena slowed her pace to match Janna's. Her shorts and shirt in day-glo orange flashed as bright as a traffic light. "Same old, same old. Your kitty meowed pitifully, but I fed him the amount you said. No more."

"Rocky would eat all day. Thanks for taking care of him."

"No prob." A sudden smile woke dimples in her cheeks. "Gotta get going before I cool off too much. Join me?"

Janna gestured to her bags. "Maybe tomorrow." The two

women often jogged together. Janna had taken up running to train for her ATSA advancement. On days she couldn't run, she swam at the nearby health club.

Jogging in place, Deena said, "Oh, new owner just moved into the townhouse across from you. Hunky single guy. You should take him some welcome-to-the-condo cookies."

Deena was constantly trying to fix Janna up with men. Janna grinned and shook her head. "Maybe *you* should."

The other woman rolled her eyes. "Girlfriend, you're hopeless." She waved and jogged off down the sidewalk toward the Maryland line and Sligo Creek Park.

Not hopeless, just in control, Janna asserted.

And she would stay that way. As soon as she could straighten out the mess Gabe had left behind. As soon as she could level off whatever relationship she now had with Simon.

The slam of a neighbor's door jerked her back to reality. Gabe was dead. She was free and independent. And safe.

And she'd stay that way.

She tugged her rolling suitcase up the brick walkway and opened her door. Tapping in the security code, she called, "Mama's home."

"Mrrr," came a plaintive voice from the living room.

Janna knelt to caress the raccoon-brown tabby that ambled over to rub himself against her.

"There you are, Rocky Raccoon. I'll feed you, and then you can help me unpack."

Crooked tail twitching with anticipation, the feline followed her into the kitchen.

An hour later, as soon as she'd stowed the suitcase in her bedroom closet, she dialed the phone.

"Hi, Janna. Just checking in?" said the cheerful voice when she identified herself.

"Dr. French," Janna said. "I'm so glad you're there."

The phone was a secure land line. Janna had swept the entire apartment. ATSA demanded it, and her tech experience made it part of her natural routine.

"I told you to phone Sunday night. How'd you get along working with Simon?"

Janna emitted her relief with a whoosh of breath. Tears welled. She finally had someone she could confide in. Dr. Marah French was her counselor. ATSA's secrets as well as hers were safe with her. Janna had done a background check before beginning to see the psychologist.

Her office appointments had dwindled to occasional ones, but the two women talked on the phone often. Dr. French's support and encouragement had bolstered her strength to leave Gabe. She needed another hefty dose of courage.

Janna stretched out on her bed. Rocky leaped up beside her, contorted his sinewy body and began washing his chest. She reached out to scratch between his silky ears.

"Simon is only one of my problems." Where should she begin? "There have been other...developments."

"Go ahead. What happened?" Dr. French's warm voice conveyed confidence and caring.

Janna couldn't tell her all the facts, even though Dr. French would hold it all in confidence. How could she reveal what she'd begged Simon to keep secret? Having the warmth of her cat tucked against her side made it easier. "Gabe's connected to this op, to the man arrested in New York. Something he was involved in just before he died."

The psychologist said, "You must've been so shocked."

"Sickened is more like it. I still feel off balance, as if I just stumbled out of a carnival fun house where all the floors and walls are askew and nothing is as it seems. Dammit, I spent the last year putting him behind me." She might never recover from the impact of seeing her husband on a tape with an international criminal.

"And how did you manage with Simon?" Dr. French knew all about her ambivalence in that department.

"Simon was a rock." If Simon hadn't been there with her, she couldn't have gotten through the weekend. What would some other operative have said? Or done? She shuddered.

"I'm going to put you on the spot, Janna," said the woman. "Why are you still keeping Gabe's pathological control and abuse secret? Especially from your family and your friend Simon?"

Her heart pounded with throbbing force and she drew a deep breath. She asked herself that question constantly. Why? "Too many reasons. How could I more than a year after his death? People wouldn't believe me. They saw only the heroic side of him, the Dr. Jekyll side. And telling people would bring back all the anger and pain—"

"And shame?"

Janna couldn't reply with tears clogging her throat.

Dr. French continued, "After all our talks and the articles I know you've read, you still blame yourself for what *he* did. You made the choice to break free. You had the courage to leave your abuser."

Only she didn't leave. He died, and she didn't have to go through with it. Fate had allowed her to avoid the horrors that other women suffered when their husbands pursued them, stalked them. "Yes, and I don't want to go there again."

When she dated Gabe, he'd been the perfect gentleman, the prince every woman longs to find. He'd looked past the social-ite history and the brainy geek to the woman beneath. He seemed to respect her work and treated her as an equal.

Until after the wedding. Then he changed. Her marriage slid from a giddy peak of new love to confusion and humiliation down to a pit of fear.

Gabe loved her so much he wanted her all to himself, he said. He isolated her from friends. He pulled strings so she worked only in the lab, never away from ATSA headquarters. She had to account for all of her time and every dollar spent. He claimed he did it to strengthen their bond as a loving couple.

Trying to find ways to convince Gabe to relax the bars he built around them, she went along at first. If she challenged him in any way, he made her feel guilty or down on herself. She was smart, a brilliant technical mind, her parents and her professors had said. She'd solved complex problems in the classroom and the ATSA lab. She ought to be able to solve her marital problems the same way.

None of her strategies helped. Not talks to Gabe the stone wall, not advice from marriage manuals.

Not even sex. But that was another story.

When she began to fear him, she sought counseling. Finally, after a year, she saw no option but to leave. She had just packed two suitcases and parked them by the front door when Simon arrived. She lied that they were a clothing donation for charity. When he told her the news of Gabe's death, she burst into sobs that Simon had interpreted as grief.

Instead, her tears had sprung from guilty relief.

Marah French's gentle voice reeled her from her thoughts. "Janna, you're not my typical client. You're more educated and stronger in many ways than most. You dealt with the trauma intellectually, but emotionally, you haven't faced the reality or its toll on your life. Beginning with one person would be a start. You need Simon's help. Why not tell him?"

Janna uttered a bitter laugh. "Simon's strong and honorable, but he wouldn't understand." He'd want to go to the AD right away and avoid conducting a private investigation. She needed to know the truth first. Truth would build the foundation of strength she'd need if they learned the worst.

"Won't the abuse come out in an investigation of Gabe?"

"I don't know. Maybe. Yes. If there's an investigation. I can handle it if I know ahead of time."

"If Gabe crossed the line, there'd be no Dr. Jekyll—only Mr. Hyde," Dr. French suggested. "Perhaps he fooled everyone. People will be understanding."

Of his control and abuse of her, she meant. "I never thought of it that way."

But nothing would absolve her guilt for allowing the abuse to happen. Nothing would prevent her from having to face pity and revulsion in people's eyes. And nothing would rid her of the shameful memories.

"I want you to think about telling Simon. You'll feel better if you do. But it's your choice, as always."

As soon as Janna said good-bye, the doorbell chimed.

Simon.

They planned to search through Gabe's effects tonight.

She gave the cat a final caress as she rose from the bed.

Rocky complained vociferously at being abandoned.

"Yowl one for me too, baby. From one emotional wringer to the next."

Chapter 5

"Nice place." Simon scoped out Janna's living room. Her new digs resembled the old about as much as a pony did a Clydesdale. Except this pony had class.

"Thanks," she said from the kitchen side of the serving bar, where she was preparing iced tea. She wore pressed jeans and a black T-shirt with the saying There Are Only 10 Kinds of People in the World: Those Who Understand Binary and Those Who Don't. He didn't get the geekspeak, but liked how the words mapped the contour of her breasts.

This was more like the old Janna—except for the damned dark-rimmed glasses. Armor or a mask?

He wandered around the room. Simple furniture in neutral colors, soothing against brick-red walls. Not too many of the puffy pillows most women liked to pile everywhere.

On the walls, paintings of the villages and mountains in Eastern Europe. Escher stylized geometric prints of fish and flowers. Both worked together. Both suited her.

A tall bookcase displayed a wide range of interests—biographies, romances, geek textbooks with titles he couldn't pronounce. Family photos—Janna with a tall, elegant couple—separated the book sections. "These your parents?"

"Yes, the newest ones were taken when I visited them last year in Prague."

No pictures of Gabe.

No wedding pictures of the happy couple. No honeymoon snapshots. Nothing.

Before he could ponder that omission, the next shelf surprised him. "Kids' books?"

"My grandmother started collecting the classics for me. She was afraid I wouldn't know them because I was living abroad."

Classics in older editions. He read the titles aloud. "*The Secret Garden, Treasure Island, Misty of Chincoteague.* I read *Treasure Island,* but *X-Men* is more my style." Unusual collection for a high-tech woman. A complex woman.

"No surprise to me, but I like *X-Men*, too." The clink of ice in glasses announced that the tea was ready.

He'd seen her house only once before—when Gabe died. That humongous McMansion could hold three of this one, not that this was a cold-water flat.

"Smaller than your Virginia house, but very nice," he added, as he returned to lean on the polished-granite countertop.

Janna handed him a glass of iced tea with lemon and two spoons of sugar, just the way he liked it. In spite of all her troubles, she took time to remember. A warm little bud sprouted in his chest, but he pinched it off before he could say anything stupid.

She sipped her iced tea and smiled. "I know what you're thinking, but Gabe had an insurance policy. That and the other house netted me enough for this, plus investments. Besides, that place was more his than mine. All those rooms echoed."

Echoed with reminders of *him.* Even if the guy was dirty,

she still loved him, Simon figured. No matter what excuses she gave him, he felt responsible for Gabe's death. That reality would gnaw at him for a long time. He glumly gulped down his iced tea. "No, I like it. Comfortable, livable, not a museum."

He got a smile out of her for that one. Small victory.

Small talk and home decor weren't why he was here. A search through Gabe's possessions ought to yield something incriminating. He'd settle for damned near anything. It didn't have to be a smoking gun. Or a confession.

Janna had nothing to do with whatever Gabe did. No way.

He wanted this spy gig over with, for her sake. And his. So he didn't feel dirty for snooping for ATSA. So he could get on with bringing down Roszca. So he didn't have to face the temptation of her day after day.

He set down his empty glass. "Ready to get to work, Q?"

She halted her glass halfway to her mouth, paused and then set it down. "I made myself wait for you. I want help and a witness. Everything's in the den." She whisked out of the U-shaped kitchen and turned left down a short hall. "This way."

To Simon, den meant fireplace, leather recliner and deep-pile carpet. Hers had the carpet, but instead of a recliner, she'd jammed three walls with components that blinked at them. "Q, you have enough electronic gear to outfit the NSA."

"A woman needs her hobbies," Janna replied. "I just got two new Zelman peripherals, a VGA Heatsink and their silent 400W power supply. I prefer listening to the newest Green Day download than the CPU hum."

Simon had no clue what she was talking about, but the enthusiasm in her voice heated his blood. "Right."

The bay window in the back wall looked out on an enclosed patio. A large mottled-brown cat lay sprawled out on the sunny window seat. Totally unimpressed with the intruders, the animal yawned before settling back into its nap.

"I've never seen a cat that big."

"I got him at the shelter. Rocky's about two years old. A Maine coon cat," Janna said. "He weighs 20 pounds, but when he snoozes on your lap, it feels like 50."

"Moby Cat." He grinned, but she was already cross-legged on the floor beside their afternoon's work.

His heart thudded. Disappointment rankled, but he should know better. Not the time to try his light-bulb riddle again. He really had to cut out the kidding around and stick with professional. Being pals wouldn't fly, and she wanted nothing from him but his help.

On the deep-green carpet sat four boxes stamped with official inspection seals and striped with tape remnants.

"ATSA sent the boxes back to me after they checked out the contents of Gabe's desk at our house. I removed bank statements, insurance and tax stuff, but I didn't bother with anything else beyond a cursory look." She untucked the folded flaps on the first box.

"Did he bring work home much?" Simon opened a second box.

"Never, as far as I know." She stiffened as if remembering something unwanted. An odd emotion that wasn't quite sorrow darkened her eyes behind the clear lenses. "But I didn't know what Gabe's desk contained. It was sacrosanct. He locked the drawers and allowed no one access."

"Not even his wife?" Simon remembered Gabe as a stickler for privacy. Maybe he had a reason beyond ATSA security.

"Not even. Gabe kept track of the finances, the checking account. Everything."

So Mr. Perfect was a damned control freak. But he said only, "Our business makes you paranoid about security."

She didn't reply and focused her attention on a trio of manila folders banded together.

Taking her cue, Simon dug into his box.

* * *

An hour later, the two of them had examined every box and file, every receipt and index card. And found nothing incriminating. Or exonerating. Just typical desk junk.

Janna sighed in exasperation. She prayed to find the answer to why Gabe had dyed his hair and met with the notorious Viktor Roszca.

"No calendar. No PDA or day planner," Simon said as he finished. "ATSA must've kept it as a security risk."

Janna nodded distractedly as she lifted a book from the last box. "What's this doing in here? I've been searching for it ever since I moved."

"What'd you find?"

"My copy of *Heidi*. I couldn't figure out why it wasn't with the other books when I unpacked."

"Your children's collection? Why would Gabe have kept *Heidi* in his desk?"

Another example of his control. She suppressed a shudder. "He didn't approve. He thought the collection was frivolous, silly. *Heidi* is my most valuable one, the only first edition."

"But why would he take it and hide it." His comment wasn't a question, but a deliberation. He scrubbed his knuckles over his shadowed chin. "May I see the book?" He held out a hand.

"What are you going to do?" Anxious for her prized possession, she clutched the volume against her breasts.

"I'll be careful. I just want to look at it."

"I'd have detected a bug." Janna handed over the book with reluctance. "You think it's booby-trapped or something?"

"Or something." He leafed through the book, but she saw that he took care not to bend or tear the fragile pages.

A taut wire of tension stretched between them as he continued paging. Janna bit her lower lip and gripped her hands tightly in her lap.

Finally, he came to the last numbered pages. "These two are stuck together."

"No. Or they shouldn't be." Janna lifted the book from his hands. She rubbed her fingers over the double thickness, peered at the edges and frowned. Her pulse kicked up a notch, the hairs on the nape of her neck rising in anticipation. "Something's sealed between them. Another piece of paper, I think."

Simon pushed to his feet and offered a hand. "It's your book. How do we separate those pages?"

She was getting used to his casual touches without an automatic fear reaction, so she allowed him to help her to her feet. "Steam. The teakettle won't take long to heat up."

Meowing, Rocky followed them to the kitchen. He twined around Janna's feet as she turned the heat on beneath the kettle. "You had your supper, Mr. Piggy. Cool your jets."

The cat twitched his tail and leaped up to the counter to glare at Simon, the apparent reason for his owner's rejection.

"Sorry, buddy," Simon said, stroking between his tufted ears. "She's cut you off. Not my fault."

Janna managed a small smile at the sight of Simon's big hand on her pet's sleek fur. And at the coon cat's reaction. Rocky purred and pushed his head into the hand. "I didn't know you liked cats."

He shrugged. "The stables at Pimlico had several cats. Some friendlier than others. I guess Gabe didn't like cats."

"He didn't like animals—period. Said they were dirty." Now why did she blurt that out? She felt too comfortable with Simon. He made it too easy to reveal too much. Shifting the conversation, she said, "I wonder what kind of glue it is."

He nodded toward the open book on the counter. "So I can assume *you* didn't do the gluing?"

Janna blinked at him in surprise when she caught his sarcastic tone. For once, she couldn't respond in kind to his dark humor and cocky attitude. "It must've been Gabe. I can't imagine why ATSA security would tamper with my book. Why, Simon? What could be hidden in there?"

The teakettle's shriek made them both jump.

"Unless you're clairvoyant, Q, there's only one way to find out."

In a few moments, steam softened the glue. Janna carried the book to the granite counter. She felt Simon's keen gaze as she plied her thinnest, sharpest kitchen knife to the paper edges. With careful precision, she peeled the two pages apart. Inside lay a folded sheet of thin paper.

"Don't touch it," Simon said. "I'll get my evidence kit."

For the first time, Janna noticed he'd brought his courier bag. He returned with latex gloves, tweezers and a plastic bag.

After they donned the gloves, he said, "Go on."

"It's tissue paper. With writing on it." She couldn't stop her hand from trembling as she lifted out the paper with the tweezers. Dread weighted her heart. Whatever Gabe had hidden wouldn't contain good news. Proof of his guilt meant divulging everything to Raines. And the risk that she couldn't continue to conceal her failed marriage.

Together, they used tweezers to unfold the paper. Janna slipped the letter into the evidence bag and sealed it before beginning to read it.

Simon shifted his feet. "What does it say? I hope to hell it's not in Cleatian or some other damned obscure language."

She unfolded the page and her gaze raced down the writing. "It's a letter. In Gabe's handwriting. To me."

Gnawing on her lower lip, she began to read.

Simon's fingers itched to grab the paper, but seeing the message first was her right. Was it Gabe's last will and testament? A confession? Evidence against Roszca?

What?

He saw Janna's face crumple. A sob tore from her throat. The thin paper in its plastic bag floated to the floor like a tiny parachute as she buried her face in her hands.

"What is it, Janna? What's wrong?" Her distress unnerved him, slipped inside his chest and squeezed. He reached out to her. Uncertain whether touching her was a good idea, he let his hands hover above her shoulders.

She shoved her glasses to the top of her head and swiped a hand across her eyes. The raw emotion—grief, anger, alarm—sparking from her flint-gray gaze set Simon back a step. "Damn him! Damn the bastard!"

She looked around frantically, then grabbed the lemon she'd sliced earlier and heaved it against the wall. The soft fruit shattered with what Simon hoped was a satisfying splat.

The big coon cat dived off the counter and disappeared with a yowl not very different from his owner's.

"Janna?" Simon scooped the all-important paper from the floor.

Fists clenched, she trembled with the rage and adrenaline that swept through her. "Gabe is guilty, Simon. He sold arms and dealt with Roszca. God knows what else he did."

He poured her a glass of iced tea and pressed her down onto the kitchen stool. Then he read the damning letter.

To my darling wife:
    If you are reading this, it means I am dead. A certain business associate has eliminated me. He pressures me too much. You don't need to know who or why, only that I have provided for you. I intended this fund for the two of us, for our future. If you hear rumors, remember I did it all for us.
    Contact Privatbank, Sarnen AG, Zurich, Switzerland. Speak only to Edouard La Casse. Give him my name and password: Hornblower.
    Yours always, your loving husband,
    Gabriel

Gabe was wrong. Roszca—if that's who he meant—didn't kill him. He died before any of his so-called associates could. *Why* was another question. "Damn. A Swiss bank account."

Swiss. Hidden in *Heidi.* And *Hornblower.* Gabriel blowing his horn. Too freaking cute. Controlling and greedy son of a bitch. Simon swallowed that and a more blistering comment.

"Blood money." Janna blew her nose on a paper napkin. Tears welled in her eyes and her nose was pink. " *'For the two of us.'* He did it all *'for us.'* That's a lie. Simon, I didn't know, I swear. I wouldn't have wanted..." She broke down in gulping sobs.

This time, he followed his instinct and enfolded her shaking shoulders.

She stiffened, then moved unresisting into his arms. Nearly his height, she buried her face in his neck.

Her warm tears soaked his T-shirt, slid past his boundary rules and right into his bloodstream. He savored her almond fragrance. The subtle throbbing at her damp temple. The ivory temptation of her skin. Need flared in him with heat like he'd never felt before.

New instincts prodded him. Unwanted primitive urges of protection and possession swamped him.

But she clung to him in her grief and anger. He could no more push her away than he could pilot her state-of-the-art electronics. He drew in a slow, careful breath and let it out. Then another. Until his traitorous arousal eased.

"He was the agency's hero. I thought—" Her muffled voice punched him in the heart.

"You didn't know, Janna. He betrayed you. He betrayed ATSA. And maybe his country." Trying to soothe her anguish, he massaged slow circles across her back. Anger and relief swarmed inside him. If he had Gabriel Harris here, the man would wish he was dead again. But thank God they'd found definite proof of Janna's innocence.

She knew nothing about her husband's moonlighting. In fact, Simon realized, she knew little of what Gabe did, neither clandestine activities nor ATSA assignments. He'd locked her out of his desk, managed the finances and kept her in the dark about everything.

He was the agency's hero. Damned odd way to phrase it. Hadn't Gabe been her hero, too? She had no pictures of him around. Granted, her bedroom could be lined with them.

Or was her marriage not the happily-ever-after he'd thought?

Janna blew her nose in her wad of tissues. Sniffling back the last of her tears, she raised her head, but didn't move away. Around eyes dark with defeat and dread, crystal droplets spiked her lashes. "Damn him! Damned—" She wagged her head and looked upward as though searching for the right epithet.

"Damned hacker," Simon finished for her.

A trembling smile lifted the corners of her mouth. "Oh, Simon, only you could make me smile at a time like this. Yes, he's a damned hacker." She paused, her watery gaze skimming his features. "Thank you."

"Anytime." Her eyes glistened like wet slate, her moist, pink lips tempted. He ought to let her go, but she made no effort to pull away. Her mouth, only inches away, beckoned. He brushed a kiss on her lips. Then another.

She didn't kiss him back, but she didn't resist, allowing him to taste her sweetness. Just closed lips, but a taste like no other, sunshine and midnight—the light and heat of the sun and the dark seduction of night. Fire surged through his veins and his body clenched.

He'd wanted to find evidence so he could get away from her, and here he was holding her and wanting more. Damn.

The longing that welled up scared the hell out of him. Unable to resist one last taste, he pressed his lips to hers before forcing himself to stop.

He saw her eyes widen as reality hit. Crimson crept up her cheeks. She jammed the glasses back on her face. "Oh. Simon. I…"

Oh, hell, now what do I do?

Stepping away with a cocky swagger, he opted for the light touch. After all, it was only a kiss.

"Thought that'd snap you out of your funk, Q." He hoisted the incriminating letter. "What do we do with this?"

The next morning, Janna and Simon briefed Raines in his office. Janna listened, hands in a white-knuckle grip in her lap, as Simon recounted their interviews in New York. She sat at attention while he slouched in his chair with his ankles crossed. His T-shirt of the day was marginally respectable, sporting a University of Maryland terrapin.

After practically throwing herself into Simon's arms yesterday, she could barely bring herself to face him.

The last-straw emotional blow had broken the backbone of her essential rule. Not only had she practically thrown herself into his arms, but she'd also allowed him to kiss her. She who couldn't tolerate anyone's touch without cringing had held on to him as the life raft in her flood of tears.

Worse, she'd liked the kiss.

Liked the light rasp of his whiskers, the resilient softness of his lips and the security of his arms around her.

And wanted more.

Inside, needs that she thought desiccated and buried had bloomed. Shock had frozen her initial response, but if he'd continued, she'd have kissed him back.

This morning, if things went as she wanted them to, she and Simon would continue to work together. She'd need strength not to break her rule again, to ignore her attraction to him, to avoid any intimacy with him.

Especially him.

She tuned in to Simon's report as his narrative arrived at the boxes from Gabe's desk. Janna had insisted on sharing everything with Raines.

He withdrew a copy of the letter from his bag. She'd let him take the original to the FBI for analysis. As a smaller agency, ATSA used the Bureau's evidence lab.

"The original had Gabriel Harris's prints all over it," Simon said as he slid it across the desktop.

She watched Raines's eyes for a reaction as he read the letter. As expected, the enigmatic assistant director betrayed no emotion.

Placing the sheet of paper on the polished mahogany surface, the AD scrutinized her for a long moment. His penetrating dark-blue stare unnerved her, but she held his gaze. "Tech Officer Harris, I'm greatly relieved your husband did not involve you in any of his criminal activities."

Simon's slow and almost-suppressed exhalation sounded like relief. When Janna glanced at him, his gaze shot down to the other papers in his lap.

The truth clicked.

And stung.

She glared at Raines. "You suspected me."

The AD steepled his fingers together. "We had to be sure about you, Janna."

"Did you know about Gabe all along? The tape. Of course. Now I see why no one in the New York office seemed to recognize him on the tape. They were in on this, too."

Raines shook his head. "New York was not in on anything. They seem oblivious. The hair dye must've altered his appearance enough for that."

The AD had sent her to view the tape to discover her reaction—

and her actions afterward. A knot twisted tightly in her stomach at what might've happened. Good God, she'd nearly incriminated herself by covering it up. If she and Simon hadn't searched the boxes, ATSA would continue to suspect her. Simon...

Then the rest of the data completed the equation. A tremor racked her body, and the other people seemed to recede. Isolation and helplessness swamped her, swirled in her head. Before Gabe, she'd have understood. She'd have accepted the agency's need to check her out. And Simon's complicity. But a year of life out of her control—of disillusionment and betrayal—had dented her and shredded her confidence.

Waves of emotion built up in her chest and rose to clutch at her throat. She had to take back control now.

She shot to her feet. "Simon, you, too? Spying on me?"

He adjusted his leather jacket and slung an arm over the chair back. His mouth quirked in cocky acknowledgment. "I had orders, Janna. I knew you hadn't done anything. But I didn't know what we'd find in New York or what Gabe might have done."

She'd asked Simon to put his job on the line to help her find out the truth about what Gabe had done, but his orders had allowed him to play along with her. ATSA had given him carte blanche. His manipulation wasn't close to what Gabe had done. She knew that, but swallowing it was bitter.

At least, Simon's betrayal enabled her to adhere to her personal rules with no temptation where he was concerned. She firmed her chin. Later, she could bawl her eyes out. At the moment, she needed professional calm. She adjusted her glasses and straightened her shoulders.

"I'm obviously not happy about ATSA suspecting me, but I understand." She deliberately addressed Raines and avoided looking at Simon. "Are the tape and letter all the evidence you have on Gabe?"

"Almost." The AD scowled at the letter. "The letter's cryptic enough, protecting himself in case someone other than you found it. But an investigation has confirmed my suspicions. In a couple of big ATF cases Harris worked on, large caches of arms stolen from military bases were never found. Some of those weapons turned up in illegal sales a few months after he met with Roszca. Unfortunately, his demise presented us with a dead end, so to speak."

Janna reeled in shock, pressing her fingertips to her throbbing temples. "That means Gabe must've hidden those arms himself. He set everything up years ahead."

"His file says he joined the ATF after not getting a partnership in a big law firm," Raines said. "Then it appears he found a new way to make money. He used his contacts in the ATF and ATSA to set up business on the other side of the law."

"He had to show his family he was doing well. To Gabe, status and success meant money and the ostentatious display of wealth."

"The Lexus sedan. The house in Virginia."

She nodded. "I didn't think we could afford that monstrosity. But he insisted. Now I know why. He had hidden assets." No wonder he'd demanded control of their finances.

"Have you contacted the Swiss bank?" the AD asked.

Since sleep had eluded her as usual, she'd phoned at three o'clock, nine o'clock Zurich time. "Once I gave Gabe's password, Mr. La Casse was most sympathetic to the bereaved widow." She couldn't prevent an edge of bitterness on her words. "The account has a little over three million dollars."

Simon and the AD both whistled.

"Our boy was busy," Raines said.

"Harris is dead," Simon said to him. "What will you do? Will you expose a hero's crimes?"

More than Simon, Janna understood the ramifications of revealing Gabe's treason. Others in the ATSA and the U.S. would be shocked. There'd probably be an internal investigation to find out how it could've happened.

But that wasn't the worst for her. If his crimes came out, she would be suspected by everyone, no matter what Raines said about her innocence. She wanted none of Gabe's taint. Having her private shame exposed would be bad enough. She would turn over his dirty money to the government as soon as possible. But she needed to do more.

What she really wanted was to demonstrate her loyalty and honesty.

Whether Simon investigated Gabe or pursued Roszca, that meant working with him.

Chapter 6

"ATSA still wants Roszca. I want to help get him," Janna said. "Let me show everyone that I had nothing to do with Gabe's illegal deals."

Simon had to admire her courage. Standing in front of Raines's desk in her nun wear pantsuit, she radiated determination and indignation. Her passionate plea kindled a hot response in his body and had his pulse jumping like a frolicking foal.

"Unnecessary. Your innocence is already proven," he said, indicating the letter. This woman who fired his blood was the last partner he wanted in his quest for Roszca.

Too much of a distraction.

Too much of a reminder of his failure.

She looked at him like he was something just shoveled out of a stable. He felt about that low. Lower. Spying on her was the least of it. She might not be in this vise if he hadn't introduced her to her traitor husband.

Another spike in his heart.

"It's not enough," she said. "I've worked hard to advance in my work, in my position in ATSA. Any hint of suspicion will ruin that. Too many people will connect me with his crimes unless I help clear up the remaining questions."

"I'll take your offer into consideration," Raines said.

Simon saw Janna's gaze shutter as she realized the subject was closed. Still on her feet, she waited quietly, chewing her lower lip, contemplating. He nearly grinned. That cyberbrain never stopped. She wasn't giving up.

The AD's gaze opaque and unreadable, he steepled his fingers again. "And you're right, Janna. There are remaining questions. ATSA has an additional reason for grabbing Roszca. We need to know more about Harris's activities."

Simon understood immediately. "The letter hints at pressure. You suspect Roszca wanted more than arms."

"If he knew Harris was ATSA, he'd have pushed for information."

Janna dropped into her seat. Her complexion paled to the color of putty. "ATSA information? *Government secrets?*"

"The fun just keeps rolling." Simon shook his head in disgust. "So you intend to keep any suspicions about Harris under wraps until we tie up all the threads?" he asked the AD.

"I don't want a witch-hunt. No questions left unanswered. No glaring headlines. But it's only a matter of time before some officer recognizes Harris on that tape or picks up intel about him. We need to bring in Roszca without delay."

"I plan to trace one of our leads this morning," Simon said. "The location of this Isla Alta where he's holed up."

"We have one more source of information—the other Cleatian knee breaker, Kravka," Janna added. "Has New York picked him up yet?"

Raines stood, indicating the end of their meeting. "In a way."

His dry tone offered no optimism. "Early this morning, the NYPD pulled his body out of the East River."

Out of the corner of her eye, Janna spied Simon by the open lab door. The hour was late and everyone else in the lab had gone home. She'd avoided him for four days and still couldn't quite shake the anger and hurt bruising her soul.

She continued adjusting the settings on the audio scanner in front of her while she waited for him to spot her. He would have to make the first move.

He hesitated, as if he suspected she might've set up booby traps. As he surveyed the room, his expression matched the darkness of his shadowed chin. In stonewashed jeans, his leather jacket and a T-shirt that read I Left Home for This? he looked as disreputable and delicious as ever. She could kick herself for reacting to his masculine appeal.

Talking to Dr. French had helped her work through the initial sting of Simon's deception. Being under suspicion had thrown her back into the same helpless frustration and isolation she'd experienced with Gabe's obsessive control.

Intellectually, she acknowledged that what Simon had done was part of his job. Her emotions took another stand.

If any other ATSA officer had been her partner, she wouldn't have felt so manipulated and misled. But Raines had sent her with Simon, who'd been her friend and very nearly more. Janna'd admitted to Dr. French—and to herself—her hypersensitivity to Simon.

She needed his support to convince the AD to assign her to the op against Roszca. Being on the team would mean working with Simon. Seeing him every day would keep her on edge.

On edge because he already questioned her relationship with Gabe. On edge because he was too charismatic, too honorable. Too sexy.

Bringing down Roszca and proving her integrity were worth new hurdles. Mostly, she needed to close the chapter on Gabe.

She glanced down at her left hand, now naked, no wedding ring. She'd continued to wear it as protection from male attention, but no more. Last night, like the abused wife in *Sleeping with the Enemy,* she'd flushed it. Except her ring disappeared and no vengeful husband would stalk her.

Her professional attire and attitude would have to serve as shields. Other team members would act as buffers. She'd make sure not to be alone with Simon, like in New York.

She could remain professional. No problem.

"It's safe, Simon." She stood and waved over the cubicle divider. "No mines or booby traps." Her voice seemed to echo with anxiety in the empty silence of the usually noisy lab.

"No forcefields?"

Of course, he'd pick up the theme. "No laser either."

He weaved his way through the equipment and cubicles to stand beside her stool. Raking a hand through his wild hair, he said, "Thought you might want to throw something at me. Like that lemon you winged at the wall."

She wrinkled her nose. "If I ever try that again, stop me. I have tennis elbow from scrubbing away the lemon goop." Then she waited, her throat tight with hope and apprehension. Why was he here?

A solemn demeanor replaced his initial brash manner and half smirk, half smile. "Janna, in New York, I wanted to level with you, but I couldn't."

"I understand," she said, setting down the scanner. "You're my superior. You were in charge." She managed a limp smile. "Just my luck you followed orders for a change."

He shifted his feet, a scowl furrowing his forehead. "For the record, I did challenge Raines on the covert nature of the investigation. Insisted he was off track. When he wouldn't budge,

I figured having me check you out meant you'd get a fair shake. Another officer might've hauled you in as soon as—"

"As soon as I asked for secrecy about Gabe being on the videotape." Her brain had skirted that notion, but hearing Simon acknowledge it soothed the last sting. This time, her smile came easier.

"Why'd Gabe do it, Janna?" Simon asked, his voice gentle, apologetic. In his brown eyes, she read controlled fury, anger at Gabe. "Was it the money?"

She'd considered it since Monday. More than she'd wanted to ponder Gabe's issues ever again. "Remember suggesting Gabe was competitive?"

"He sure as hell hated to lose at racquetball. I had the ball bruises on my back to prove it. But competitive doesn't cut it. The man had a whole side to him that no one knew." The familiar sexy smirk was back, but with a wry cant.

More than one side. "You're right. He wasn't just competitive. He was the *ultimate* competitive guy from a long line of hard-nosed businessmen. His mother needled him constantly about his failed businesses and law career. Every time he talked to her, she'd mention his father's or brother's latest business coup. That's why he constantly sought the spotlight—for approval and advancement. It didn't work. He was too rash."

"Ironic that hotdogging is what roadblocked his advancement."

"I tried to tell him that, but he wouldn't listen." No, he'd belittled her suggestion as he had any of her ideas. "Instead of a promotion, his heroics got him killed."

He shook his head. "For what it's worth, Gabe's tackling of that terrorist saved a lot of lives. Whatever else he did, he died a hero. Remember that."

For her, that sacrificial flash didn't burn hot enough to purify the rest of the darkness that had been Gabriel Harris. Simon was trying to comfort the bereaved widow, but he hadn't seen deeper into Gabe's soul.

Apparently, neither had she.

"I'll try. Thank you for telling me that." Attempting nonchalance, she fiddled with the audio scanner again. "Have you made any headway in finding Roszca's location?"

Amusement glinted in his eyes. "Two bucks says you found it, too, Q."

"You know me too well, Simon. A cheap win. You should've bet at the ten-dollar window."

"So give. What do you know about Isla Alta?"

"It's a small island between Jamaica and Cuba. Three hundred years ago, it was a pirate stronghold, with tunnels for escape in case of attack. Today, both neighboring countries claim sovereignty. As a result, the island is a sort of no-man's-land."

"And a safe retreat for crooks like international arms brokers."

"Like Viktor Roszca."

"Unfortunately, since the two governments dispute ownership, neither of them will give the U.S. permission to launch an operation. Surveillance is all they'll go for."

His confident tone hinted at more. A plan must be in the works. "But ATSA won't let that stop us, right?"

"The general idea is to trick Roszca into leaving the island's protection. Once in open waters, ATSA and the U.S. Coast Guard can board his boat." Stopping at that, he shrugged. Either the plans weren't set or more information was on a need-to-know basis.

She drew a deep breath. "Let me help, Simon. Security, surveillance—I can give you better eyes and ears on that island." Dammit. Her voice sounded shamefully needy. She didn't intend to beg or plead, but he had to understand.

"You're too emotionally involved. Taking part would be too dangerous." He hooked a hip on the worktable and propped an elbow on his knee.

She tensed, feeling caged, but his familiar leather scent relaxed her, and his gaze pinned her.

"You trying to prove yourself or prove that Gabe didn't expose ATSA secrets?"

Her temples ached with those same questions. She'd level with him as much as she could. "I'm not sure. I feel I can't put all that—Gabe—behind me until I know the whole story. If I don't participate in the op, official channels could lock me out. Proving myself is part of it. I admit that."

He eased to his feet. "Raines said he'd think about it. You'll have to talk to him."

That meant Simon wouldn't help her. Now what chance did she have of convincing Raines? "Fine."

He grinned, back in cocky mode. "You never did answer my riddle, Q. How many software engineers does it take to screw in a lightbulb?"

If he thought he could kid her away from her goal, he was wrong. The jangling of the telephone caught her with her mouth open, ready to accuse him of sidetracking her. "One sec." She dashed to a desk in the back and picked up.

"Tech Officer Harris," said the smooth male voice. "Assistant Director Raines would like to see you in his office. Is Officer Byrne there with you?"

"He is."

"Please ask him to accompany you. In five minutes, if that's convenient."

She assured the AD's assistant it was and disconnected. Her heart hammered with anticipation. "Simon, your riddle can wait. We have an appointment."

Simon strained to focus his mind on the AD's update and not on the possible reason he'd summoned Janna. He figured proof of Gabe's guilt would be enough to disillusion her, but no. Her wanting to probe deeper meant she still clung to some feelings for the treasonous son of a bitch. Did she hope to find that he'd been undercover after all?

Damn. He wanted to leave her behind so he could leave behind his confusion about her. For all her geek expertise, intelligence and determination, she was a gentle, vulnerable woman who deserved better than a raw deal. Better than Gabe.

Better than Simon and his love-'em-and-leave-'em rules.

She sure as hell didn't deserve the danger and heartache of further investigation. No way should she be part of any op against Roszca.

He cast a glance her way. No electronic recording devices were allowed in secure ATSA meetings. He noted the intent expression on her face as, head bent, she recorded notes with a ballpoint pen, an alien low-tech device.

Her left hand was bare of a wedding ring. About damn time. Because of Gabe's treason, not because she was available.

A shining veil of buckskin-blond hair feathered across her satin cheeks. Their chairs were close enough for him to inhale her scent—almond shampoo and woman—as he forced his attention back to the AD.

"Since we know where Roszca's base is," Raines said, "we've been intercepting phone calls and e-mails from Isla Alta. His computer system has firewalls, but his satellite phone and e-mails are vulnerable to EARS41."

Simon perked up at the mention of eavesdropping on the arms broker. "EARS41?"

"Electronic Acquiring Reconnaissance System," Janna said, removing her glasses and rubbing the bridge of her nose. "When I interned at the National Security Agency, we tested EARS38. This version must be even more advanced." She smiled brightly at Raines.

The man's usual poker face softened as his lips curved to match her smile. Simon's gaze whipped to Janna. Her sexy gray eyes with that witchy tilt were working their magic on the hardcase assistant director. On purpose.

A knot cinched Simon's stomach muscles. Using feminine

wiles to get her way wasn't like her. And the AD's hot-eyed ogling ground his gears. Simon had five years on Janna, but Raines had at least ten. Too many. Simon could swear the man's nostrils flared like a damn stallion scenting a mare.

He itched to slap those ugly dark-rimmed glasses back on her face and snap his fingers in front of Raines. "Messages and intercepted conversations you were saying, *sir?*"

That shocked the man out of his trance. Simon never called his superiors *sir.* Raines slowly turned his attention away from Janna. "Interceptions, yes. To potential buyers for his cache of weapons-grade uranium."

With relief, Simon saw Janna slip on her glasses and bend her head toward her notes.

Raines explained that the auction summit Roszca was organizing would take place in three weeks. So far, three bidders had confirmed their interest. Ahmed Saar, an exiled Yamari fronting for more than one extremist group, was the first. A diamonds-for-arms trader with too many aliases to identify was the second. And an ATSA officer, masquerading as Leo Wharton in U.S. custody, was the third. ATSA would go after the bidders once they were en route to Isla Alta.

"Except for 'Wharton,'" Simon said. "That'll be our in."

Raines nodded. " 'Wharton' informed Roszca that U.S. pressure was forcing him to keep a low profile. He would send a trusted lieutenant in his place," the AD continued. "We need more than EARS41 on that island. We need to roll up Roszca before he can sell his nukes."

Janna leaned forward. "And we need to find out what Gabe might have leaked about ATSA plans?"

"Exactly." Raines continued, "The U.S. Coast Guard will transport Wharton's motor yacht, the *Horizon,* from St. Thomas to Guantanamo Bay."

"Gitmo's only about 45 miles from Isla Alta, an easy two- or three-hour trip for the undercover officer." Adrenaline pumped as Simon imagined the possibilities. Undercover in the middle of Roszca and his entourage of thugs would be damned hazardous, like juggling nitroglycerin.

Raines's gaze veered from Simon to Janna and back again. He flattened his palms on the desk. "I see I didn't make myself clear. Officer Byrne, I'm assigning you this undercover op. *You* are Wharton's trusted lieutenant. Are you up to it?"

Jackpot.

Simon shot to his feet. "More than up to it." Challenging and dangerous, but bringing down the slimy arms broker would help avenge the deaths of ATSA officers and many other innocents. "One problem, though. I'm no more the crewcut G.I. Joe type than Janna. Roszca won't believe I'm Wharton's man."

Still wondering why Raines had included Janna in this meeting, he slid a glance her way. When Raines added nothing, Simon hoped that meant he just wanted her informed.

"Then you missed some research on Wharton," Raines said. "He has a small cadre of trusted men. Some are streetwise gangsters with long hair and tattoos. And earrings."

"In that case, I'm your man."

"I knew you'd want this chance."

Simon slugged his hands in his jacket pockets so he wouldn't rub them together in glee. "One other thing. Put me on any horse with four feet or behind the steering wheel of any land vehicle, and I'm good to go. But the only boating I ever did was in the Tunnel of Love. Can I assume I'll have a captain and crew?"

"And a tech officer. All rolled into one." When Raines sent Janna another hint of a smile, Simon felt an iron-shod kick in the gut. He should've known. "I'm assigning Harris."

Eyes bright with excitement, Janna sat at attention. "Oh, thank you, sir. You won't regret this."

"But Raines," Simon said, avoiding Janna's glare, "this is a delicate and dangerous mission. Janna's too emotionally involved to be detached."

The AD arched a blond eyebrow. "And you're not, Byrne? You're practically salivating at the prospect of confronting Viktor Roszca." He held up a hand to stay Simon's next protest. "She has the technical and language expertise. And she knows the *Horizon*'s design and navigation systems."

"Then it must be a Caretti," Janna said. "Simon, my family used to vacation on my uncle Dean's Caretti. I did the navigation and manned the helm. She's a sweet yacht." She drilled Simon with a pointed stare. "With *three* staterooms."

"Enough room for more crew." Simon was growing desperate. A vision of the two of them on a luxury yacht in the sultry tropics beaded sweat on his temples. How could he concentrate on his undercover op with this woman as his only companion?

Raines's stern expression said he was adamant. "The boat's designed for a couple to man. More crew would arouse suspicions. Roszca won't suspect a beautiful female in a bikini of being anything but a…companion."

"Yeah, who would?" Seeing the intensity on Janna's face squelched Simon's lame excuses. He gave in.

"Don't worry, Simon," Janna said. "We have time for me to teach you how to handle the *Horizon.* Uncle Dean docks his Caretti in Annapolis." Beneath the satisfaction in her soft voice, he heard the strain of apprehension.

Damn right, she should be scared.

Raines stood. "Get going then, officers. You have two weeks to prepare. I want a detailed outline of your operation plans in eight days."

A shiver skittered up Simon's spine as he saw the week in the Caribbean looming ahead of him. Where Janna was involved, his protective instincts kicked into a flat-out gallop. He couldn't figure it out. He'd worked with plenty of female officers in the DEA and ATSA without the anxiety knotting his gut about tandem time with Janna. He trusted her competence, her excellence. She was too sharp and stubborn not to excel.

So why did he feel that this op just got a whole hell of a lot more dangerous?

For him.

For the next several days, Simon and Janna studied and plotted their operation. CIA spy satellites provided detailed photographs of Roszca's compound. Operatives found the builder and decorator in Jamaica and sent drawings that aided Janna in designing surveillance equipment.

Simon researched Wharton's habits and dealings further to support his cover story as the arms buyer's man. "Wharton" had told Roszca his man was arriving a week early for preliminary talks. Then Wharton would participate later by satellite phone. Since the rogue American's paranoia and attention to detail were well known, Roszca accepted the story.

Janna's cover was simple. She was a "boat bunny," one of many anonymous females who hopped from yacht to yacht as cook, crew and/or "companion." Her job of monitoring their eyes and ears meant remaining on the *Horizon* when Simon went ashore to meet with their quarry.

Simon breathed easier once Raines agreed to that rule.

Janna would breathe easier once Simon's yachting lessons ended.

With only a few days to go until their lift-off for Guantanamo Bay, she watched as he slowed the twin 700-hp, V-drive engines. With his weed-whacked hair and bristly jaw, and sitting on the well-cushioned helm seat in his torn cutoffs, Simon resembled a pirate more than a legitimate yacht owner. He wore a *Pirates of the Caribbean* T-shirt and a boyish grin that she tried and failed not to respond to.

Once Raines finalized their assignment, Simon had stifled his objections. Thank goodness. And he'd said nothing about her shameful lapse in professionalism. Flirting with the AD had been born of desperation and a mistake in judgment. And unnecessary. Raines had given her the assignment because of her expertise, not her sexy eyes.

Sexy eyes she would continue to hide—today behind sunglasses.

Keeping her independence meant sticking to her rules. Only professional contacts with men meant less chance of endangering her goals, less chance of panic reactions that would leak her shame. This mission could threaten that secrecy, but she had to know. And she had to prove herself.

She watched as Simon slowed the powerful engines.

Open-water navigation wasn't his problem. He still needed practice docking the 60-foot cruiser. Rather than take a chance with her uncle's yacht or his boat slip, they were using a couple of orange buoys as a target for docking.

Dented and drowned buoys at this point.

On the third try, he approached too fast. Again.

"Simon, think of it as taking a horse into his stall. You wouldn't canter or trot in. You'd slow him to a walk." She tried to keep her voice calm and patient, but her jaw clenched.

"Got it."

She held her breath as he jockeyed the engines into reverse and applied the bowthruster. He turned the wheel. The *Horizon* eased closer to the two buoys. Closer.

Then the orange cones disappeared beneath the broad hull.

"Damn," Simon said without heat. "Thought I had her that time."

Janna sighed, but couldn't help smiling at his unrelenting good cheer. "Me, too. You're getting better. But that's enough for today."

"Sweet." He shrugged. "Docking's the least of our problems.

Anchoring offshore is more secure where we're going anyway. Easier for you to stay under Roszca's radar."

Simon gave her the helm and watched as she expertly maneuvered for him to retrieve the buoys. As she steered the yacht back toward the Annapolis marina, he relaxed on the companion seat beside her. He savored the ocean's salty air and her profile-thick eyelashes that nearly brushed the lenses of her sunglasses and full mouth pursed in concentration. Thanks to sultry May weather, white shorts showed off her long, tanned legs.

"I agree on the safety issue," she said, chewing her lip, "but you still ought to be able to dock her. Who knows what we'll face."

So right. And he wanted her kept out of danger as much as possible. "Don't worry. I'll keep practicing."

Janna nodded absently as the Bay Marina hove into view. A forest of bobbing masts and flying bridges spread across the sunlit water and into the docks. And beyond, the brick facade and dome of the state capitol building dominated the quaint old town. Slowing to the required five-mile-per-hour no-wake speed in the harbor, she brought them toward the boat slip.

"You're a good teacher, Q. I know a great place right on the Severn River. I'll spring for soft-shell crabs and beer on the way home."

"Thanks, Simon. I'd like that, but I'll pay my way." She tilted her head. Pushing her sunglasses up on her head, she studied him oddly. "My showing you how to maeuver the boat doesn't bother you?"

"Bother me? Why should it?"

A pink flush crept up her cheeks. "I mean, having a woman know more than you. That doesn't threaten your…your…?"

He burst out laughing. "Threaten my male ego, you mean? No way. I'm fine with anything you can do better than me. Your geek brain fascinates me." *And turns me on as much as your witchy eyes and perfect butt.* But he couldn't say that aloud.

"Good. I didn't want a problem between us."

"We have plenty of other problems. Our biggest is the hole in our strategy. I have no idea how to trick Roszca into leaving that island so ATSA can nab him."

"Fast thinking on your feet is what you're known for. Something will come up after we get to Isla Alta."

"Yeah, maybe. But Raines wants a plan now."

Janna slowed the engine and applied the bowthrusters as she jockeyed the boat into its narrow space.

Simon observed with admiration. He did want to do that. Speed and power thrilled him big-time, but finesse could also bring a major rush. He knew that from horse training.

And sex.

A grin curved his lips, but he stifled his libido as her strange concern came back to him. "Janna, did Gabe have a problem with your intelligence?"

But she'd already jumped out of earshot onto the dock with the bowline.

Chapter 7

"Don't wiggle so much, Simon." Janna took a step back and stood with her arm propped on one hip and her other hand holding what appeared to be tiny felt circles. "I can't attach these bugs if you don't stand still."

She wore two blue scraps that passed for a bikini and a sleeveless white cotton shirt. Unbuttoned, it flapped in the tropical breeze. His mouth went dry at every glimpse of the lightly tanned skin at her small waist.

"Sweetheart, you can bug me anytime. But tell the boat to stand still," he said through gritted teeth. The gentle motion didn't rock him nearly as much as having her hands roam over his chest. If her warm fingers drifted below his belt, she'd discover exactly how much. "I'll try."

With a huff that said she doubted his compliance, she stepped close enough for him to savor her female scent. "You don't have enough buttons on this shirt. I'll have to slip some of the devices into the waistband of your trousers."

Simon nearly groaned.

Deftly slitting the waistband seam with a sharp tool like a scalpel, she didn't seem to realize his predicament. In fact, ever since they'd stepped on board, she'd been nothing but professional. As if they hardly knew each other.

Concealing her mesmerizing eyes and slim but curvy figure behind dark-framed sunglasses and the flimsy white shirt worked as well as hiding an AK-47 in a shoulder holster—it didn't.

When she slid her soft hands across his stomach, his pulse skipped, and heat blasted his lower body. The tropical furnace couldn't compare. Sweat trickled down his spine.

Suck it up, Byrne.

Professional. Right. They'd both be better off. Safer.

Trying to ignore her touch, he stared out the *Horizon*'s tall windshield at the tropical lushness of Isla Alta.

Behind a strip of spun-sugar sand and palm trees rose the jungle-covered heights that gave the island its name. Birdsong floated to the yacht on the light breeze.

What appeared to be paradise was a predator's lair. Viktor Roszca's white stucco compound squatted almost hidden among flowering shrubbery at the hill's base.

Simon knew the estate consisted of a main house that horseshoed around a central courtyard. Four smaller guest cottages buttressed the open end. The builder's wiring diagrams indicated that the security base and Roszca's office, with its all-important computer, occupied two rooms on the long land side of the main house.

His eventual goal was twofold: dupe Roszca into leaving his sanctuary and invade his computer. But not today.

Today, his objectives were to plant as many of Janna's minilistening devices as possible and to convince Roszca he was who he purported to be—Leo Wharton's emissary.

They'd arrived late yesterday, ostensibly at the end of a voyage from St. Thomas, a hell of a lot farther across the impossibly turquoise Caribbean than the 45 miles from Gitmo. He'd spoken with Roszca's assistant on the satellite phone and arranged an appointment for today at one-thirty.

Simon's gaze turned to the boat dock, where a gleaming white three-decker motor yacht and four other smaller boats bobbed. Nearby, three brown pelicans were taking turns diving for fish.

One of the smaller boats was a Cigarette-type speedboat, a fast and sleek Checkmate, Janna had informed him. Probably the tender to the big yacht. Another was maybe brought over from Jamaica, a Bertram fishing boat with rods sticking up from her like porcupine quills. The last two were smaller, rigid inflatable outboards.

Roszca's yacht stretched half again as long as the *Horizon* and boasted about the same horsepower. Could a world-stage player like the arms broker resist a race?

In half an hour, the man's bodyguards would meet Simon there to escort him to the house. At the prospect of a face-to-face confrontation with the man responsible for arming countless terrorists and killing thousands more—including Simon's ATSA colleagues and friends—a pure rush of adrenaline whipped his pulse.

He couldn't wait.

"Okay, that does it. Even a strip search shouldn't find those." Her voice—oddly breathless, though cool in tone—jolted him as much as her warm hands.

"They'll pat me down. No strip search." He hoped to hell not. "Talk me through the electronics one last time."

She gave a sharp nod and crossed her arms, the motion plumping her breasts in the tiny swimsuit bra. Her breasts weren't large, but high and enough to fill his hands.

He swallowed and willed away his growing arousal.

"First, the security," she said. "You have a GPS button implanted in one of your shirt buttons. I can track you room to room on the floor plan."

He could handle himself with Roszca, but fear for Janna tied sailor's knots in his guts. The damned sunglasses blocked him from reading her intent. He shouldn't, but he reached out to snatch them.

"Hey, what are you doing?" She blinked in confusion, and tiny lines formed between her brows.

He dangled the glasses by one earpiece. Her mesmerizing, silvery eyes worked their magic, but he steeled himself. "We've discussed contingencies. If something happens to me, if the GPS goes down, you are not—I repeat *not*—to go ashore or try to confront Roszca."

Her chin shot up. "I know what to do. I call Jack Thorne on the contact boat. ATSA operatives will handle extraction. I'm not stupid, Simon."

He handed back her sunglasses. "An understatement if ever I heard one, Q. I know you're capable, but we're outnumbered. And outgunned." He grinned. "Don't tell anybody you heard this from me, but stick to the rules and regs on this one."

She lifted one shoulder in too-deliberate nonchalance as she replaced her dark-tinted shield. "No problem because nothing will happen. You'll be fine."

"Keep a good thought. Okay, the surveillance toys?"

"You have a sensitive mike in your earring in case I have to contact you."

He tugged at his left earlobe, which still tingled from her warm touch. "Sweet. That's set. I don't have to do anything with the mike."

"You also have listening chips wired into small felt circles. Scraping the shiny side activates the adhesive as well as the unit itself. Then you can attach them to the backs of pictures or the bottoms of lamps."

"And anyone looking at them will think they're those doo-dads that protect surfaces."

"Right." Her expression softened as she warmed to her favorite subject. "It's new technology, completely undetectable by any countersurveillance devices they might have. You have seven of them. Three behind the buttons on your Henley and four in your waistband. That's it."

"You're amazing, Q." He ached to kiss those bee-stung lips for luck. The danger of the mission and the temptation of her nearness streaked excitement and desire through him with a flash as hot as the tropical sun. She stood close. He could pull her into his embrace.

Her cheeks flushed as if she knew what he was thinking. Then she lowered her chin and averted her gaze.

Instead of kissing her, he edged away. Clenching his fists, he willed himself calm and into his undercover role. He stopped his progress toward the salon when he saw her stiffen and focus on the island.

"Your escorts have arrived." Janna pointed at two large men on the dock. "Mr. Clean guys on steroids. The twins that Thorne's snitch told us about, Stepan and Sergiy." She grimaced.

"Okay, Q. Let's do it." He slipped on Oakleys, quantum leaps above the knock-off sunglasses he'd bought on a Manhattan street corner, and jammed his bare feet into Italian kidskin loafers.

"I'll be listening. Be careful."

He stared at her grimly. "Listening is all you *can* do, Janna. They'll be watching the boat. Stay below if you can. Out of sight."

She sucked in a quick breath as she shoved her sunglasses up on her head. "Nagging, Simon, or ordering? I know my job. You do yours and you can trust me to do mine."

His gut clenched at the resentment flaming in her eyes. Dammit, he didn't intend to give orders. He just wanted her safe.

Hell, he just wanted her—period.

What could he say? He couldn't tease her, and his fear for

her made him say the wrong things. They weren't exactly friends, and professional concern didn't quite cover it. Her ire and his protectiveness tied his tongue and clamped his jaw.

More reasons he was better off alone.

No matter if the prospect of being alone was beginning to ream an emptiness in his chest.

So he merely waved and climbed into the yacht's tender, a fiberglass dinghy lowered from the stern and tied to the port side. At this point, he'd rather face Roszca and an army of bodyguards.

When the inboard engine didn't start at the first key turn, he hoped that wasn't an omen.

Janna watched through binoculars as Simon zipped across the smooth water of the protected cove.

Her cheeks still felt flushed from her overreaction to Simon's reminder to stay out of sight. Yes, she needed to be in control of her life, to stand up for herself, but this was not the time. Simon didn't issue arbitrary orders. He only expressed concern about security—for all the *Horizon*'s surveillance instruments—and for her safety.

She needed to stop reacting so harshly. Being strung out from lack of sleep was no excuse. She hadn't slept well in two years.

Simon wasn't her husband. He wasn't Gabe.

Not even close. He wouldn't berate her in the middle of the night. He respected her abilities and worked with her as an equal. It wasn't an act.

She had to resist the sensual appeal and cocky grin that curled her toes. Even the earring seemed to wink at her. Had to resist the bone-deep integrity and audacity that drew her to him. Next time, he could conceal his own electronic bugs.

The feel of his hard body and the scent of his sunbaked skin had stolen her breath away. And not with fear.

Nothing she should or would explore further.

This duet on the luxury yacht was only temporary. Maintaining a professional outlook was the only way to guard her heart and her secret shame.

She glanced down at her attire. Being professional in a pantsuit was a lot easier than in a bikini. But ATSA had mandated her wardrobe, including shorts and some sexy dresses to fit her undercover identity.

The roar of a motor drew her attention back outside. Simon had shoved the throttle forward. Too much speed. Again. She sighed. At least this boat shouldn't take out the dock.

The pelicans wisely flew away.

She held her breath as he approached.

She scrutinized the twin escorts awaiting Simon. Shaved heads. Weight lifter bodies with triceps and lats that forced them to stand with their arms jutting out like small children wrapped in thick snowsuits. Their untucked tropical shirts probably hid sidearms tucked into their shorts. Reflective sunglasses concealed their eyes.

Simon's boat rammed a piling. The entire dock shook and the hulks staggered. Janna expelled her breath in a muffled laugh. Okay, a little ramming's not bad. A show of force could intimidate enough to give Simon an edge.

As long as the bodyguards didn't catch on to his ineptness as a boat handler.

She adjusted the binoculars to focus on Simon as he climbed onto the dock. He'd dressed for image in cream-colored linen trousers and a sleeveless black Henley knit that displayed hard shoulders and arms that had smooth strength, not grotesque bulges. A gust of wind lifted his thick shag of hair, the only softness detectable.

He looked exactly like a street hood who'd moved up in the ranks to be second in command. She had to admit, he looked incredibly sexy. Janna pushed away that notion along with the current of heat rippling through her.

Simon slipped his sunglasses into a trouser pocket and waited for the men to approach. Tense and tautly coiled, as if he could erupt in violence at any moment, he projected power.

He'd need intimidation as well if they suspected a ruse. Roszca's men stood a head taller and had a good thirty pounds on him.

Unsmiling, the bodyguard twins exchanged a look, then ambled toward the visitor.

They came to him. A good sign. Although the thugs must know Simon was also an underling, apparently they accepted his position as superior to theirs. Simon's attention to image and his contemptuous demeanor worked.

The first Mr. Clean twin—Stepan or Sergiy?—made exaggerated gestures with his ham-sized hands.

Janna frowned. "Ah, they don't speak English." Their linguistic limitations might mean Roszca would keep them in the room for the meeting. Three sets of eyes on Simon gave him less of a chance to plant the bugs.

Simon nodded and held out his arms for a pat-down. When he turned toward her, her stomach tightened and her heart lurched. She saw not the cocky, irreverent man she knew, but the guarded, remote mask of a predator.

Janna had barely shaken off her sensual reaction when the second Mr. Clean twin's next move tripped her pulse in fear. He slid off Simon's belt and examined it.

"Not the waistband, please, oh please," she whispered.

But a moment later, the thug handed back the belt with a curt bow. Apparently satisfied with the search, the men gestured for Simon to accompany them to shore.

After the three disappeared through the shrubbery, Janna lowered the binoculars. She peeled the damp cotton shirt away from her hot skin and wished she could dive into the cove's water to clear her head and cool her body. Since she couldn't run, she'd swim for exercise. Snorkeling would be good here, she speculated. There were a couple of small reefs and an area under the cliffs where fish would congregate.

When she peered into the water, two long, sinewy forms gliding out of the white hull's shadow changed her mind.

Barracudas.

A light shudder rippled through her. Swim with predators? Barracudas usually didn't attack humans, but the island's human predators were quite enough for now.

She turned to the ship's computer and the bank of surveillance monitors concealed in the navigation panels.

Time to do her job. To wait and listen.

And stay out of sight, she reminded herself with a pang.

Simon observed cameras eyeing him from the white stone wall surrounding the estate. He downshifted his overt swagger to a confident stride. In spite of his hatred for Roszca, whose weapons had killed without mercy, he had to show respect, like Wharton. On the tapes of the arms broker's conversations with Simon's supposed boss, Wharton displayed the deference he'd once owed to his U.S. Marine-Corps superiors.

Just before they reached the iron gate to enter the compound, Simon heard a crackle in his earring receiver.

"Simon," said Janna softly, "this is a test. If you can hear me, scratch the top of your head."

After he complied, she said, "A-okay. Be careful." Silence.

No surprise, an electronic panel beside the gate controlled entry. The bodyguard on Simon's left blocked his view as he punched in a code. Janna could get him past that if necessary, but they ought to be more subtle than a B and E.

The gate swung open without a sound.

Inside the compound, other guards patrolled. Three or four, Simon wasn't sure yet.

With its massive mahogany door and windowless facade, the house's front looked more like a white stone fortress than a classy estate. They entered a cavernous foyer dominated by a polished table and a floral centerpiece as big as the ones in hotel lobbies. Simon caught himself before he whistled in awe.

An arched doorway led to a two-story-high living room with beamed ceilings. His brief glance took in marble floors, dark wood and French antiques. Tall arches opened to a flower-filled courtyard. Silent fans circulated the salty trade wind.

And on each wall, covering all angles, Simon noted electronic eyes. Openness to the outdoors didn't mean freedom. He glanced past the teak benches and kidney-shaped pool to the far wing containing the security headquarters. Someone was always watching. He suppressed the urge to give a middle-finger salute.

His escorts ushered him down a hall and through another carved mahogany door into a smaller, private parlor that also opened onto the courtyard.

"You wait," one stone-faced hulk said in an accent similar to that of the New York Cleatian informer.

Simon nodded, expecting the two to leave him alone, but they stood unsmiling and watchful, one by the only door, the other by the courtyard arch. For all their animation, they could've been stone statues.

The small sitting room was less formal than the parlor, but no less luxurious. Bright paintings of Caribbean gardens and marketplaces added color to the otherwise all-white room with silk-upholstered bamboo furniture. A wide-screen television occupied one wall, a bookcase another. A computer monitor took up a corner. A chess game covered an inlaid marble-topped table. An informal game room where Roszca apparently spent leisure time, he concluded.

With good places to plant bugs.

Sticking the felt-camouflaged bugs behind paintings or beneath lamps would require speed and dexterity. He glanced at the hulking twins standing opposite each other.

And subterfuge.

He surreptitiously checked his hands as he strolled around the room. Sweaty smudges on his host's white silk would not be cool.

"You guys know if this island gets Playboy TV?" He picked up the remote from an end table.

The bodyguards' eyes shifted to each other in puzzlement. Either they didn't understand enough English, or they had to figure out the answer.

Simon slid a felt circle from beneath his top shirt button.

Stepan—or Sergiy—shrugged. He frowned, the expression scrunching his single black eyebrow into a caterpillar-like curl. "No TV."

"No problem." Simon replaced the remote, now with its fake furniture protector beneath it. *One down, six to go.*

The carved door swung open into the room, and the bodyguards stood aside deferentially.

The man Simon had been waiting to meet marched in.

"Welcome to my island, Mr. Simon." Viktor Roszca's lightly accented voice rumbled with the confidence of power even though his tone remained soft. He shifted his cigar—Cuban, at a guess—to his left hand and held out his right.

Simon clasped his enemy's hand in a firm grip. Soft palms, he noted, a man who had others to do his dirty work. He swallowed nausea at the cloying combo of cigar smoke and heavy cologne. "Thank you, Mr. Roszca. It's a pleasure to be here. Colonel Wharton is eager to do business with you. He regrets that he couldn't come in person."

Like Wharton, Roszca looked like a former military man, even in his tailored white slacks and open-collared shirt. His unnaturally black hair, dark brows and mustache bristled with energy and strength. Unlike Wharton, prosperity and power had padded a barrel chest with more than muscle.

Seeing the arms broker countless times on tape and in news

footage hadn't prepared Simon for the impact of the man's intensity. A few inches taller than Simon, Roszca seemed to dominate the room. He commanded all the attention of those in it. Eyes as blue as the seawater in the cove bored into Simon like laser beams.

"Make yourself comfortable," Roszca said, settling onto one end of a silk-covered loveseat.

One hulk rushed to his boss with an ashtray before a curl of cigar ash could fall.

"Thanks." Simon sank onto an armchair beside the loveseat.

But comfortable? Not until this parasite living off the deaths of others was in custody. Or dead. To achieve that, Simon had to be very convincing and very clever. Adrenaline thumped his heart in a slow, steady beat as he immersed himself further into his role.

"Colonel Wharton gave me only the one name. Do you have another?"

Simon smiled, but with no hint of humor or good will. He needed to be nonthreatening, but, in a subtle way, a man who gave away only what he wanted. "Just Simon."

"A surname or a given name?"

He had to show Roszca that he, too, was dangerous, that he was a man who revealed only what he wanted to. "Suit yourself."

It was Roszca's turn to smile, a grim curve of lips. "I see. You have power to negotiate for your boss."

"Exactly."

Roszca leaned back against the plush cushions and aimed smoke circles at the rotating fan over his head. "Wharton and I have a long association. We met in Moscow at a Cleatian embassy function." He launched into a rambling tale of diplomatic finagling and financial wrangling.

Simon kept an interested mask as he sorted out what was going on. Janna must be biting her lip with anxiety. At this rate, he wouldn't make it into other rooms to plant bugs. Apparently, Roszca liked to take both his time and the measure of the man he'd negotiate with.

As the involved tale wound down, a maid brought in a tray with coffee and small cakes.

Over refreshments, conversation ranged from news from the States to film festivals to horse racing. Simon held his own on current politics and thanked the luck of the draw that Roszca was a track fan and stable owner.

Simon had left the track world years ago, but he still kept up with his friends among the jockeys and trainers. He followed the new horses and attended races whenever he could.

"Assad's Silver Bullet is the horse to watch next year," Roszca asserted. "I am considering buying him."

Simon set his coffee cup gingerly on its china saucer. He shook his head, warming to the topic. "He'll do, but the Saudi prince who owns him doesn't appreciate the better talent in his stables. Silver Bullet may have great bloodlines, but Immediate Delivery has been cleaning up in early races."

"I shall look into it," Roszca said, coming to his feet. "You are a complex man, Simon. Do you play chess?"

Matching wits with his adversary in a civilized form of warfare held an irresistible challenge and might lead to other opportunities.

"I'd enjoy a game of chess with you, Mr. Roszca." Simon stood as well, realizing the interview had reached its end.

"Then you will return tomorrow morning for a game or two. We shall discuss our business over lunch. Ten o'clock."

"I look forward to it." A game wouldn't give him access to more rooms since the chess table sat in here. Planting bugs just became harder. He glanced around with an admiring expression. "You have a beautiful home here."

"Tomorrow, I shall give you a tour."

They shook hands, and the bodyguards escorted Simon back to the dock.

Disappointment itched between his shoulder blades that he'd been able to plant only two of Janna's bugs. He'd slipped the second behind a painting in the foyer. They had only five days to find the scoop on the nuclear material before more potential buyers arrived. Five days to trick Roszca into leaving the island so ATSA could pick him up. And he'd had no opportunity to hint at a yacht race.

Every second wasted ratcheted up the pressure.

Chapter 8

As Simon pulled away from the dock, the three pelicans eyed him from perches atop the pilings. The bodyguards had disappeared by the time he had tied up the dinghy at the *Horizon*'s stern. He congratulated himself on avoiding bumping the swim platform.

Relieved to escape the oppressive atmosphere of Isla Alta, he sucked in the clean sea air as he climbed the short gangway. A small gray gull, or maybe a tern, dipped down to skim along the surface.

Too bad this beautiful place had a history of such corrupt owners. First pirates and now a criminal selling pricey contraband. A modern-day pirate on an international scale.

Where was Janna? He expected her to meet him on deck.

"Janna? Where are you?"

Only silence and the gentle lapping of waves answered his call.

Alarm kicked his heartbeat into a gallop. What if something had happened to her? While Roszca kept Simon occupied, some of his goons could've sneaked onto the yacht. Her cover was good. So why take her?

Another idea reined him in.

Someone could still be on board. Waiting.

He had no gun, no weapon of any kind. Tension hardened a tight ball in his gut as he edged toward the companionway. If he could make it down to the salon, he could grab his Glock from where he'd stashed it behind the fire extinguisher. From now on, he'd stow it on deck when he went ashore.

He flattened himself beside the open hatch and listened. An electronic hum was the only sound from below. The familiar smell of morning coffee drifted toward him. He sensed no movement, nothing out of order except the unnatural quiet.

Silently, he grasped the railings and slid down the companionway steps in one motion. He reached to the right behind the fire extinguisher. Cold steel fit his palm. At least nobody had found that.

Gun in hand, he scanned the salon's blue carpet and leather-upholstered seating forward to the captain's console.

Janna sat in the swivel chair, her head on the helm desk. She'd shucked the white shirt, but wore headphones for monitoring the listening devices.

His breath hitched and cold sweat beaded his skin. Was she hurt? Drugged?

Or worse?

His brain screamed denial, and he could no longer keep silent. No one else seemed to be here.

"*Janna!* Janna, are you all right?" He hurried through the salon toward her.

She stirred, dumping the headphones on the console. Then she sat up with a jerk of alarm. "Oh, God!"

That's when he saw the scars.

As many as nine or ten livid vertical stripes branded the middle of her back, new pink growth over seared skin.

Burn scars in a distinct grill pattern.

His nostrils constricted at the imagined smell of seared flesh. His brain spun in a sickening spiral. His heart slammed against his chest wall. *What the hell?*

Janna popped from her seat and faced him, alarm on her ashen face. She snatched up the white shirt from the floor and jammed her arms into the holes, nearly ripping the garment in her haste.

Too late. Simon had seen the reason for the shirt.

His head swam with questions, but before he could sort them out, Janna began.

"Oh, Simon, I'm *so* sorry! I don't know how it could've happened. I didn't sleep much the past few nights. I know that's no excuse."

"It's okay. I—" He took a step toward her.

She raised trembling hands as if to ward off blows as she backed against the console. "I'm sorry. I was listening to the conversation—Roszca's long story—and, well, I just couldn't keep my eyes open."

Simon halted, shocked at the fear in her eyes and defensive stance. "Janna, take it easy. It's not the end of the world." But she babbled on.

"I've always tried to be professional. Falling asleep on the job is disgraceful. It's unprofessional. I never… I promise it'll never happen again. You'd be justified in sending me back to the control boat. You can request another tech officer. I should be reprimanded."

She continued, repeating the same self-accusations in whispery tones. Tears welled up in her beautiful eyes. Crimson flagged her cheeks, and her breathing became rapid and shallow.

She was hyperventilating. Panicking.

To help her, he needed calm. He held out his hands, palms up, and spoke in what he hoped was a reassuring tone. "We're cool, sweetheart. Let's go sit down in the salon."

"No, I don't want…I should check the settings…" A sob caught in her throat, and he thought she might keel over.

He snagged her water bottle from the console as he grasped her hand and led her to the leather sofa. "Here, take a good, long drink and try to relax."

"But I—"

"Shh, no more buts. Sit. Drink."

He watched as she sipped water. Her breathing regulated, still rapid but deeper. Janna settled against the sofa back and closed her eyes.

The time had come to confront what he'd only just begun to suspect.

Fragments of memory hammered at him.

The unnecessary glasses and loose pantsuits meant to conceal her beauty, her femininity.

Janna flinching when any man put his hands on her.

No pictures of Gabe. Not even a wedding picture. Gabe, who kept the finances and the key to his desk secret.

Leave my marriage out of it. You have no idea what my marriage was like.

Finally, there were the telltale marks on her back. And today's panic attack when she woke up groggy. She had been afraid of Simon, terrified he would strike her.

But the person she really feared wasn't Simon.

Gabriel Harris had been more of a control freak than Simon realized. *Much more.*

Pain chewed a path to his brain. Fury burned as hot as the cruel grill that had branded Janna's smooth skin.

He clenched and unclenched his fists as he sought control. The last emotion Janna needed to see was anger, even if the anger wasn't aimed at her.

"How did you get those scars?"

She raised her head from the cushion and opened her eyes. A tear trickled down her cheek. "You weren't supposed to see them."

"How, Janna? What exactly burned you?"

"I'm okay now. The gas-grill cooktop. In the kitchen. It was a long time ago. I…fell. I was clumsy."

"Clumsy." He shook his head. "No way. I observed you whiz through the obstacle course during training. Clumsy you're not. What happened? *The truth.*"

"It's not important. It doesn't matter." She started to push to her feet, but he laid a hand on her knee. She startled at his touch but didn't move away.

"It matters to *me.* And I think what happened matters to you or you wouldn't hide the scars. You recoil from even a gentle touch. Your condo has no pictures of your hero husband. You hide behind nun suits and frames with clear glass."

At his words, a flush rose to her cheeks. Her chin firmed, but she wouldn't look him in the eye. "That's my business, not yours."

"When your 'business' spills into our work and our friendship, it becomes mine. You're not sleeping, you say. I bet you haven't slept well in a long time."

When her mouth tightened, he knew he'd hit a nerve. She shook her head, and tears streamed down her face.

Keeping the truth locked inside was eating away at her like a cancerous growth. She needed cut it out.

And Simon needed to help.

He'd introduced her to Gabe. Then he'd abandoned their friendship. Abandoned her to the son of a bitch who'd hurt her. Who'd burned her. God knew what else he'd done to her. Simon felt guilt about Gabe's death, but this was somehow worse. Guilt pounded him, hardening the tight lump in his gut to lead.

Since she wouldn't open up, he'd have to pry for the truth. "You can't keep this all inside, Janna. Don't deny the truth. Gabe was worse than a traitor to his country and a control freak. The bastard abused you. How can you protect him? *He* gave you those scars. *He* branded you."

"Yes! Yes! Are you satisfied now?" She scooted away and shot to her feet. She stood trembling at the end of the cocktail table, her hands in a white-knuckle grip. "He hit me. He knocked me onto the grill and held me down until I could smell my skin burning."

The agony in her eyes would haunt Simon forever.

He rose slowly to his feet and started toward her.

She backed up a step, and his throat constricted in pain. He swallowed down the bitter bile of guilt.

"Janna," he said, approaching slowly as he would soothe a frightened filly, "I'm not Gabe. I won't hit you. I won't hurt you. Let me help."

A sob tore from her throat, a raw feral cry that slashed his heart. She buried her face in her hands. "I didn't want you to know. I'm so ashamed."

She'd been protecting *herself,* not her bastard of a husband. The realization slugged him, shaming him and easing the unreasonable envy that had tightened his chest.

He crossed to her in two strides. Gently drawing her into his arms, he made comforting noises. When she rested her cheek on his shoulder, he kissed her hair, tangled and damp but silky and sweet-smelling, and laid his cheek against her head.

"No, sweetheart," he said, "I'm the one who's ashamed. I should've been more of a friend. I should've known. I should've stopped him from hurting you."

More to the point, what should he do now while they were in the middle of a deadly game with Viktor Roszca?

Janna opened her eyes to darkness. The smell of a charcoal fire drifted through her cabin's porthole.

She rolled over on the sheets, remembering. After her appalling lapse and panic attack, Simon had herded her to her bunk for some rest. She hadn't thought she could sleep, but apparently exhaustion had overruled her nerves.

So now Simon knew.

He didn't know the whole story. But enough. The worst part. Raw anguish filled her, an ocean of tears and pain, until it overflowed in another flood of tears. She rolled into a ball and let the shame and sorrow soak her pillow.

Now that he knew, what did that mean? She had to decide whether to tell him the rest.

When the tears subsided, she went to wash up. A cold wet cloth on her eyes allowed her to see what she hadn't before. Simon hadn't been repulsed. He hadn't berated her for allowing Gabe to abuse her.

Instead, he blamed Gabe.

And he blamed himself for not intervening.

He was right about the fault being Gabe's. And Marah French was right that Janna had accepted that intellectually, but not emotionally. Before he left her in her cabin, he announced that he wanted the whole story.

Telling him more might help heal her damaged soul.

But what damage would the shameful truth about her disastrous marriage do to their tentative new friendship?

When she came up on deck, in clean white shorts and a tank top, she was still pondering.

Beyond *Horizon*, the velvety night was broken only by the lights from Isla Alta. On board, tiny white lights circled the afterdeck. A glowing hurricane lantern sat on a low table between two padded deck chairs.

Simon was just laying two juicy steaks on a hibachi. He'd changed from his natty mobster attire into cargo shorts and a palm-tree-decorated shirt. The light breeze scents of the sea and hibiscus blooms blended with the charcoal smell.

"I heard you moving around, so I figured it was safe to start dinner. My mouth's been watering for these babies since we left Gitmo yesterday." His face fell. "You ordered veggies in New York. You're not a vegan, are you?"

She shook her head, amused at his horrified expression. "Still a carnivore. Make mine medium rare."

"A woman after my own heart." He beamed his cocky grin as though nothing had happened, as though a time warp had hurtled them back two years.

"I'll see about a salad," she offered, turning back to the companionway.

"All done. Baked potatoes, too." He gestured at a small table where a bottle of red wine and two goblets sat. "Open the wine and relax."

"Aye, aye, captain." She eased into the deck chair beside the table and picked up the corkscrew.

Conversation remained light during their delicious dinner. Simon coaxed her to talk about her travels with her diplomat parents. In turn, he regaled her with stories about his days at the Baltimore track.

"Did you want to be a jockey?" she asked over coffee.

He shrugged. "Yeah, but then I grew and it wasn't an option. Doc insisted I go to college."

"He's the stable manager who helped you." When he nodded, she continued, "Why law enforcement, the DEA?"

"Old buddies from my days on the street were dropping like proverbial flies. Some to crack cocaine. Some to drug-related gang violence. Without Doc, I could've met the same end. I wanted to make a difference." Zeal sharpening his gaze, he leaned forward and flattened one hand on the table.

"Were you stationed in Baltimore?"

"Miami for a time, then the Northeast, Boston. My last case was stopping heroin traffic. We took down the gang of a Colombian drug lord named El Halcón. I never learned if they rolled up the big guy though."

She laid a hand on his and forced herself to leave it there a beat, to show him—and herself—that she trusted him. "Then you *have* made a difference. You should be proud."

His brown eyes softened with sadness. "Maybe. But I screwed up. I failed to make a difference when a friend ran into trouble."

He meant *her*. Her stomach clenched. Confession time. Simon wouldn't back down or give up. He'd made the decision for her. "I didn't run into trouble. Trouble crept up on me so stealthily that I didn't know what was happening."

Simon poured more wine for them and leaned back in his deck chair. "Gabe had the charm and ego of a confidence man."

Reflecting on the emotional prison she'd existed in—still existed in—squeezed her throat and chest with a strong fist. Unable to swallow even a sip, she set down her goblet. "He swept me off my feet. He was the perfect gentleman before we were married."

He'd seemed like the responsible, reliable type she ought to marry, not an unconventional rebel like Simon, who challenged her studious nature and teased her and lured her to the wild side. But she couldn't say that to Simon.

A motor started up at the island dock. A moment later, a speedboat rumbled past, headed toward the mouth of the cove.

"Regular patrol," Janna said when Simon stood with his hand on the gun in his belt holster.

"You heard them, too? They circled the island three different times last night. Roszca takes no chances." Simon subsided into his chair and rescued his wine as the boat's wake rocked the *Horizon*.

Her tank top and shorts should've had him ogling her breasts and long legs. But her pinched mouth and hunched shoulders grabbed him more. "You really don't sleep, huh?"

"Not for a long time."

Gabe had controlled and abused Janna. He'd ground her self-confidence under his heel and turned her nerves into Mexican jumping beans.

Bastard! If only... But Gabe was dead, out of reach of retribution except in whatever flaming maw of hell had swallowed him.

Like steam forming in a kettle, rage heated inside Simon, but found no outlet. He clenched his fists and willed his voice steady and soothing. "Can you tell me? About how Gabe changed, what he did to you?"

Pain darkened her silver-gray eyes to pewter. "I'll try. Marah French—that's my counselor—advised me to talk, but I couldn't tell anyone. Until now."

He scooted his chair beside hers and took her trembling hand in his. "Go ahead."

She swallowed, a strained gulp, as if emotion had tightened the muscles of her throat. "You know most of it. He exerted more and more control."

"How? I want to know what the bastard did."

"I had to go home directly from work or with him. He went with me to shop. He wouldn't let me see my friends. I don't know how, but he arranged something with the tech lab chief to not assign me any work outside the lab itself. I had to account for every penny and every minute. He isolated me."

As she talked, the rage built to a boiling point within Simon until his vision blurred with a red haze. Every new detail slugged him with guilt for not having seen, for not remaining her friend, for not saving her.

Keeping hold of her soft hand, he struggled to maintain a gentle grip—on her and on himself. "This didn't seem weird?"

"I knew he was a domineering kind of guy, but I went along at first because he insisted his demands were to bond us as a couple."

"At first. What changed your mind?"

"He became jealous. I had to wear shapeless pantsuits so I was unattractive to the hordes of men in his imagination. He'd wake me up in the middle of the night to berate me about who

I'd been with or where I'd gone." She closed her eyes and her shoulders shook. "Then he'd…he'd want…"

"Sex," he finished for her. Her shudder told him how pleasant the sex had been. No wonder she couldn't sleep. Simon felt sick at her so-called loving husband's perversity. "What did you do about it?"

She ducked her head, the silky layers of her gold-highlighted hair dipping onto her cheeks. She shed no tears, but perspiration sheened her face in the warm night. She gripped his hand tightly.

She raised her gaze to his. "Simon, remember who I am. I'm supposed to be this brilliant geek, but coping with my husband's demands stumped me. I kept trying to solve the problem, to find the answers."

He should've realized. His lips curved with bitter humor at her unique approach. "Like you'd tackle a tough technical glitch in a surveillance camera or a—"

"Main frame. Exactly." The corners of her full lips quirked but didn't form a smile.

He held up a hand. "Don't tell me. You researched it."

Finally, she awarded him a tiny smile. "All the data I found online described the controlling behavior, but the solution was always counseling. So when persuasion and compliance didn't work, I sought help—from Dr. French."

"Private counseling so the agency wouldn't know."

She nodded. "And so Gabe wouldn't know. First, I begged him to go to marriage counseling, but he scoffed."

Teeth gritted, he said, "Was that before or after he burned you?"

Her breath hitched. "Before. His need for control escalated. He became almost desperate. Do you think it was when Roszca started pressuring him for agency information?"

He dropped her hand and shoved to his feet. *Do you still love the bastard? How could you?* But that might be too harsh. "Dammit, Janna, are you still making excuses for him?"

"I just want to understand." She rose and stood at the railing beside him. The light breeze lifted her hair. Beneath the thin tank top, her nipples budded.

He lifted his gaze. She needed comfort, not lust. Her plaintive plea squeezed his heart. He understood. This woman, curious above all else, would naturally want answers. "Aw, hell, sweetheart, why did you stay with him?"

"Do you remember when you came to tell me Gabe was dead?"

"Yeah, but what—?"

"Bear with me. That was two days after the hospital released me from the burn unit—a week after he accused me of flirting with a lab colleague and shoved me onto the gas grill. I told you the two suitcases by the door were clothing for charity. That was a lie."

"You were leaving him."

"What Dr. French had been saying finally sank in. He wasn't going to change, except to become more violent. She arranged for me to stay at a women's shelter until I found a place."

Simon suddenly saw Janna's actions and reactions in a new light. "But his death as a hero changed everything."

"I unpacked my bags and pretended to grieve. What I really felt was profound relief." She paused, sobs choking her voice. "And shame."

Once again, she was crying. And once again, he drew her into his arms for comfort. This time, her arms came around him, and she held on like a bareback rider on a runaway horse.

"You couldn't bring yourself to shatter the hero's image. I get it." The burden of his abuse had lifted, but a new burden weighed her down.

The hero's brave widow.

She didn't reply, but clung to him with breathy sighs, surrounding him with heat and softness, igniting his senses and arousing possessive instincts. Her sultry breath feathered against his neck. Her breasts rose and fell against his chest in rhythm with the boat's rocking. The pulses of the tropical night throbbed in his blood.

When she lifted her face, he saw the same heat in her eyes. "Simon."

"Janna, I..." His words trailed off as his body thrummed with need for her. She'd suffered more than he'd ever know and had remade herself with courage and determination. He didn't deserve to touch her, but he couldn't help himself.

He lowered his mouth to hers, and they met with heated urgency. Compassion, fear and fury for what she'd suffered slid into tenderness and then into passion.

Heat simmered between them, and her sweetness flooded him with the rich flavor of wine and the sizzle of the tropical sun at high noon. The possessive urges he'd fought for weeks—months—flared from banked coals into flaming arousal.

He had no right to make love to her, to even kiss her and hold her. He'd failed her. He should stop. But he wanted her with an ache greater than any need he'd ever known.

If she made any move to withdraw, he'd back off even if it gelded him.

Chapter 9

Janna held herself stiff in Simon's arms, expecting the panic to tighten her chest and race her heart. But instead, his touch made her senses reel. She'd existed in a state of numbness for so long that the lush sensations surprised her.

The gentle circle of his arms and the firmness of his hard body against her softer one. The hot, wild taste of his mouth, enriched with the wine they'd shared.

The brush of his whiskers against her cheek and chin. His heartbeat, steady and strong, against her breast as he deepened the kiss.

Excitement streaked through Janna, leaving a long, soft ripple of pleasure in its wake.

Currents of desire sluiced through her, loosening her thigh muscles to putty and pulsing dampness between her legs. She thought she'd never feel arousal again, but this was Simon. Simon, whose gentle caring had opened her soul enough to trust him with her shameful confession.

She heard him whisper her name and sighed in response. The exhalation passed from her parted lips into the warm, moist cavern of his mouth. Feeling bold, she probed his tongue.

He emitted a low, inarticulate sound of satisfaction. When his thumb brushed across the tight pinnacles of her breasts, heat spiraled through her body. He caressed her, massaging one hand down the full curves of her breasts and drawing a fingertip across the budding nipples. The hard ridge of his arousal surged against her belly.

Steamy heat enveloped her, licked through her. She pressed closer, rubbing her fingertips over the contours of his muscles through the thin shirt fabric. At last free to explore his taut body, she caressed his smooth shoulders, slid her palms down his firm biceps. She lost herself in him, in feelings, her mind emptied of thought.

"Simon," she whispered against his mouth.

Abruptly, his lips left hers and he ended the embrace.

Bereft, she nearly moaned. "What's the ma—?"

The low rumble of a boat engine penetrated her sensual fog. She sought air to clear her head.

"The patrol. Keep back." He grabbed her by the shoulders and tucked her beneath the shadow of the flying bridge.

"But why? They'd see your boat bunny." From her protected position behind him, she watched the running lights as Roszca's guards reduced speed to return to the cove.

Silhouetted against the dock lights, the boat and its occupants flickered like an old black-and-white movie. One man jumped out to tie up the motorboat. After the engine noise and the boat lights died, two more men climbed out. In another moment, the dock emptied.

"You're safer if they don't see you at all. That was a whisker too close." Simon turned to her, his dark eyes unreadable in the dim light. His lips, taut with tension, still glistened from their kiss. Sweat beaded his forehead. "Besides, I forgot where I was. That can't happen again. It's too dangerous."

"What can't happen again? Forgetting? Or kissing?" Her uncharacteristic boldness shocked her, but she liked feeling again and wanted more.

As insane as it was, she wanted Simon.

He dragged a hand through his wild shock of hair. An exasperated sigh escaped him, and he stepped farther away. "Either. Both. Aw, Janna, you and me, together—it's not a good idea. And not just because of this gig."

She folded her arms, trying not to tremble. How could she explain what she barely understood? "You may be right. We're very different. I have some heavy baggage. I just know that talking to you about my marriage has freed a part of me that's been frozen harder than a crashed PC. Then kissing you...well, I *felt* again."

"Q, I'm not the one to help you heal. Go back to your counselor." His lashes lowered, shuttering his expression, but his husky voice betrayed emotion.

He usually called her Q to put professional distance between them. It wasn't working. For either of them.

"Kissing Dr. French won't have the same effect." She gave him a shaky smile.

"You don't want me, not really." He stood legs apart, hands fisted at his side in a combat-ready pose. "It's just a reaction, a rebound thing. You don't want a guy who doesn't do relationships. I screwed up our friendship the last time. I'd only hurt you again. No. No way. It won't work."

Screwed up the last time. Did he mean backing off after she'd scared him off? Or was it something else? His desire had been obvious. He wanted her, and she wanted...she wasn't sure what. Yet.

This time, Dr. French couldn't help her. She had to sort through her maze of feelings and thoughts alone.

But the hour was late, and she felt as though her system had lost all GHz and her RAM was overloaded. Something her neighbor Deena, an experienced man magnet, had told her popped into her head. *Always leave 'em guessing.*

Summoning her strength, Janna affected a nonchalant shrug. "Then let's be friends again. *If* you think we can."

"Friends," he repeated, his gaze searching the yacht as though counting the days they must remain alone together. "Yeah. Friends it is."

"Thanks for a great dinner. See you in the morning." She summoned a bright smile and a wave.

She paused at the companionway bottom to look back.

He stood where she'd left him, planted in the middle of the deck, brow furrowed, gaze unfocused and the fingers of one hand on his lips.

Late the next morning, Simon prepared to motor to the island compound with more bugs to plant, along with a miniature camera.

Standing beneath the flying bridge, Janna looked delectable in another bikini, an eye-popping pink, flowered number. The sight was enough to roast him more than the white-hot sun searing his head and shoulders. The breeze hadn't come up, and sultry air blanketed him like a fever.

Last night's amazing and confusing encounter had him on edge. He felt like a stallion around her, testosterone on the hoof. But no horse was ever burdened with the guilt and misgivings that had kept him awake for hours in the sauna his cabin had become.

Dammit. He couldn't deal with that now. He had a job to do. No time for distractions.

Thinking of Janna as his tech officer would help him put a lid on last night. And douse his hots for her. For now. Consulting her expertise—the incredible woman knew just about everything—reined him in.

"The chess game should open the door to more competition," Janna said, pulling him back to reality.

"Like a yacht race," he said. "Roszca's keeping a poker face on that notion. I can't read him. Got any other ideas for tricking him into leaving the island?"

"He seems hunkered down until after his nuke summit. Too bad the AD couldn't come up with an old map of the pirate tunnels. A team could sneak inside in the middle of the night." She twirled an imaginary pirate mustache.

He considered the suggestion. "Not a good idea, even if they had a map. If the tunnels exist, he has them wired for security. He'd have time to wipe out the computer."

"Too bad. You have to admit, it'd make for a terrific headline. Are you all set then?"

"About the chess game," Simon said. "I'm only a fair chess player. My instincts say to give Roszca a challenge, but to let him win in the end. Thorne agreed."

"And you're not sure you're up to it? After your sit rep, what did he say about Roszca's game?" Late last night, Simon had given a situation report to the contact on the other boat.

He flopped down on a deck chair. "Roszca plays in tournaments. Has trophies."

Janna grinned. "I know some Internet chess sites. Roszca will use the algebraic chess notation. Do you know it?"

"Algebraic? Oh, yeah. Coordinates for the squares, like a1 and e5, instead of the old descriptions, like Queen's Knight 1. I know it. What will you do, talk me through the moves?" He hoped like hell that would work.

"Exactly." She hesitated, biting her lip. "Um, that is, if you want." She ducked her head and averted her gaze to the sun-dappled water.

Her trapped look and shrinking-violet reaction made Simon blink. After a moment, he got it. *Saint Gabriel strikes again.*

Rage seared him like a red-hot brand.

He spoke in a low voice, but with a knife-sharp edge. "Janna, did Gabe resent your brains?"

She inhaled, dragging in the heavy air bit by bit as if fear was suffocating her. Finally, her response threaded out on a fine strand of nerves. "He said that a wife should defer to her husband's authority. At first, he claimed to admire my intelligence and my degrees. He was no slouch in the brains department."

"If your abilities threatened him, his own are sure as hell in question." Simon crossed the deck and gently turned her to face him. "But go on. What did he do?"

"He'd say that I was acting like a know-it-all. That I was only a geek and knew nothing about real life. He'd yell and…" Her breath hitched and tears glistened, but she blinked them away.

"It's all right, Janna. You can say it."

"Sometimes, he would grab me by my braid and throw me down." She reached a tentative hand to her short hair. "Once, he dragged me across the bedroom floor."

"For the record, in my mind, intelligence is a turn-on, not a threat." He skated a palm over her hair and down the curved layers, sleeker than a filly's flank. To soothe, not to intimidate. "So after he died, you cut your braid."

"I'll never again let anyone use my hair as a weapon against me."

"I like your hair this way, a short, silky mane."

She chuckled. "Oh, Simon, only you could compare me with a horse and make it a compliment."

Her laugh reassured him. When she turned around, he saw amusement and desire in her eyes.

She swayed toward him, her full lips parted for his kiss. Need burned him. His body hardened in three heartbeats. What choice did he have—spending the day sweaty and naked with her or playing games with a slimy international arms dealer?

No choice. And even if he could scratch Roszca from the race, he needed to resist. He'd only hurt her again, not the way her son of a bitch husband had hurt her, but he had nothing of himself to give her.

Bonds, even romantic ones, were temporary. He'd learned that the hard way. She had packed to leave Gabe. She would leave Simon. If he was dumb enough to let her get close.

Besides, he had the twitchy feeling that, in spite of everything, she still loved the bastard. Mourned him, at least. Why else did finding out what he'd told Roszca obsess her?

He backed away. "Time to go. During the chess game, I'll describe the moves. Roszca will believe I'm thinking out loud. If I need help, I'll give a 'hmm.'"

On a shaky smile, she flipped him a mock salute. "Yes, sir. I'll be ready with cyber strategies."

Afraid she'd kiss him for luck, he stalked to the stern and scooted down the gangway to the dinghy.

Janna pressed the headphones to her ears as Roszca showed Simon around the sprawling estate. She grinned at Simon's hyperbole over this exquisite vase or that pricey painting. Lights blinked green on the monitor's house diagram as Simon planted bugs in the dining room and formal living room.

Perfect.

If the hulking bodyguards were watching, Simon's sleight of hand escaped their scrutiny. She clicked the mouse to connect each device to its voice-activated recorder.

The camera, Simon, where will you put that?

As the two men lingered outside near the guest cottages, she tapped on the computer keyboard to find the chess site that would guide her. Once she found the page, her attention turned inward.

Friends with Simon? Maybe.

Maybe more.

He was romantic, tender, funny and sexy. Simon respected her, even asked her for help. His openness reassured her that not all men wanted to control a woman's life.

She could trust him, even if he did have that streak of macho protectiveness. He tempted her to consider breaking her solitary, no-men rule. But Simon had his rules, too, and relationships didn't fit in.

They were alike in that way. As a boy, he'd had to become a loner to survive hurt and loss. The man used his rebel cockiness to protect himself from more hurt, much the same way Janna used the boring pantsuits and glasses she'd had to leave behind for this mission.

Did the chemistry between them threaten the mission and the independence each guarded?

Maybe. Maybe not.

The tension between them—whether they acted on their desires or not—was a distraction in itself.

On the personal side, more than healing, her attraction to him was morphing into more than caring, more than friendship.

Having her heart broken would be worth the chance to feel again, to be a normal woman.

For Simon, sex with her would mean a fling. He'd move on once he returned to the States and his normal routine. So why was he resisting so? When he said he'd screwed up their friendship before, he meant more than backing off. She was sure of it. When he'd coaxed her to reveal the truth about her marriage, what was it he'd said?

I failed to make a difference when a friend ran into trouble.

Guilt. *There* was the reason. She'd wallowed in guilt for not fixing her marriage and for allowing the abuse. Now Simon took on the burden of guilt because he hadn't saved her. Simon, her protector, felt he'd failed her.

For so long, she'd felt nothing. Only emptiness punctuated by the occasional panic reaction. But now a sense of euphoria and a warm flutter in her stomach made her giddy.

Simon's unfounded guilt was a problem she could solve. Tonight—

"Pawn to e4," Simon said, jerking her from her thoughts to the first move of the chess game.

"Interesting opening." Viktor Roszca's accented voice came farther from Simon's collar microphone but clear enough.

So Simon's host had adhered to etiquette and allowed him the white pieces and first move. She waited, hands poised on the keyboard, for Roszca's countermove.

A moment later, she heard Simon's commentary. "Black pawn to c5. Hmm."

So soon? First move? Janna straightened at her monitor.

She pictured him leaning thoughtfully over the board as he contemplated his next move. Janna keyed in the two moves and waited for the computer to offer a strategy.

The next move came with a link that read Sicilian Defense. When she scanned the paragraph of notation that popped up, she nearly fell out of her seat.

"Okay, Simon, hang on to your hat. Your move is c3," she said into his earring receiver.

For the next hour, the game followed the pattern and strategy set by the Website. With two exceptions, when Simon's host veered from the expected. But each time, the chess website came up with a countermove.

When Simon conveyed to Janna that each player was down to a small number of pieces, she said, "Time to lose, Simon."

Simon's competitive equality had done the job of raising Roszca's respect level. If they played again, Simon could win, but this game belonged to his host.

But not by much, she vowed, giving Simon the next move for white.

In a few more moves, black had maneuvered so that he had several ways to defeat white. As she'd planned, white had no real way to attack black.

"Well played, sir," Simon said, conceding defeat.

Chairs scraped on the marble floor as the men stood.

"An impressive game, Simon," Roszca said, his booming voice layered with esteem. "I see you are a student of the game as well as a fine player. You must join me in one of the little tournaments I enter from time to time. For amusement only, you understand."

"I'd be honored." There was a pause. "I see you're a man who enjoys competition. Even a small wager. Your yacht, the *Prowler,* looks like a fast boat."

There was silence as Roszca apparently weighed Simon's implication. "I have had occasional need to move fast in her. Yours—that is, your employer's boat—is a Caretti design, no?"

"Twin 700-hp MAN engines. V-drives. More responsive than most women." She pictured the cocky grin on Simon's face.

Roszca laughed, but didn't bite as they left the room.

Opening up the subject was enough of a start, Janna thought. She slumped, exhausted, in the captain's chair at the console. Simon sounded positively chipper. Easy for him. She'd done the heavy lifting.

Chagrin heated her cheeks. She'd directed him, but he'd performed with flair and confidence. He would be impressed when he heard exactly what they'd accomplished.

She couldn't wait to tell him.

Roszca ushered his guest through the courtyard on their way to the dining room. She could hear him pointing out a fountain and various plants to Simon.

Suddenly, a second monitor flickered from a GPS chart to a full-color live shot of two men.

"Holy cow!" Simon had planted the mini-cam. Hooting at the irony of the location, Janna wheeled closer. "Welcome to *Candid Camera.* Stare into the potted palm, please."

"You've brought island nature in to protect your privacy. Impressive," Simon said as he maneuvered Roszca to a better camera angle.

"Some are unique to this small island. Others are imported. Here is one of my particular favorites."

Janna recognized the arms broker from the videos. Dressed in pressed slacks and a khaki shirt with epaulets and flap pockets, Roszca carried himself with military bearing. His black hair, dark brows and mustache bristled with intensity.

"You bastard," she murmured. "We're going to bring you down and stop the nuke sale." And fulfill her personal quest—to find out what official secrets Gabe might have given him.

During their luncheon, Janna used her time to begin trying to hack into Roszca's well-protected computer system. She needed more than intercepted e-mails to find out where the uranium was and what information Gabe might've given him. She needed access to the hard drive.

As she reached for her bottle of water, she heard an odd noise. Her hand stilled. She listened, her heart tripping on itself.

Voices. Footfalls on the deck.

Simon tried not to yawn as Roszca tested his stamina and good nature with yet another long yarn, this one about a chess tournament in Monaco. Thanks to Janna, Simon had acquitted himself well against the big man.

The image of her talking him through the game rose to his inner eye. Leaning forward in rapt attention, her breasts nearly spilling out of her bikini bra. Staring at a chess site, her incredible silvery eyes glittering with excitement. Wheeling from monitor to monitor, her long, tanned legs propelling her.

Simon shook his head and made interested noises as Roszca concluded his story. His libido was interfering with his concentration. Just the sound of her low voice, breathy in his ear, giving him the chess moves had been enough to stir his juices. And now his overactive imagination was distracting him from the mission. Man, he had to stop thinking about Janna as anybody but his tech officer.

Roszca set down his coffee cup and stood. "I have enjoyed our time together today, Simon. Come tomorrow at one o'clock and we will talk business."

The dismissal came sugarcoated, but as subtle as a shark bite. Today's social time and the chess game had apparently satisfied some unknown criteria, and Roszca was ready to deal. So was Simon. "Thank you for a stimulating game, Mr. Roszca, and for the delicious lunch. I'll see you tomorrow."

Roszca gestured toward the bodyguard standing at the courtyard door. "Ivan will see you to the dock."

As Simon wended his way outside and to the dock, he considered Roszca's security force. At least four other men carrying Heckler & Koch 9 mm semiautomatics guarded the compound. Plus the hulking twins, who were nowhere in sight.

Ivan, although fit, was small, wiry. The captain of Roszca's yacht, his intellect made him more dangerous than the muscular but slow-witted twins. Ivan watched Simon's every move through alert, black-button eyes in a leathery face.

The trade winds were blowing again, cooling the afternoon air. In spite of the ceiling fans, the full weight of the tropical heat had blanketed him inside the house. Or maybe it was the cloying scents of the many flowering plants and the heavy tension of the situation. Sweat pooled in his armpits and streamed down his spine. He longed to open his shirt and kick off his shoes.

At the dock, Ivan untied the line as Simon clambered down into the yacht's tender.

Simon noticed that one of Roszca's smaller boats was missing. Stepan and Sergiy probably went out on patrol, he decided.

Ivan turned to stare at the piling where the missing boat was usually tied. His confused gaze shot down to Simon. He appeared about to say something but clamped his mouth shut and hustled back toward the estate.

Probably ticked he missed the outing. Simon figured the guards were probably in the habit of sneaking some extra time for fishing or swimming.

"So long, Ivan ol' buddy," Simon called as he started the motor. "Catch you tomorrow."

As he neared the *Horizon,* he saw the missing motorboat tied up at the stern. His pulse kicked into a gallop.

Janna!

He nearly rammed the swim platform as he pulled up. Had the bastards seen her? Hassled her? Where was she?

In two steps up the gangway, he knew the answers.

He saw the Mr. Clean twins on the deck, waiting for him. Dammit, he should've suspected something like this when the boat and these two guys were missing. *Cool stealth approach, Byrne.* They couldn't have missed the roar of his motor and the clunk of his landing.

Expressionless behind dark sunglasses, one man waved a Glock semiautomatic at him. "You come. Woman here."

Arms folded, Janna glared at her captors from a deck chair. "Simon, tell them I'm not here to attack their boss. I tried to make them understand that I'm just the cook and first mate. But they don't seem to speak English."

"Have these goons touched you?"

"They…grabbed me." A bruise purpled her right forearm. "But I'm fine."

Anger furnace-blasted Simon. But they hadn't molested her, thank God. Relief swept away some of the heat.

He could've kissed her. After all she'd been through with her louse of a husband, she was facing down these goons with bravery and sticking to her undercover role. Even pretending she couldn't understand their language.

Crossing the deck to stand at her side, Simon had no trouble working up a furious scowl. "You guys know a little English. Listen up. You have insulted my woman. Get off my boat." He ignored the pistol's menace and jerked a thumb toward the stern. "Go."

Janna jumped to her feet. "Yes, shoo." She made the appropriate hand motions.

The two men exchanged perplexed glances but stayed put.

Simon guessed they had orders to search the yacht while he lunched with their boss. Nobody had suspected Janna was aboard, so her presence had thrown them off. Their steroid-dulled brains didn't work fast.

A rumble signaling the approach of another motorboat sent Simon to the rail. "What now? Did somebody send out party invitations?"

"It's Roszca. And another man," Janna whispered. "What—?"

"Good," Simon said in a loud voice, snaking an arm around her shoulders and tugging her close. He understood the other bodyguard's behavior on the dock. Ivan had seen the problem and had gone to get his boss.

Simon would have to improvise. Fast. "Now we'll get some results."

As soon as Roszca stepped on board, he barked an order.

His men's guns immediately disappeared into their pockets. The two stood aside.

"Mr. Roszca, your men boarded this yacht without permission. They scared the hell out of my…friend."

The arms broker removed his sunglasses. His avid gaze browsed Janna's assets like a prospective buyer examining a promising filly. "The fault is mine. I sent Stepan and Sergiy for security purposes. In my business, one cannot be too careful. You understand."

Simon should've expected a search. His preoccupation with Janna had scrambled his instincts. "They had no right to frighten Janna here. Or touch her. She has a bruise."

Janna affected a sexy pout. "They…they searched my things. My *personal* things." Her shoulders quivered to indicate her sense of violation. She held the white shirt closed across her breasts.

"They were crude." Roszca made a small bow. "Once they saw you were on board, they should have left." He turned to his men and, in a flurry of Cleatian, gave more orders.

The two chastened bodyguards bowed briefly to Janna, climbed into their boat and sped away.

Once the motor noise diminished, Roszca said to Simon, "I would apologize properly, but we have not been introduced."

Simon released his vise grip on Janna's shoulders and slid a hand down to clasp hers. Her fingers were icicles. "Janna, I'd like you to meet our host, Viktor Roszca." *International arms broker and courtly thug.*

With a tentative look at Simon as if for confidence or approval, she held out a hand to Roszca.

He took her proffered hand and bowed over it. Simon noted with satisfaction that he stopped short of kissing it. "I am honored, Janna. Please accept my deepest apologies for my men's actions. They are loyal, but not refined or clever. I hope you were not harmed."

She shook her head. "Just scared."

"You will both come to dinner tomorrow night at my house. It would please me to show you my island hospitality. Seven o'clock."

At Roszca's invitation, Simon's throat convulsed. His first thought was hell no. How could he do his job and keep her safe at the same time? But this was an offer he couldn't refuse without insulting their host.

Their quarry.

Chapter 10

"We'd be delighted. Right, Janna?"

"Absolutely." Her pout returned, and Simon thought she even batted her lashes. "Will *they* be there?"

"For you, lovely Janna, I shall banish my men." On another small bow, he left.

As Simon watched Roszca speed to the dock, he unclenched his fists finger by finger so he wouldn't punch holes in the fiberglass. Exerting control, he went to Janna and placed his hands gingerly on her shoulders.

"You're sure you're all right? They didn't hurt you?"

"I'm fine. One of them clamped down on my arm while the other one searched." She rubbed the bruise.

"Are we still secure?"

"I heard them on deck in time to mask the monitors. All they saw in the console was the normal nav gear. The other weapons and our IDs are still behind the panel in the galley."

"First undercover test and right out of the starting gate you went for the rail. Great work, Janna." He planted a quick kiss on her forehead.

She beamed. "Thanks. I guess we're okay then."

"Okay? Not by a long shot." Swearing under his breath, he stalked back and forth on the deck. "Hell, I should've anticipated a search. My neglect put you in danger. You have to get away. I won't let you go into that animal's lair."

Hands on hips, she glared at him. "*You* won't let me? Simon, you may be my superior, but the mission leaves you no choice. I can be another set of eyes and ears on the island."

"No way, Q. You're my second set of eyes and ears already. Now that the bugs are in place and working, you can monitor them from the control boat as well as from here."

He hadn't protected her from Gabe, but dammit he'd protect her now. He cared too much for her to chance Roszca getting his paws on her. A glimpse of her bruise at the hands of those thugs roused anger in him all over again. The thought of her chatting with that slime clawed at his chest. Fury drummed down his nerve endings.

Her sharp intake of breath stopped him in his pacing. "You *can't* send me away! Don't try to control me, Simon. You can't order me around. You don't own—" Cheeks painted red with indignation, she stopped mid-sentence, shook her head and put a hand to her mouth.

The bottom dropped out of his fury, eclipsed by bewilderment. He closed the distance between them to a step. "What is it? What's the matter?"

"Oh, Simon, forgive me. That was unprofessional." Her chin trembled, and she gazed upward at a single, high cloud. When she focused on Simon again, her eyes were clear, but with pain in their storm-sky depths. "First, those…twin thugs and then you ordering me…I lost it. I apologize."

Her distress wrenched at his heart. His arms ached to enfold her, but he wouldn't start something he shouldn't finish. He'd failed her again, but had no clue how to make things right. Other than to leave her the hell alone.

"Hey, you have every right to be upset. They hurt you, and then Roszca…" He stopped as he felt anger heating him.

"It's more than that. Loss of control over my life terrifies me. My therapist has helped me become more assertive, but I have to temper my panic and anger so I don't overreact."

The low, shaky sound of her voice found resonance in the hollow inside him. Emotional fallout from her husband's abuse, yet she still looked to vindicate him. An emotional tangle that didn't leave room for another man. Not Simon, of course.

"Saint Gabriel again, the bastard. He did a number on you. I overreacted, too." *Out of fear for you.*

She tugged her shirttail smooth in an apparent effort at calm. The action didn't hide the swell of her breasts or the dip of her waist, bared by the bikini. The scent of her sun-warmed skin teased him. If he couldn't touch, he'd torture himself with the sight and scent.

"Simon, let's look at this logically." Her witchy gray eyes held him—steady, no flirting, no fear. "You *had* to accept Roszca's invitation to dinner, didn't you?"

"Right. Refusing would've slapped him in the face."

"And slammed the door on our mission."

"Exactly."

"Sending me away would accomplish exactly the same end. Roszca would see my absence as an insult. We'd have no choice but to fold. Roszca might even spot the contact boat. ATSA wouldn't find out where the stolen nukes are or learn what government secrets Gabe might have told Roszca."

"Or roll up the man who armed the New Dawn Warriors." Simon pushed at the shock of hair on his forehead and sank into the nearest deck chair. "Man, when you argue with logic, Q, you're a pistol. I bull ahead on instinct and intuition."

"Don't knock intuition. You saw the situation, thought on your feet and went with Roszca's change of program."

He shrugged, making light of her compliment. "We'll see how switching gears pans out. Tech officers are supposed to stay in the background. Another rule broken, but it can't be helped. I'll advise Thorne."

"Simon, the chess game—"

His smile nearly blinded her. "Hey, Q, you really came through on that one. I felt like a grand master."

"You were channeling one. The opening moves were right out of Kasparov's first game against Deep Blue. I took it from there."

He stared at her as though she'd grown another head. "You mean when the chess champ played the IBM computer? That's what we did?"

She chuckled at his shock. "I used a Website that guided your moves to match Kasparov's in that famous game. I'm not sure I could do as well a second time."

He gave a long, low whistle. "Better avoid more chess. I've dangled the yacht-race bait a little more. He'll calculate the bigger *Prowler*'s chances against the *Horizon*'s before he goes for it, but I'll have him."

He stood, headed in to call the command boat. "You up for a whole evening of the boat bunny act?"

"I can play my part. I learned to be very good at playing a part. At least, this one's temporary."

He saw her wry grin as he slid down the companionway into the saloon. With Gabe, she meant, playing the Stepford wife he'd tried to mold her into.

Two sets of talons scraped at Simon's chest—guilt and fear. Guilt at failing her. Fear he couldn't keep her safe this time, either. As a trained operative, she had to face the same risks any ATSA officer faced. He had to think of her as a colleague only.

No. Hell, he had to think of her as a boat bunny.

* * *

"Great chicken," Simon said.

Janna couldn't take her eyes from the flex of his muscled forearms as he wiped down the kitchen counter. "Thanks. I'm limited to the galley's ingredients. I adapted the recipe from one I got from my family's cook." She picked up her wineglass and followed him out of the galley.

They settled side by side on the foredeck, bare legs hanging over the side. Some of the day's heat had dissipated in the evening breeze, perfumed with the small island's hibiscus and frangipani.

The gibbous moon—their only light—dappled stars on the water and heightened Simon's thoughtful expression. "A recipe from a cook. We had very different childhoods. You had your parents and God knows how many servants, and I had… myself."

She knew only bits and pieces about Simon's rough beginnings in Baltimore. "Was it before or after you lost your mom that the Pimlico stable manager took you in?"

He took a long drink of wine. "Both. Long before Mom died, I lost her to her pills. She had a bad back from the car crash that killed my dad. She swallowed painkillers like candy. One night, the older guys I ran with broke into the vet office at the track. Looking for drugs. When the lights came on, they got away. I didn't."

The rumble of a motor announced the return of the nightly patrol. In the boat's wake, tiny lights danced, the output of microscopic, luminescent marine creatures. Janna and Simon didn't wave as the guards passed. Neither did the guards.

"How old were you?"

"Thirteen. And small for my age. With a big mouth." He grinned. "Doc nabbed me and put me to work cleaning stables."

"Instead of jail. He did you a big favor." Simon had once told her that the other guys had gone on to bigger crimes. But he didn't.

"More than that. He saved my life." His voice hitched, betraying his love for his mentor.

"I remember." Doc became the father that Simon had lost so young. "You had an aunt, I recall. Why didn't you go to her after you lost your mom?"

"Aunt Minnie. She was willing, but her drunken husband wasn't. I was better off with Doc."

No blood relative to want him, to care for him. Her heart ached for him. "Do you still keep in touch with him?"

A muscle tightened in his jaw, and he directed his gaze toward the horizon. "Doc died my junior year at UM. Heart attack."

"Oh, Simon, I'm so sorry. That must've been rough."

"Yeah. People die. Things change. That's life. I married Summer soon after that. Mistake." He downed the last of his wine and leaned back on his elbows.

She twisted to face him so her bare knee rested against his thigh. His body heat seemed concentrated in that single point, jolting her temperature. His unbuttoned shirt fell open and tempted her to thread her fingers through the dark hairs dusting his chest and arrowing down to his shorts.

Janna averted her gaze to his face. She remembered the brush of his whiskers on her cheek, her lips, imagined their rasp against her breasts, her belly.

She'd never known his wife's name, only that he'd been married and divorced. This was the most he'd ever shared without using humor to be evasive. She'd sensed the hurt behind his cocky mask, but hadn't understood enough. "You met your wife in college."

"We had a good couple of years, but she couldn't take the life of a DEA agent. The absences, the secrecy, the danger." He tipped his head, the mocking grin in place. "But, hey, once a loner, always a loner. If I want to spend a week at my cabin in the western Maryland woods, I do it. I got nobody to answer to but ATSA."

Nobody to answer to. Nobody to love. Both parents. His mentor. His wife. Janna's heart ached for Simon as she added up his losses. He'd lost everyone he'd ever been close to. Even his hoodlum friends. The realization stunned her.

Breathing in the subtle scent of Simon's soap and the more distinctive one of his skin, she felt a rush at the sense of connectedness. A wave of longing swept through her.

"Hey, now that you don't have to hide from Roszca, how about a moonlight swim?" Simon was on his feet before she could blink.

"You got it." She'd let him change the subject, but not for long. "I didn't get to go snorkeling today, so I need a good swim. Last one in is a rotten hacker."

"Q, your numero-uno job on this gig is as a hacker. Rotten is no option. Looks like I lose the dare before post time."

She laughed as they headed to their cabins to change.

Janna stripped off her tank top and shorts. Being a loner was an act for Simon. He used devil-may-care charm as a cover for loneliness. The cocky rule-breaker facade masked a disappointed idealist who was fiercely honest and loyal. He'd transferred her guilt to himself—but at what cost?

No wonder he avoided relationships. Caring meant being hurt again.

Exactly *her* reason for keeping people at arm's length. And no less valid.

Her insights into Simon's soul melted the hardened boundaries of her heart. It gave a hard kick against the wall of her chest before taking off like one of Simon's beloved racehorses.

No. The last thing she needed was to fall for Simon.

She doubted he'd ever hurt or betray her, but she couldn't take that chance. Never again would she put herself in the trap of a relationship. Never again would she give up her self, give control of her life to a man. Even to a good man. Not in this lifetime.

Could she leave her heart out of the equation if they gave in to the desire hovering between them on the tropical air? Could they simply enjoy each other?

She didn't know. But perhaps they could help each other heal. She hadn't had that many sexual experiences before her marriage. Gabe's attentions had been demands rather than love-making. The desire Simon sparked was reviving a part of her she'd thought was dead. He could bring her senses alive again and make new memories to shut out the bad ones—if he'd stop piling on the guilt.

She might have to make the first move. Seduction was not her forte. But making the first move put her in control. Where she needed to be.

A scene in one of her favorite romance novels occurred to her. Something she'd never dared to do with Gabe, who had no sense of humor. Uncertain of Simon's reaction, she placed a hand over her stomach, where a school of the coral reef's blue tangs was swirling. No, she wouldn't be afraid. Simon wouldn't hurt her.

If she could pull it off, the ploy might just work.

Janna tossed her cover-up shirt aside. He'd already seen her scars, hadn't he? She dug through her swimwear for the skimpiest bikini her boat bunny wardrobe included.

Simon knew the moment Janna came back up on deck because his temperature climbed like a flu victim's.

Carrying two white fluffy towels, she sauntered toward him. The light from the companionway behind her silhouetted every undulation of her hips in the bikini bottom, made of some kind of wet-looking stuff. *Whoa, mama.*

His mouth tasted as dry as sand. The tiny pink triangle rode high above her tanned, taut thighs and low on her smooth belly. Her legs stretched into next week. And oh, man, the bra—a misnomer—barely covered her nipples. He imagined her legs wrapped around him, how sweet her nipples would taste.

His body reacted, shooting lust through him so he could barely breathe. Good thing he'd nixed bikinis for himself in favor of trunk-style suits, or his condition would be tent-pole obvious.

Janna slung the towels over the aft rail and joined him on the swim platform. Her slow smile seemed to tilt her witchy eyes so he felt like he was falling into them, into silver clouds.

"How nice," she said. "You've secured the tender on the star-board side, clear of the platform. You're getting the hang of boat life, Simon." Her voice flowed low and warm right into his bloodstream.

"Starboard. Uh, yeah." He could see her nipples bud against the thin bra. He stifled a groan. Sweat streamed down his torso, and he backed toward the outer edge of the platform.

Swinging her hips, she closed the space between them. One cool finger burned a trail down his temple. She tossed the sweat she'd gathered to the breeze. "Ooh, poor baby. Are you *hot,* Simon?"

"*Hot?* Oh, yeah. Hot." But the heat shimmering between them sure as hell had nothing to do with the tropical night. He inhaled her almond scent and ached to taste her silky skin, like dark honey in the scant light. His pulse throbbed to the beat of the water slapping against the hull.

"I thought so."

Her husky laugh curled tingles through him. The moonlight painted shades of platinum and wheat on her flirty hair. That same cool finger, now damp with his sweat, danced over his shoulder and down his chest. He'd give up breathing, give *anything* if she'd continue downward.

Her hand stopped at the base of his sternum. "Then you need to cool off."

She pushed.

Air rushed past Simon as he flopped backward with a splash. An instant before the bathwater-warm Caribbean closed over his head, he saw Janna dive. Her slender body, straight as an arrow, sliced the water beside him.

They bobbed to the surface at the same time.

Simon watched Janna swim away a few feet as he shook back his hair. With her wet hair sleeked back, she belonged in the water, a mermaid.

He spouted a fountain of salty water. "Yuck. This stuff tastes saltier than my aunt Minnie's fried chicken. Way saltier than Chesapeake Bay. Hey, but I barely have to work to float." He'd swum every day, but hadn't noticed. Worry about leaving Janna alone had curtailed his enjoyment.

"You're okay then?" she asked.

The tight set of her mouth meant worry that he'd be angry. His gut clenched. *Gabe strikes again, the bastard.* At least she'd had the gumption to take a chance on teasing him. He sent her a grin of reassurance. "Okay? Come here and I'll show you how *okay* I am."

She shook her head, spraying droplets onto the surface. A smile twitched up the corners of her mouth. "No way. You'll dunk me or something."

Or something. Smart woman. The dunking she'd given him might've cooled his skin, but not the furnace inside him. If he got his hands on her wet, bare skin, he might be tempted to sample the salt on her neck, her breasts, her belly. He might have to taste every inch.

Wiser to keep temptation farther than arm's length. He'd failed her more than once. She didn't need a loner like him. He sure as hell didn't need another woman who'd leave. A woman who might still love a ghost. Why that notion carved another empty space in his chest, he refused to examine.

For her, he manufactured a gasp of shock. "Never. Would I do that?" He placed a hand over his heart and gazed skyward.

Laughing, she hit her palms on the surface and splashed him. "We could race around the boat. One, two, three, go!" Without waiting for his response, she took off with a strong overhand. All he could see as she splashed toward the bow was a flash of stroking arms and her perfect heart-shaped butt.

Racing in this bathwater seemed like too much work to Simon. Floating on his back, he paddled to the right—correction, starboard—corner of the swim platform. He had only to wait.

When Janna touched the platform, he popped up in her face. "What took you so long?"

She sank, splashing and sputtering.

Simon slung an arm around her waist and yanked her back to the surface. He tethered them with one hand on the yacht. "I didn't mean to scare you."

Coughing, she clung to his shoulders.

With her this close, he could barely think. He felt his heart knocking against his sternum.

She was breathtaking. Water beaded her lashes. The moon shone in her pupils, dilated so there was almost no silvery gray. Water streamed down her cleavage.

She pulled closer.

As they bobbed together in the water, her breasts brushed his chest. The barely-a-bra slipped, and one shell-pink, pebbled nipple peeked at him.

Every molecule in his body stood at attention. His pulse sprinted and his entire body clenched. Intense as a volcano, desire blasted through him.

He sucked in a heated breath.

Her gray eyes turned smoky. Her wet lips parted. "Just what *did* you mean to do, Simon?"

Not this.

His mouth took hers with a fierceness he'd never felt before. A raw jolt of electricity shot to his belly as he tasted her, sweet and salt and Janna. She sighed into his mouth and ran her hands over his shoulders and down his back. Her taut, slender body fit against him perfectly, her skin soft as flower petals to the touch.

He eased her closer, pillowing her breasts against him. When her erect nipples tickled his chest, he saw that the bikini top had slipped to her waist. Her high, perfect breasts glistening in the moonlight was the most beautiful sight he'd ever seen.

The weightless buoying of the bathwater-warm Caribbean, the wet slide of their heated bodies, the tropical canopy overhead—surreal seduction he couldn't deny.

He kissed and licked his way down her slender neck, down the upper swells of her breasts, to the nipples that begged for his tongue to taste them.

When he drew first one, then the other nipple into his mouth, she shuddered with delight.

He nearly lost it right there.

Sweet, so sweet and warm. Salted almonds. His body throbbed with need. A need to possess this brave and beautiful woman, a need that burned a direct fuse to desperate.

He drew her closer, massaged his aching shaft against the softness of her flat belly.

Her hands on his shoulders tightened. Her sweet breath puffed against his lips. In her wide eyes, he saw a glimmer of doubt, of fear.

He swallowed, shuddered, as he controlled his straining body. *Damn Gabriel Harris.* She would set the boundaries, the pace. If it killed him, he would never cause her fear.

And holding back just might kill him.

Chapter 11

Panic stiffened Janna in Simon's arms for only a brief moment. He was only a few inches taller than she, but much, much stronger. He could overpower her, hurt her if he wanted.

She felt his powerful need for her. She felt his arms encircling her, but they were supporting her. He posed no threat. No smothering trap. He would free her if she chose.

The old fear evaporated. Only warmth and arousal pervaded her. She snuggled closer into his gentle embrace, made even more tender by the obvious strain in his body and his words.

Desire burned in his chocolate-brown eyes, but tension crinkled their edges. His muscles flexed as he started to release her. "Janna, do you want me to stop?"

She released a sigh and melted against him. "Don't stop."

She wrapped a leg around his thigh, pressing her belly against his arousal.

He groaned and took her mouth again. Deep, delicious kisses that poured heat into her body and sizzled her blood. His wet beard stubble prickled softly against her cheek, against her breasts. She greedily inhaled his scent—seawater and hot skin and male musk.

She rubbed her fingertips over the muscled contours of his chest. She nibbled at his earlobe and the earring that so intrigued her—the real diamond, not the communicator. She slid downward, the seawater sluicing around them, between their stroking bodies.

Her flesh tingled at the sensation.

With the recognition of freedom, her soul rejoiced. Simon didn't trap her beneath him. Buoyed by the salt water, they held each other, gave pleasure to each other as equals.

She wasn't helpless, but empowered. Free.

A soft, vibrant warmth uncurled inside her, and desire returned, in currents that swirled inside her stronger than ever before.

When her hand closed over his straining shaft, he groaned and peeled off his trunks to give her better access. He shuddered against her hand, not driving into her, but allowing her to explore and stroke.

"Sadist," he gritted out against her mouth.

She smiled. "Your turn."

His hand slid across her abdomen, inside her bikini and between her legs. With his thumb, he stroked her most sensitive spot. Her flesh felt tight and wild. Sensation plucked at her nerve endings, licking her with a flame just out of reach.

"*Simon*," she cried, shimmying out of the tiny swimsuit.

He withdrew his hand slowly and held her hips. "No protection." His voice cracked with agonized restraint.

Passion fogged her brain, saturating her senses, so his meaning didn't click immediately. "Protection. Oh, I'm on the pill. ATSA regs for undercover."

He flashed a whiter-than-white pirate grin. "Now that's one rule I approve of."

His lightning bolt of a kiss sent shock waves through her.

He followed it with a knowing hand that sought and stroked and brought gasping moans of pleasure from her lips.

She opened to him, wrapping her legs around his body and arching backward. Sensations sparked as though falling stars had entered her body.

Then his hand withdrew and he pushed solidly into her. At the spiraling heat of his invasion, she clenched and unclenched her muscles around him. They surged together, waves of pleasure rippling through her, around her, between them, until the flood rolled through her from the deep recesses of her body, swamping her with spasms of molten sensation and swirling her into oblivion.

He stiffened against her as his climax took him. He shouted an incoherent cry of pleasure as he followed her into the whirlpool.

Long moments later, Simon peeled her legs from around his taut flanks. He set her away from him. "Are you all right?"

His impersonal tone and shuttered expression drove a knifepoint into Janna. The edge of the swim platform cut into her hand as she sought calm. "Never better. Simon, what—?"

"This was a mistake. You don't really want me." He pushed himself up onto the swim platform and offered her a hand.

Her arms were empty, but her body ached for him. The water that had felt warm earlier now chilled her skin.

She let him hoist her onto the boat.

"I believe I do, but *you* seem to know what I want more than I," she snapped. "You wanted me a few minutes ago. We gave in to chemistry. Was that wrong or misguided?"

He finger-combed his hair away from his face. It was the first time she'd seen it stay in place. Dripping water on the deck, he stood there apparently unconcerned about his nakedness. "Yeah, I want you. I've always wanted you. But anything more than a one-time thing won't fly, and we still have to work together. Not cool."

She snatched a towel from the stern rail and wrapped it around her. "It wouldn't work out? Do you mean the sex?"

"You're not making this easy."

"Darn right." Her heart clattered in her chest like an overworked hard drive, but she kept her face impassive. Gripping the towel around her held her hands steady.

He huffed out an exasperated sigh. "Not the sex. We sizzled the water to a boil back there."

"What then? You afraid I'll cling?"

From his deer-in-the-headlights look, she knew she'd hit it. That, and his guilt about not rescuing her from Gabe.

"Janna, I don't do relationships. They don't pan out for me. And you're working your way out of a deep pit." Finally, he slapped the other towel around his hips. Too late. She'd seen exactly how much he still wanted her.

"Oh, you think it's a rebound thing." She marched across the deck and poked an index finger at his bare chest. "Let me tell you something. I'm done with relationships myself. Been there, done that. Once burned, if you get my drift."

He winced, as well he should. "It's not the same thing."

She jabbed him again. "No matter. You feel guilty you didn't save me from my abusive husband. So you took your chance to help out the poor widow."

He grabbed her hand. "Janna, for the love of—"

"Will you stop interrupting me!" Flattening her palm against his chest, she felt his heart racing as fast as hers.

She could see in his eyes when he yielded, but just as quickly, he masked his emotion, masked his renewed desire for her. Anxiety shivered through her and tightened her chest. She had to make him understand.

His big hand curled around hers. "Okay. I'm listening."

"Simon," she said in a gentler tone, "love has nothing to do with it. Being human again is what I want. To regain my sense of self, to feel an emotion other than fear. To live without jumping out of my skin every time someone touches me. When you kiss me, when you hold me, I'm not afraid. This time was wonderful, but it was a beginning. You can help me heal."

And maybe we can heal each other.

When she finished, he remained silent. His brown eyes, dark and brooding, hid his thoughts. Shadows and moonlight scored his face into harsh planes and sharp angles. Only the leap of a jaw muscle beneath his whiskers betrayed the emotional battle within.

Simon lifted her hand to his mouth. He pressed a moist kiss to her palm, a kiss so tender she nearly wept. "You're forgetting we have a mission. A dangerous mission that distraction could crash and burn. No, this ends it, Janna. You'd regret more. And so would I."

He turned and went below without another word.

After the negotiating session the next morning with Viktor Roszca, Simon loosened the dinghy's line from the dock. That knot slipped free, but Janna still had him tied up so tight that every muscle in his body ached.

She filled his mind and soul with longing. Dark, bottomless kisses. Supple skin and the sensuous weight of her breasts in his hands. Her unique scent, laced last night with salt. She was a wonder—sleek femininity, an incisive mind, strength and vulnerability.

He wanted her with heart-stopping hunger. When they merely brushed in passing, his body hummed with arousal. The dual needs to protect and possess burned in his heart. One time with her and he was in big trouble.

Help her heal? How could he help her heal without scarring himself? Without sinking in deeper? She was already special to him. She might not hate him for failing her about Gabe, but one day she'd see how vast their differences were. He was a street tough. She was a socialite with a brilliant mind.

When that day came, she'd want out. She'd leave.

Tension pounded in his temples and shafted pain in his chest. He fought the urge to howl in protest. No, he wouldn't set himself up for that fall again.

Then there was the mission to bring down Roszca. His preoccupation with Janna threatened his alertness, his focus. He had to fight his lightning-hot reactions to her. Fight his mind from drifting to her.

He turned the key to start the engine. When the motor rumbled to life, he steered for the *Horizon*. Terns dipped and dived at the water's surface, their aerodynamic bodies like bullets through the air.

Pulse thrumming in anticipation, he looked for Janna on the deck. When she waved from the flying bridge, his soul sang at the sight.

Keeping his mind and hands off her for the next few days might kill him.

When he tied up at the yacht's stern, he congratulated himself on bringing the dinghy in smoothly. Especially in his delicate condition.

The first things he saw were their swimsuits from last night. Seeming to mock him, they hung on the stern rail to dry. Janna must've done some diving to retrieve what he'd racked up as lost. He wouldn't consider what else that meant.

"That went well," Janna said, as she met him on the afterdeck. She wore a swimsuit that covered up most of the eye-popping parts and her sleeveless white shirt, which hid the burn scars.

His body clenched with craving anyway. *Down, boy.*

He coughed, aiming for control. "Not bad. Room to maneuver on both sides. Roszca's not going to commit until he talks to all the contenders."

"He seemed closer to taking the bait on a race, too."

"Wary son of a bitch. Circling the proposition to check all the angles. He didn't reach the top of his game acting on impulse."

Janna sighed. "Too bad your tour didn't take you into private quarters and the offices. I wish our electronics were picking up more juicy info than what's on the dinner menu. Once I thought I heard a woman's voice, but I wasn't sure."

"I haven't seen any females. The cook is male, but maybe the maids are women. Roszca's musclemen ferry over a cleaning crew once a week from Montego Bay."

"Maybe." She leaned a hip against the rail. The breeze lifted her hair, sunlit to white gold and wheat. Strands caught in her mouth, but she didn't seem to notice. "You arranged for more discussions in the next couple of days. That should give me enough time to find what we need in his computer system before we have to scram."

"How's that going?"

He couldn't take his eyes off the corner of her luscious mouth, where wheat-colored strands were caught. As if on its own, his hand reached out to tug the hair loose. His finger trailed across her soft cheek before he withdrew.

Hands off, remember?

She smiled and lowered her sunglasses. Her witchy eyes held him. "Slow but sure. He has more firewalls than the NSA, but I'm getting there. Firewalls are just packet filters and can be bypassed using techniques like fragmented packets. Then once I break the password, I'll send in a sniffer and—"

His mind fogged. "Whoa, Q. That's more techspeak than this boy's brain can wrap itself around. Just go for it. Find the location of his nuclear material before he moves it."

She laughed, a husky refrain that curled around inside his chest. "I'll get back to it now. Let's go below. Jack Thorne's waiting for you to check in." She turned and ambled toward the companionway.

Simon pulled his gaze from her swaying behind and stared at the deck. Why was she so damned cheerful? As if he hadn't pushed her away after the best sex he'd ever experienced, after more than sex. As if his rejection bothered her less than a mosquito bite. Worry crimped his brow.

"What's the matter, Simon?"

The touch of her soft hand on his forearm streaked wild currents through him. He jerked to attention. "Oh, nothing, just planning my report."

She turned again, but waited at the companionway.

He'd have to squeeze past her if she didn't move, feel that tautly curved body against him, inhale her almond scent. "Ladies first."

She rolled her eyes, but started forward. When she stumbled at the lip of the opening, he put out a hand to steady her.

"Thanks." She beamed a smile over her shoulder.

She seemed okay, but he kept a hand on the small of her back until she started down the short set of steps.

Didn't count as touching. He was just being a gentleman.

At the helm, they sat side by side. Janna sent stealth UDP scans as part of her probe into their quarry's household network. Concentrating was tough. Her pulse wouldn't settle. She couldn't help but be constantly aware of Simon as he reported to the control officer. And she knew from his sideways glances that he was just as aware of her.

A good reason not to give up on reaching him.

Their lovemaking last night had given her more pleasure than she'd ever felt in Gabe's arms. Simon's uptight reaction convinced her he was trapped in the same kind of emotional prison as she was. He needed her, even if he didn't know it. Their being together could be no more distracting from the mission than the magnetic field arcing between them already.

They would walk away when their fling ended, that was a given. Normal for him. The prospect wrenched at her heart, but there was no other choice. She'd at least have good memories to replace the bad.

She'd have to keep reminding him of what he was missing.

When he ended the secure transmission, he said, "Thorne wants you to put a rush on the hacking. He has three techs on board ready to copy the entire hard drive once you get in. There's a rumor the nuclear material will be moved in a day or two, ready for the sale. Losing it could be disastrous."

"The so-called summit starts Thursday. We need to be out of here by Wednesday—that's only three days. And Roszca's not close enough to agreeing to a race." She leaned back in her swivel chair, contemplating the urgency. And a possibility. "I'm getting there. If I could insert an open-sesame monitor directly into his hard drive from any one of the stations, that would do it. Tonight—"

Simon shot to his feet. "No. Uh-uh, no way. Tonight you're playing Janna the boat bunny, not the spy. Don't even think about putting your hot little hands on his computer. You could get us both killed."

She held up her hands in surrender. "You're probably right. Guess I've broken enough ATSA rules."

He flopped into the captain's chair again. "Sorry, Q, but wild chances are out of the question. If this doesn't work, we'll find another way."

"You mean Roszca and his enriched uranium sale, not what secrets Gabe might've spilled."

Simon regarded her oddly, silently, as if weighing her words. "Once you crack the network, the techs will find out what Gabe revealed later. Finding the nukes is priority."

Priority for ATSA, but Janna needed to know the full story on her husband's nefarious activities.

Essential for closing that book.

Then maybe she could sleep soundly again. Maybe she could hear his name without feeling a tight pain in her chest. Maybe she could move on. But until she hacked into Roszca's system, what Gabe had done was a moot point.

Hands on the keyboard, she asked, "How much damage can a small amount of enriched uranium do?"

"You mean you haven't researched it?" He sent her a teasing smile.

"No time. Had to refine my hacking skills."

"You're in luck because I have. Depends on how small the amount we're talking about is. Intel says Roszca's stash is about five kilos, or a little more than ten pounds. Even so, five kilos could net him up to a hundred million in his private black-market auction. And five kilos is plenty to make a small nuclear bomb or arm a shoulder-fired missile."

"Or a dirty bomb?"

"Death and destruction almost anywhere. If terrorists get their hands on nuclear weapons, no telling what catastrophes they could dream up. ATSA's immediate problem is that because of its density, five kilos of uranium takes up less room than a can of beer, even in a secure canister."

"Easy to transport."

"And we don't know if a buyer might already have a stash to add it to."

Every aspect of this mission seemed more urgent with each passing day. Her shoulders quivered with a shudder. "I'll probe more after lunch. You up for a sandwich?"

"My stomach is scraping my backbone. Last night's chicken should make dynamite sandwiches. I'll slice." Simon watched as she made her way through the saloon to the galley. The boat's gentle rocking seemed to require more hip action when she walked. Not that he was complaining.

At the steps that led down to the tiny galley, she stopped so suddenly that he nearly crashed into her.

She leaned against the rail to gaze up at him. "Simon, it feels good to kid around again, to be friends. Maybe being more than that wouldn't work for us, but we're not as different as you think."

"What do you mean?" In his view, they were as different as Arabians and Holsteins.

"Your mom wasn't there for you, but neither were my parents. They'd dress me up to show me off at parties, but otherwise left me alone with my studies. They were distant, indifferent. Almost…ashamed. As though my intelligence were a dirty secret to keep in the closet."

"They didn't *get* you." Simon's grin slid into a wistful smile. "No dirty secret, your brain is your secret weapon. The hottest geek I know."

"I've struggled to be taken seriously. People stereotype me by my outside."

"Beauty queens have no brains, huh? That your reason for the goggles and the nun suits, even after Gabe's death?"

"Partly. I wore the glasses through college and grad school, but dropped them once I established myself in ATSA. Wearing them interfered with close work."

He reached up to flick the hair over her ear. The feathery strands slipped through his fingers. Mentally slapping himself for forgetting his hands-off rule, he jerked his hand away.

Realizing that she no longer flinched when he touched her gave him an idea. "Gabe had you wear the nun suits to keep men away. Then you chose to wear that armor for protection."

"Thank you, Simon, for *getting* me." She stretched up and pressed her lips to his.

The kiss shot a raw bolt of lightning through Simon's bloodstream. His lips tingled and his body tightened, even as she was pulling away.

She beamed him a sunny smile, apparently unaffected. "One thing I missed about being friends was your riddles."

Riddles? He could barely get a grip on reality. But geek humor had kept the relationship light, just what he needed. "Um, how many software engineers does it take to change a lightbulb?" Same old joke, but she'd never answered it.

Mischief glinted in her beautiful eyes. "You can't come up with a geek joke that'll stump me. We techs trade them on-line every day."

"Quit stalling, Q. So how many software engineers to change a lightbulb?"

Smiling, she let her gaze meander meaningfully down his body. Her sultry regard enveloped him like a steam bath.

"It can't be done," she said, with enough heat to thaw the galley's Sub-Zero fridge. "It's a…*hard*ware problem."

His pulse took a thrill ride. He watched her dance away, down to the galley as if nothing had happened.

Sizzling kisses. Double entendre in the geek riddle's answer. Not what he'd had in mind to lighten things up.

Just what did *she* have in mind?

Chapter 12

"Welcome to my humble home." Viktor Roszca was resplendent in pale-yellow crepe trousers and a paneled dress shirt to match. Janna'd expected a sophisticated world traveler to be beyond outdated Cleatian fashion. But no. He looked like an underworld character from another era.

The gracious welcome came from his lips only. His sharp blue eyes had the mien of a hunter—merciless, cold and probing for weakness.

As his gaze undressed her, she felt sullied and cheap in her slip dress, cut up to here and down to there. At least, the high back covered the burn scars.

She must've hesitated because she felt Simon's hand at the small of her back giving her a slight push, as though to remind her that cheap was her persona.

"Your house is beautiful." She forced herself to smile at Roszca's welcome. She'd be sure to wash off his sweaty handshake later. For now, she folded her hands in front of her to keep them from shaking.

"A high compliment indeed coming from such a lovely lady." He preened as he shook Simon's hand. "Do come into the living room. My chef has prepared appetizers and a rum punch."

She and Simon sat on a snowy damask loveseat as they chatted with their host. In his own way, Simon had the underworld look, though a trendier one. Black silk mesh shirt and white slacks, woven slip-ons without socks. And, of course, the earring. Baltimore street tough goes South Beach. She would've giggled if his nearness didn't have her on edge.

He was constantly touching her with one hand on her back or her arm or her knee. Meaningless, only a demonstration of possession, she reminded herself. But she welcomed the solid and secure feel he gave her.

"And what do you do all day, Janna," Roszca asked, "while we men talk business?" He passed her a tall, frosty glass garnished with a pick of fruit chunks.

Small sips of the powerful rum drink were all she allowed herself. She needed all her wits tonight.

Simon squeezed her knee in subtle reassurance.

She gave a toss of her head, mimicking Deena. Her neighbor knew just what moves would show off feminine assets. "Oh, I'm a bit of an amateur bird-watcher. I've done some sketches of the pelicans and gulls."

"Janna's a great artist," Simon said. "You expect her pelican to splash into the water."

"That's *so* not true, Simon. But thanks." Pure hyperbole. With a pencil she wasn't much, but ATSA had insisted on a plausible, nontechnical pastime in case she was noticed.

"Sketching?" Their host gazed upward as if pondering the possibility. "I believe Stepan mentioned seeing a sketchbook on the yacht."

Her lower lip jutted out in a pout. "Yes, he tore one of the pages. I'd love to get a look at an orangequit. Are there any on Isla Alta?"

Roszca regarded her with a patronizing smile. "Alas, I regret I know little about the wildlife here. But Ivan tells me hummingbirds come to the flowers in the courtyard."

"Ooh, there are three different species in Cuba and Jamaica. If you have hummingbirds, you must have wonderful flowers in your courtyard."

"I have several rare species," the arms dealer said. "Cultivated, of course. Not wild, like your birds."

More compliments might win her a tour and access to computer terminals. With only three days left, she needed to get into that system, in spite of Simon's dire warning. With all the rule breaking, she hardly recognized herself.

As though he'd read her mind, Simon squeezed her knee. "Mr. Roszca is prouder of his small armada. His yacht's horsepower rivals *Horizon'*s."

"*Prowler* is such a pretty boat." She gave him a wide smile. "So big and sleek. I'll bet she cuts through the water like a knife."

A careless wave of her hand jangled her clunky bracelet. One of the rectangular beads contained a miniature USB flash drive with her open-sesame monitor program. Undetectable in most cases. All she needed was a moment alone with one of the computer terminals.

"What a coincidence," said Roszca. "Simon and I have been discussing the idea of—" He stopped suddenly and stood.

She followed his gaze. A woman stood in the arched entry, a tentative smile on her delicate face. Dark-haired, she wore a banana-yellow strapless sarong-style dress that set off her vivid coloring and voluptuous curves.

Was this woman Roszca's wife? Research hadn't mentioned a new wife since his third divorce. She looked in her early thirties, only a few years older than Janna, a couple of decades younger than Viktor Roszca. From Roszca's ardent reaction, not his daughter. A mistress then.

Holding out both hands, he said, "Ah, my dear, I am so pleased you felt well enough to join us."

His profile was to Janna, but she saw concern and something like warning flit across his bold features.

The woman took his hands and stepped into the room. "I want to meet our guests." Her Cleatian-accented English was more hesitant than Roszca's. "I so seldom see another woman."

"This is Yelena," Roszca said, a minimal introduction, to Janna's mind. "Simon is the man with whom I have been meeting this week. And Janna is his…"

"Crew." Simon stood and shook Yelena's hand. "I'm pleased to meet you." He stood aside for Janna to greet the woman.

"How do you do?" Janna said. "Crew, yes. I do the navigation and some of the cooking. And…whatever else might be required." She loaded the last words with innuendo and tucked her hand in the crook of Simon's arm. She wasn't sure, but he might've blushed.

Roszca brought a chair beside him for the newcomer. "Yelena has not been well, or you would have met her sooner. You will have her to thank for tonight's excellent menu."

"You cooked for us?" Janna asked.

Yelena held up a hand in denial. "*Nich,* I did not cook. Viktor's chef is talented, but only at preparing the food, not the menu. How do you say—" She looked to Roszca.

"Coordinating the dishes," he finished for her.

"Time is also a problem for him," Yelena said, her eyes downcast. "Dinner will not be ready for a little moment." She twisted her hands together in her lap.

Their host's black brows drew together in displeasure. He rose. "I will go speak to him. Please excuse me." A general's set to his shoulders, he strode from the room.

Yelena's gaze followed him. She murmured a Cleatian idiom that Janna recognized as the equivalent of "Oh, dear."

She could only speculate about the reasons for the other woman's concern. But with Roszca out of the room, she had her opportunity. "Yelena, would you mind directing me to the powder room?"

At the woman's confused expression, she wished she could speak in Cleatian. They might learn something key. Instead, she added, "I need to freshen up. Use the toilet?"

"Ah, I understand." Yelena pushed slowly to her feet as if she were stiff. "Follow me."

Simon stood, but placed a hand on Janna's arm. "You'll come *right* back, won't you." His tone meant that it wasn't a question or a request, but an order. *No snooping allowed.*

She gave him an obsequious smile. "I'll be back before you can miss me, honey." As she turned her back, she could almost hear his teeth clench.

Yelena led her down the hall. The two women's heels clattered across the marble floor in staccato rhythm, echoing in the silence. True to Roszca's word, none of the bodyguards was around. Janna fingered the flash drive on her bracelet.

They passed a small sitting room. She recognized it as the game room where Simon and Roszca had played chess. A computer terminal sat on a Louis XIV-style table in the corner. The screensaver scrolled a field of stars.

This could be her chance. Her pulse skipped a beat.

At the very next door, Yelena stopped. "Here is…" The Cleatian woman paused, searching for the English word. She opened the wooden door to show a sink and commode.

"Powder room?" Janna supplied. How could she get away alone? Was the woman going to guard the door?

"*Dak!* Powder room." Yelena's rouged lips tilted in an off-center smile. "I return one moment. Check on cook."

Relieved, Janna thanked her, went in and closed the door.

She listened until she no longer heard the tapping of the woman's heels. No telling how long Yelena would be gone. She might have to pacify either Roszca or the cook. Or both.

Janna had to hurry.

She peered out. No one in sight. She knew Roszca had surveillance cameras all around the outside of his compound, but none inside. Once inside his castle, he wanted privacy.

Slipping off her heeled sandals, she tiptoed back the way she'd come and into the game room. She touched a finger to a key, but drew it back. For sure, Roszca had a security device. But what? She knelt down and peered at the back of the CPU. The two-inch-long plastic device plugged into the back meant her flash drive was useless. Disappointment sagged her shoulders.

At the sound of heels clicking on marble, she shot to her feet. Too late to return to the powder room. She dashed to the loveseat and waited, dangling her high heels from one hand.

"Ah, there you are, Yelena." She gave the surprised woman an airhead smile. "You caught me. I simply *had* to sink my tootsies into this *heavenly* carpet." She wriggled her toes in the thick white shag in front of the loveseat.

"No matter." Yelena's brow furrowed as her gaze darted around the room. She apparently didn't know whether to be suspicious or not. "Come. We eat now."

"Oh, good. I'm famished." After stepping into her shoes, Janna slipped her arm through Yelena's.

The woman seemed almost grateful for the feminine connection. Arm in arm, they hurried down the hall.

To Janna, their clicking heels sounded no louder than her pounding heart. "Everything okay with the cook?"

"*Dak,* um, yes. Okay." A heavy accent didn't disguise the anxious edge on Yelena's words.

Scrutinizing her, Janna blinked in shock. Up close, she saw that everything was *not* okay with Roszca's mistress. She owed her vivid coloring in part to heavy makeup.

Makeup meant to cover the fading yellow of large bruises.

Janna's heart hammered, and she fought to even her breathing. She gripped the other woman's arm and pulled her to the courtyard side of the passageway. "Yelena, how did you get those bruises?"

Color drained from the woman's face. Even with her heavy makeup, she looked ashen. "Is nothing. I fall. It heals."

A bird chirped in the potted palm standing in the courtyard. The perfume of frangipani blossoms floated on the light breeze. But all Janna smelled was the stench of abuse.

"No, Yelena. You didn't fall. I know because I've been there." She tried to sound confident and soothing, but couldn't keep her voice from shaking.

Yelena averted her eyes and shook her head.

"A fist made the bruises on your cheeks. Your mouth is swollen, too. A man's open hands squeezed the bruises into your neck. Roszca did this to you, didn't he?"

"It was my fault. I displeased him."

Janna squeezed her eyes closed as she sought strength. How many times had she said the same thing? How many other women had made excuses for their abusers?

She took Yelena's trembling hands in hers. "He has no right to beat you. I—"

"Come along, ladies. Dinner is now being served."

Janna looked up sharply to see Roszca standing in the foyer. His penetrating blue eyes seemed to bore into her soul.

How long had he been there? What had he heard?

Yelena squeezed Janna's hand before releasing her, a silent plea for silence. In her eyes was a mirror of Janna's old fears. Color had returned to her cheeks in crimson flags of alarm. Or shame. Or guilt.

Facing the truth and what Janna had to do about it had taken her months. Yelena needed time, a limited commodity given the circumstances.

But this was not the end of their conversation. Janna would make certain they would talk again.

"Thank you, Yelena," she said brightly, "for showing me these *gorgeous* plants. I may start sketching flowers as well as birds."

"It was my pleasure," Roszca's mistress said as she allowed him to take her elbow and lead her to the dining room.

When the two women returned with Roszca, Simon suspected from the high color on Janna's cheeks that she'd been up to something. She confirmed his worst suspicions when she wouldn't look him in the eye and chewed her lower lip.

The glass-topped table could've accommodated ten easily, but was set for the four of them. Roszca and his mistress sat on the ends. That left Janna and Simon facing each other between silver candelabra. When she finally met his gaze, the haunted look darkening her eyes to pewter nearly made him lose his cool.

What the hell had happened in the short time she'd vanished with Yelena?

Simon had no choice but to wait until they returned to the *Horizon* to find out. He shuttered his expression and murmured an appropriate response to his host's change of topic. They were back to horse racing again.

Roszca hadn't leaped aboard the yacht-race proposition at the beginning and still wasn't warming to it. Did he suspect a trap? Or did he simply doubt his boat's speed? Whatever the reason, his mistress's arrival had given him the opportunity to avoid the topic.

Simon's jaw tightened with frustration. He had to come up with an alternate plan to lure the arms broker off his island sanctuary. And he had little time to do it.

The evening took longer than any surveillance detail Simon could recall. Thank God he could discuss horse racing without having to concentrate.

When a clock chimed the witching hour, Simon took the reins and made their excuses. But he didn't make it out the door without Janna wangling an invitation from her new best friend. Amazing, but she orchestrated it so that Roszca thought it was his idea.

Yelena agreed to fix a picnic lunch so the two of them could roam the island to look for the elusive orangequit.

What the hell was Janna up to? She didn't have time to go looking for a damn bird—if orangequits even existed.

Simon ground his teeth as he hustled her down the path to the dock. He'd started the evening twisted in knots, and his condition only got worse. Seeing her in that nothing of a dress and the kicky heels that showed off her world-class legs had set a match to his tinder.

He'd felt like pawing the ground as he watched Roszca ogle her. Asserting his possession, Simon had remained as near as possible—touching distance.

Touching her knee, her arm, the arch of her neck. Inhaling her scent—sun-warmed skin and almond. Silken skin made golden in the sun, the sensuous curve of her cheek, the silvery gray of her huge eyes. Strength and brilliance, softened by vulnerability. Simon appreciated her depths, but their slimy host saw only the beautiful exterior.

As ATSA intended. The concession made him feel no better.

He fired up the boat's motor and watched as she slipped off her sandals and climbed into the dinghy. She avoided his eyes and stared into the darkness.

She'd snooped. A sure bet. But he kept his accusation to himself until they reached the privacy of the *Horizon*'s salon.

At the foot of the companionway, he spun her around and grabbed her shoulders. "Give, Q. What did you do to Roszca's computers? Did Yelena see anything?"

She clutched his arms with the same vehemence. "We have to get her out of there, Simon. He beat her. And not for the first time, I think."

He shook his head. Her words made no sense. "My nerves are jumping like ants on a summer sidewalk. You scared the crap out of me going off alone like that. The computer. What did you do?"

She cleared her throat, but emotion still plucked at her voice. "Nothing. I couldn't. But Simon, you have to listen. She needs help. *Our* help."

Maybe she *didn't* mess with the computer. He'd get to that, but the anxiety tightening her mouth and the corners of her eyes had him kicking at his stall. "Okay, tell me."

Janna gripped his arms so tightly he could feel each fingertip. "Roszca beat her. He's abusing Yelena. She's afraid of him. We have to get her out of there."

He saw moisture sheening over the fear he'd glimpsed in her eyes. "Janna, couldn't you be mistaken? Not every woman—"

"Didn't you notice how stiffly she got out of her seat? Who knows what he did to her?"

This was a complication they didn't need. "We can't help her, Janna. It would blow the mission. You could be wrong. Roszca said she hasn't been well. That's all."

"No. She has bruises. The heavy makeup almost concealed them, but I saw. Fading yellow bruises on her face and neck. He probably choked her, too. And her lip was swollen."

"Maybe she fell." The words sounded hollow and false, even to his own ears.

Janna hooted, a bitter laugh with no humor or music. "That's the classic excuse. Covering up. 'I fell down the stairs. Clumsy me.' No, I'm certain. She admitted it, even blamed herself, the typical abused woman's excuse. I need to talk with her, to convince her to leave Isla Alta with us."

"The picnic." When she nodded, he said, "Roszca's not going to let you two women traipse off alone. He'll send one of the twins to watch you, or Ivan."

"I'll find a way, a few moments alone. Please, Simon."

"I can't commit to helping this woman. It could trash the mission." The trembling through her body seemed to burn his hands. He pulled her into his arms. For reassurance and comfort this time, not sex.

"We have to get her away from that monster. He must be keeping her a virtual prisoner. We're her only chance." Tears trickled down her cheeks. Her eyes were fathomless gray pools of fear and sadness.

"Getting in and getting her out of Isla Alta without being detected or caught? A tough call. Besides, once Roszca is in ATSA custody, she'll be fine."

"Will you at least think about it?"

At the end of his arguments, he shook his head in frustration. "You're asking the impossible. Our only chance might be those mythical pirate tunnels."

He expected her to escape his arms, but she stayed put. Fine with him. He wanted more, a hell of a lot more, but just holding her while they talked was all he allowed himself.

"Pirate tunnels? I'd forgotten about them." Her gaze grew unfocused, a sure sign of deep thought.

Simon kissed her nose. "I do love to watch your brainiac mind go into action, Q, but this one will stump you. Now tell me about the computer system."

"I didn't tamper with the computer. Remember?"

He exhaled his relief. "Start at the beginning. Where did Yelena take you?"

"Across the foyer and along the passageway to a powder room."

"The green one beside the game room?"

"It's pale turquoise, but yes."

"The game room with the computer in the corner."

She nodded, finally stepping out of his embrace. "Yelena left me to go check on the chef. I think she kept Roszca from breaking something."

"Who knows? Go on." His arms felt as empty as his heart. He backed away and sat on the arm of the white leather sofa.

"I went into the game room, as you assumed. But I couldn't touch a thing. The drive has a key katcher."

"Which is? Don't get too tech on me, Q."

She appeared to relax, too, dropping her sandals and coming to stand before him. Close enough that he could pull her between his spread legs, feel her warmth again and breathe in her womanly scent. Her skirt barely fell to mid-thigh.

He could... He shook off the image before it took root.

"A key katcher is a small device to capture keystrokes. Roszca or whoever monitors the network would know what keys were pressed, what programs were accessed, e-mails, anything."

Keystrokes. *Key strokes* on her toned thighs would open her to him. She wanted him. Why not? But at the moment, she was serious, professional. And fragile enough to shatter. Reaction to Yelena's predicament.

He forced his attention away from sexual possibilities. "Ah, I've heard of those keystroke grabbers. Other missions have used them for surveillance."

"Not all that high-tech but effective. I couldn't remove it without their knowing. I'm back to hacking." She sighed.

"Yeah, hacking, not bird-watching. Is an orangequit a real bird?"

"Of course, *Euneornis campestris.* It's native to Jamaica. A rare songbird."

Unable to resist her nearness, he clasped her hand and savored the soft skin of her palm. "I should probably be grateful you didn't recite the Latin name to Roszca. He might've suspected that sexy dress disguised more than your average boat bunny."

She laughed, familiar music that stirred his already-heated blood. "Thanks for agreeing to consider helping Yelena. And thanks for cheering me up." After covering a yawn, she said,

"I'm going to make some coffee and boot up. There's one more strategy I want to try."

Simon slid onto the leather cushion. Abandoned. She'd gone off to work at her precious computer. No sex. He should be grateful. Relieved. Hell, wasn't that what he wanted?

Instead, he wasn't sure how he felt. Except for one thing. He needed a cold shower.

The yacht chronometer rang four times as Janna signed off with Jack Thorne. Cracking the last barrier into Viktor Roszca's files had nearly taken her until morning, but she couldn't have slept anyway. Not after the emotional upheaval of knowing the arms broker was also an abuser. And not after that encounter with Simon.

Simon had been as seduced by the evening's pretense as she had. His constant caresses had sensitized her to his touch. He held her as she poured out her worries for Yelena. Then he argued and resisted helping the woman, but he would yield. He was too honorable not to.

He'd wanted to make love to her again. She'd seen it in his eyes, sensed it in his touch and felt it in the urgent arousal pressing against her. The same desire had streaked down her spine and swirled in her belly.

But the time hadn't been right. He might've thought she was giving herself to him to persuade him to help Yelena. Besides, time was running out on their mission.

And time was running out on them.

One more night. Maybe two. A little food, a little wine, a little breeze, and his shaky barrier should crumble. Being in his arms would heal her soul, and she could move on. Simon would see that she was fine, so he could release his misplaced guilt. They could remain friends afterward. She repeated it aloud to block the twinge of pain in her heart.

But for now, she needed to close her aching eyes. Still in her shorts and T-shirt, she fell, face first, onto her bunk. She drifted to sleep resolving to tell Simon about her big breakthroughs first thing in the morning. Then she would find a way to persuade Yelena to leave.

Chapter 13

Janna awoke smothered by a wet towel of tropical heat. Through her porthole, she saw the sun shimmering its fire from high in the bright, blue sky.

The yacht was silent, except for the constant hum of the generator. Oh, no, Simon had left for further negotiations on Isla Alta. This was the first time she'd missed listening in on his talks with Roszca.

She raced to the captain's console, where she found a note in Simon's slapdash scrawl.

Get some sleep. No prob about not monitoring. A-okay.
Will return in time for picnic.

She glanced at her watch. Eleven-thirty. Not much time to get ready.

After a shower, she searched her undercover wardrobe for something more modest than shorts that barely concealed the color of her underwear. She settled on a scoop-neck T-shirt. But the only pair of shorts with slightly longer legs rode low on her hips.

When Simon tied up the dinghy at the stern, she hurried to the rail. Back at the dock, three pelicans settled back on the waters now that all was quiet again.

"Great steering," she said. "You haven't bumped the dock or the boat since the first day."

Tight with Roszca, Simon had apparently chosen to dress more casually. The sleeveless Henley and the khaki walking shorts allowed her a clear view of his smoothly muscled biceps and corded legs as he tied up and climbed aboard the yacht.

"I'm ready to try docking something bigger." He shot her a crooked pirate grin that curled her toes in her sandals.

The sun flashed off his earring, and she wanted to put her tongue there where it rested on his earlobe. In his mobster persona, he intrigued her more, seemed more dangerously seductive. Daydreaming like this wasn't like her. She shook away her sensual thoughts.

"Like the *Horizon?*" she said. "Mmm, maybe, but it would be the difference between parking a sub-compact and a semi. You can try docking this boat when we get back to Gitmo."

Stepping aboard, he lowered his sunglasses and swept her with an appreciative eye. "Would you say that if it was your uncle's boat and not Wharton's?"

She laughed. "We may get back to Gitmo soon. During the nigh, I cracked through Roszca's defenses. Thorne's techs are copying the server's hard drive. They should have something for us later."

His broad smile heated her insides to match her sunbaked skin. "Q, I knew you could do it. It's the winner's circle for you. I'll check in with Thorne right now."

Donning her sunglasses, she pointed at her watch. "Time to

go. I don't want to blow my chance to talk to Yelena." She started down the gangway to the swim platform.

A hand on her arm stopped her. "Don't." His teasing grin morphed into a grim line.

She felt her heart stutter in dread. "What happened? What's wrong?"

He scrubbed his beard-shadowed chin with one fist. "Maybe nothing. Maybe something. I don't know. Roszca said to make Yelena's apologies. She isn't feeling well today and can't make the picnic."

Tears stung her eyes and a vise banded her chest. She flung away her sunglasses to get a better look at the island house. Willing Yelena to appear well and whole didn't conjure the woman. Only blank windows stared back. The sun's rays flashed on them with blinding intensity. "Damn him! If he's hurt her again, it's my fault. I shouldn't have—"

"Stop, sweetheart." Simon turned her toward him and chafed her upper arms in soothing strokes. "Do you hear yourself? Whatever happened is not your fault. Or Yelena's."

The old fear cinched her throat as she fought to breathe, to free herself from the vise. She let Simon draw her into the shelter of his arms. When the strength of his body and the feel of his strong, steady heartbeat calmed her, she said, "I know. It's hard to erad-icate the victim mind-set. My knee-jerk reaction shocks me."

"If Roszca beat her or locked her up, it was for his own de-praved reasons."

The low velvet of his voice smoothed her ragged-edged nerves. Deep breaths calmed her panic attack, and she managed a wobbly smile. "Some undercover agent I am, falling apart on a mission."

"You had cause. No harm done."

She cocked her head, intrigued by Simon's insight. "You knew about the guilt reflex. How'd you get to be so smart about domestic abuse?"

He kissed her forehead and released her. With a wink, he said, "I did a little research after you told me...about Gabe. I'm not a total wipeout on the computer."

He'd investigated abuse because he cared about her. Sensitive, intuitive and totally denying both. "Thanks, Simon, for caring."

"No problem, Q." He ruffled her hair, letting his hand linger a little too long to be strictly playful. "I'll go rustle up something for lunch."

In silence, she watched him disappear below as she accepted what her heart already knew. She'd moved past the barrier of her self-imposed rules, beyond friendship and caring. Her heart hiccuped with a shock wave of realization.

Between them was a chemistry that set her on fire. A longing for connection in every way possible. A comfortable warmth that could turn to jagged need with a touch or a look. A magical fluttering in her heart and in her stomach. Her heart and soul yearned for him.

But she wouldn't utter the word, even to herself.

Heart thundering and knees liquifying, she sank onto a deck chair. How did this happen? How could she fall for Simon? Simon who ran from relationships. And she who wouldn't allow herself to be trapped again.

Just sex between friends, she'd thought two days ago. No strings, no commitment.

But that was when real danger to her heart seemed remote. If they became intimate again now, she wouldn't have the strength to fight her feelings for him. Her heart and her emotions were still too brittle, too fragile. She pressed both hands to her chest in an effort to calm her racing heart.

Two years ago, his rejection had forced her away from a walk on the wild side with Simon. If she wanted to survive, she had to walk away again.

* * *

At dusk, Simon found Janna sitting cross-legged on the swim platform and staring toward Roszca's dock. The setting sun silhouetting her slim form made her skin seem to glow. A soft breeze lifted her silky hair off her neck just enough for a man's lips to press a kiss there.

Man, he had it bad for her. The woman was making him a poetry freak.

Or maybe he was just tired. Tired of sucking up to his enemy. Tired of playing his hoodlum role. And tired of not letting anyone in—especially Janna.

Enough of that. She was plotting something after hours on the computer. He knew her long silences, muttered words and furrowed brow meant her geek brain was onto something.

"Gold doubloon for your thoughts," he said, joining her on the platform.

She blinked in surprise. "Whoa. You reading my mind?" She nodded toward Roszca's yacht at the island's dock. "Look beyond *Prowler* there, to that point of the shore beyond."

Simon turned to scan the shoreline, only a dark blob against the sunset's glare. Small forms winged up from the point and vanished into the coming night. "I see it. You've done some snorkeling over there."

"There's a ledge just above the water level. And a cave beneath it partly concealed by overhanging plants."

"Bats," he said, recognizing the winged silhouettes rising from the point. His shoulders shook with an involuntary shudder of revulsion. "Those were bats I saw flying out."

"I watched them the other night and went to investigate the next time I swam. I believe it's the entrance to one of the old pirate tunnels."

He opened his mouth to argue with her, then closed it again. All that time she'd spent researching on the computer. If anybody could find the pirate tunnels, it was Janna. "Argh, me hearty, tell me more. How do you know it's more than a shallow cave?"

She grinned, warming to her topic. "I found geological reports on the Internet. Old geological surveys of this island show that it's similar to Jamaica. Jamaica is riddled with limestone caves. Some are horizontal, tunnels scraped out by changing sea levels. A sea-carved cave would logically open onto the water."

Simon pictured her venturing inside the black hole. He shuddered again. "How far inside have you gone?"

"I didn't try. It's dark even at noon, and I didn't want to enter alone. The whole island is no more than two miles long. If that tunnel reaches into Roszca's compound, it must be no more than half a mile, maybe less. Will you go with me?"

He scraped back his hair. "I set that up when I said a tunnel was the only way to get to Yelena."

"I have tools to make sure the cave's not booby-trapped or bugged. You can figure out a plan to rescue her. You've done some spelunking, haven't you?"

"You got me. Upstate in Maryland near my cabin. There are lots of sinkholes and caves in those foothills. But you gotta know I hate bats. I *hate* the freaking things."

"The bats'll be gone if we go at night."

He saw the commitment and hope shining in her mesmerizing eyes, and his heart melted. How could he deny her?

She'd asked him to make love to help her heal. He saw compassion in her determination to free another woman from abuse, but maybe it was also a track to healing. The way things were going, rolling up the arms broker with a bogus boat race was in doubt.

Then a different possibility glimmered in his mind. A possibility that involved Yelena. Janna wouldn't understand, and his wild idea might not work anyway. The cave might lead nowhere. If it did, Roszca probably had it blocked.

But for her, he'd give it a shot.

He smoothed her kitten-soft hair with one hand, then lifted her chin. "We don't have much to work with on this yacht, but I'll see if I can put some equipment together. If we find a us-able tunnel, I'll think of a plan. Whatever we do means exceed-ing our orders. And involving a civilian. Breaking more rules, you copy?"

Topsy-turvy. Little Miss Rule Book was asking *him* to break more rules. He'd broken his own, getting involved with her be-yond friendship. And damn if her sexy eyes and sexy brain weren't tempting him to do it again.

A bright smile lifted her lips. "Thank you, Simon. Tonight then, so Roszca's goons can't see us. There's no time to waste." Her soft voice slipped into his bloodstream and dived to his groin.

Time, a scarce commodity. "Tonight," he agreed and knew he meant more than caving and plotting a rescue.

Janna was careful to avoid making a splash as she led Simon to the cave entrance, a shallow, black eyebrow of an arch. She looked at the lighted dial of her watch. Ten-thirty. They'd waited a while after the patrol boat's return before swimming from the *Horizon* using fins and their snorkel masks.

"Damn, it's as dark as that New York bar," Simon said as he helped her climb into the opening. His voice reverberated in an eerie echo.

"The Danube? This place smells a thousand times worse." Janna wrinkled her nose. The black cavity emitted the com-bined stench of guano, moldy seaweed and unidentifiable filth. "Ugh. The tides here are too shallow to wash it clean."

She pulled off her fins and snorkel equipment and put them on the cave floor. Then she opened her waterproof knapsack by feel and dug out her headlamp and water sandals. She slipped the straps of her lamp on her head. The cone of light projecting before her cheered her immediately.

A second later, Simon's lamp illuminated. He crouched beside her as he removed his fins and mask.

"If I'd known we'd be caving, I'd have brought equipment. Caves are cold, even in the tropics. Hey, but guano between our toes might warm our feet." He shrugged into his pack. "Okay, Q, let's see where this baby leads."

His lazy wink rippled warmth low in her body. His cocky attitude banished her incipient dread. Simon always made her feel better, as though she could do anything. One of the things she… No, she wasn't going there. No warm and fuzzy feelings. No relationship trap. No more rules broken. She felt the pang of loss clutch her chest.

Rotating her head to move the lamp, Janna could see that the cavity was indeed tunnel-shaped. Inside, the rocky walls arched high enough that they could stand bent over.

In addition to a lamp and sandals, Simon's pack contained what he'd put together for cave gear. He fished out a small compass and examined it under his headlamp. "Looks like we're heading north. Minerals in the rock could skew the reading. No telling how deep the tunnel goes, either. Wish we had some way to measure distance."

"Or a roll of string like in the mythical labyrinth," Janna said. "We can't get too lost on a small island."

"Unless the cave goes under the sea."

She hadn't considered the cave going deep. Before she could reconsider, a movement ahead caught her eye. Dark wings materialized out of the tunnel's fathomless maw. The tiny brown bat zigzagged to avoid them as it streaked by.

Simon jumped aside and slipped. He sat down hard on the rocky floor. "Damned flying rodent," was the mildest phrase he muttered as he pushed to his feet.

Janna pinched her lips together to keep from laughing. "Poor Simon. I don't know who was more scared—you or the bat. The little guy just wanted to get out."

"He's damned late. Aren't they supposed to go out as soon as it's dark?" He rubbed his behind, and his hand came away covered with guano. He glared at it in disgust.

"Apparently not." There were twenty-one species of bats on these islands, but mentioning that bit of research didn't seem wise at the moment.

As they moved on, he wiped his filthy hand on the side of his swim trunks. His shoulders shook in a shudder.

In spite of the tragic losses in Simon's life, he always projected strength and stoicism. Allowing Janna to see his fear meant he trusted her. That realization kindled more unwanted inner warmth against the tunnel's chilly dampness. She shook her head at *her* weakness for him.

A few feet farther, Janna's light beam caught on small creatures on the cave floor. She gasped and stumbled backward.

"It's okay," Simon said, holding out a hand. Moisture seeped from the limestone above, forming lumpy structures of minerals on the floor. "Only stalagmites. Bet they're more scared than you."

"Touché." Janna's pulse slowed from panicky to merely nervous. "A trick of the light. They looked grotesque, like slimy cave creatures."

Simon twirled an invisible mustache. "Argh. Or the horrible ghost of a tortured pirate."

She swatted at him, but he cackled a maniacal laugh and hustled ahead out of reach. "Now we're even."

The tunnel bored into the island in a more or less straight course. As they went deeper into the heart of the earth, the temperature dropped. They hadn't room in their small packs for shirts or jackets.

Shivering, Janna rubbed her arms. She saw Simon do the same up ahead.

They descended steadily, walking slowly on the wet rock, made slipperier with occasional bat droppings. Finally, the tunnel floor began to climb. The only sounds were their footfalls, echoing the crunch of gravel underneath.

Janna checked her watch. "Ten minutes. Simon, we've been in here ten minutes."

From ahead of her, Simon said, "A hell of a cave, Q. We've inched along. This tunnel just might reach all the way."

He sounded more positive than earlier, downright jaunty to her anxious ears.

Tears stung her eyes with the renewed hope they'd be able to help save Yelena. Getting inside and back out and even persuading the frightened woman to go with them weren't insurmountable problems. Just difficult ones to puzzle out later. She trusted Simon to devise a strategy.

He stopped so suddenly ahead of her that she ran into his back.

Simon snapped on the light and waved it ahead. "Something up there."

Janna peered around his shoulder. "Oh, no."

Two equally black, yawning passages diverged before them.

He lifted one shoulder. "As Yogi Berra said, 'When you come to a fork in the road, take it.'"

She edged closer to his warmth and strength. Sharing body heat wasn't a bad way to banish the chills. "Very funny, but what does your compass say?"

His brow meshing in thought, he studied the disk. "Looks like the main tunnel's meandered west too far. Let's try the right fork."

As they proceeded in the new direction, the rocky ceiling lowered until they were trudging ahead bent over.

"Smell's worse in here," he said.

"The guano fumes are making my eyes water," Janna said. "All that ammonia. No wonder you dislike bats."

Over the next few feet, the tunnel walls and ceiling expanded out of their lamps' reach.

"Hey, a cavern room, like Mammoth Cave," he said, straightening to his full height.

Suddenly, Simon saw a black, whirring cloud descend toward them.

Damn! He dived to the cave floor, as he pulled Janna down with him. *"Down! Bats."*

The creatures objected to the invasion with a chorus of high-pitched squeaks. Wings brushed his back and stirred a noxious breeze as the flapping cloud rushed past toward the distant cave opening.

His heartbeat thundered in his ears, but he realized he'd reacted more to protect Janna than out of his irrational fear. The fleeing bats had stirred up an awful stink, but they were gone. Thank God.

Both headlamps had fallen off. One lay at a crazy angle beside them in inch-thick dung. He couldn't see Janna's face, but he felt the tension in her body.

Beneath him, she lay as rigid as the rock under her back. He felt the racing tattoo of her heart against his chest, the too-rapid gasp of shallow breaths.

She hadn't shown fear earlier—not of the cave itself or the bat that had, um, surprised him. When she started pushing at his chest and whimpering, he knew.

He'd trapped her. He'd revived her old fears. The last thing he ever wanted to do.

There'd been a horse once that had been terrified of blankets because some idiot had snapped one at him as a colt. The trainer'd needed buckets of TLC and patience to desensitize that horse. With Janna, Simon calculated that humor was what the doctor ordered.

He rolled to the side and freed her.

Gasping, Janna leaped to her feet. She stood trembling, her hands fisted.

Letting her stand over him and get her bearings, he sat up and dusted his hands together. "In other circumstances, sweetheart, having your hot body beneath me in that painted-on one-piece would jump-start my hormones. But a bed of guano-covered limestone is not my idea of a turn-on."

The fallen headlamp shined enough light that he could see when her shoulders relaxed and she eased from fight-or-flight mode.

Her lips curved in a small, wavering smile. "Mine, neither." She bent to retrieve her light.

Simon found his lamp against the cave wall. "Busted." He held up the useless light, its wires dangling. "Sorry I jumped you, but the bats…" His skin twitched as if the ugly beasts were crawling all over him, and he shuddered.

"No, you were right. That was too many bats for me, too. Ick, my back feels worse than the time my cousins buried me in the sand." She pivoted to shine her light around the cavern room.

"Hey, over there!" Simon urged her to the right.

On that side of the cavern, they found rotted staves of a wooden barrel and more boards with metal straps attached.

"An old chest," Janna said. "Pirate booty *was* stored here on Isla Alta after all."

Simon heaved an exaggerated sigh. "Long gone. Too bad." Looks like this is a dead end. Let's try the other passage."

"The compass must've thrown us off. As you said."

Arm in arm to share the lamp's illumination and their body heat, they trudged back to the fork and headed down the left passage. That tunnel had a higher ceiling, but moisture dripped from everywhere. Guano and mineral slime plastered their skin and belongings. Now they were wet, too. Cold seeped into their bones, and they shivered as they picked their way over the slippery rock floor.

The reek of bat guano diminished the farther they got from the cavern room, but a new odor began to permeate the stale air. Metallic and sweet, yet sharp and nauseating. Simon breathed through his mouth, but it didn't help much.

Up ahead, Janna's light reflected on metal. A flat metal plate in a heavy wooden door. Her bug detector was dormant—no blinking lights, no hum.

"No electronics?" he whispered, afraid that someone on the other side could hear.

"None. Simon, we've done it," she whispered back, "Roszca must've built this."

Hand outstretched, she started forward.

Simon spotted something ahead that he didn't like. A firm hand on her upper arm stopped her. "Not another step."

She looked at him questioningly.

"Let's take it slow. Shine your lamp on the floor there." He pointed to a black area five feet in front of the door.

As they approached, he saw that the black area was a hole. His heart stuttered, then sprinted at the image of Janna's body lying broken at the bottom.

"I could've fallen in there. Oh, Simon!"

"You didn't. We're okay." He squatted beside the stygian hole. "Hand me the lamp, would you?"

"Here you go." Janna knelt beside him and watched as he aimed the beam downward.

"It's like a well," Simon said. "Something's there."

He bent over to peer downward. The faint beam flickered across something white. An arm in a white jacket came into view. A leg in dark trousers. The head of a dark-skinned man bent at an unnatural angle.

Janna gasped and sat back.

"He's dead. It's the Jamaican chef," Simon said, ice-edged horror sawing at his nerves. "I saw him the other day. He could've been dead since last night."

"Oh, the poor man." Her voice wavered. "Roszca killed him because dinner was late?"

"Or had him killed." He uttered a harsh laugh. "I doubt he does his own dirty work."

"*Yelena*. We have to get Yelena out." She clutched at his arm. "I know Roszca divorced two wives, but I bet he beat them, too. His level of violence is escalating. I know the signs. Simon, Yelena could die."

He patted her hand on his arm, then smoothed back her hair at her temples. With the single light aimed away from her, he couldn't see into her eyes, but knew they were wide with fear and worry.

She'd been through hell and back. She was wet and cold and plastered with bat dung, but he was the only one who'd complained. A hell of a woman. More than a lug like him deserved. And now she wanted to throw herself in the lion's den to save a woman she'd met only once.

"Q, take a gander at that door. There's no handle of any kind. No lock on this side. Not even hinges. How do you figure we get through without blasting it open?" He hated telling her, but rescue looked less possible than ever.

Chapter 14

Janna aimed the handheld showerhead at her back for the third rinse. When they'd emerged from the refrigerated cave, the tropical steam bath had leached the cold from her bones. The swim back to the *Horizon* had rinsed off most of the gluelike guano, but the stink lingered like a bad memory.

Worse was the memory of finding the dead cook at the pit's bottom. She'd never forget his misshapen sprawl, like a broken puppet. But all too real, all too human.

She could've fallen on top of him if she'd taken two more steps. Her chest tightened around the fear. She squeezed her eyes shut against the nightmare vision of what could've happened if Simon hadn't stopped her.

But Simon *had* stopped her.

Another memory clogged her throat with tenderness. Simon had ignored his own fears to protect her when the bats swarmed past them. He'd sensed her panic at being trapped beneath him and defused it with humor. He'd considered her pride as well as her fear.

More emotion jolted her as waves of memory fanned through her—the strength of him against her, the insight and caring in his eyes, the way he held her gently so she wanted to melt into him. She leaned against the shower stall.

But she couldn't let herself love him. She couldn't.

No relationship was worth losing control of her life. How could she trust anyone, even Simon?

He would run from a relationship anyway.

Hot water wouldn't wash away the jumbled thoughts that clamped her throat. She turned off the shower and dried off with one of the yacht's plush towels.

No more flogging herself with the impossible. Instead, she had to focus on the immediate problem. The tunnel door.

After pulling on clean shorts and a tank top, Janna hit the computer. It was just after midnight, but the night's excitement had her too wired to sleep.

A while later, she was just finishing an e-mail when Simon joined her at the helm. He postponed his shower and waited on deck while she showered to make sure none of Roszca's goons had observed or followed them. The scent of oatmeal soap wafted toward her as he settled into the swivel chair.

But she shouldn't notice such intimate details.

"Man, I feel three hundred percent better." He nabbed the satellite phone from its charger and flipped it open, but his finger hovered over the speed dial. "Q, you working on busting that door? If anybody can solve that puzzle, it's you."

Simon was the only person who truly appreciated her abilities, especially her persistence. She smiled. "Can't do it alone this time. The lock needs Houdini."

Propping his bare feet on the console, Simon leaned back in the cushioned chair. He wore only frayed cutoffs—sneaked into his luggage, not ATSA approved, she knew. She ought to

be accustomed to seeing his bare torso, but his smoothly muscled chest dusted with silky, dark hairs drew her gaze.

He regarded her with heavy-lidded eyes, a look that made
her toes curl. The cocky quirk to his lips told her he was working up a smart-mouth crack.

He snapped the phone closed and crossed his arms. "The Internet reaches far and wide, but beyond the grave to dead ma-
gicians? Do you have powers I don't know about, or have you
lost your mind?"

Janna slapped her forehead. "Ah, my mind! But I couldn't
have lost my mind. I have it backed up on a CD somewhere."
She searched around on the console.

Laughing, Simon shook his head. "I must be hanging out
with you too much. I actually understood that one." He eyed
her pointedly. "Houdini? Seriously?"

She grinned back at him, noting how good it felt to laugh
together. "Seriously, Houdini is the nickname for my FBI lock
wizard. His real name is Harry Demers. The metal plate in that
door has to be the back of an electronic lock panel. When I
couldn't find what I needed to crack it anywhere else, I e-mailed
him."

Simon's expression turned serious as his feet hit the floor.
"Hope he checks e-mail first thing in the morning. We don't
have much time. It's the wee hours of Tuesday already. Roszca
will expect his nuke-buying bidders on Thursday."

"But ATSA's going to head them off."

"When they don't arrive, he'll get suspicious of us. We have
to hightail it by tomorrow night—whether or not I can lure
Roszca into a yacht race."

Janna considered the consequences of failing to capture the
arms broker and didn't like her conclusions. "His computer system might tell us where the nuclear material is, but he could
set up other sales."

"Exactly. We need the man. I want him where he can't sell

arms to kill more innocents," he said in a dry, disgusted voice. No longer softened by joking, his face was all hard planes and uncompromising angles.

When the satellite phone jangled in his hand, he stared at it in surprise. Then he flipped it open and punched in the security code.

"Yo, yacht *Horizon.* I have news for you."

At Thorne's voice, Simon activated the speaker.

Janna swiveled her chair toward Simon. "Maybe about Roszca's files." The uranium. And Gabe's involvement. She leaned forward, scarcely taking a breath.

Simon settled back into his seat. "I copy. What's up?"

"You're not going to like this. It may mean we'll have to abort the mission. Yesterday, Wharton escaped from custody."

Simon and Janna exchanged shocked looks.

"How?" Simon barked into the mike. "What happened?"

"His watchers were moving him from the safe house to the correction center. Some of his cohorts set up an ambush and sprung him. I don't know the whole story."

"Any idea where he went?"

Static briefly interrupted Thorne's reply. "…people watching for him at ports and airports. If he's spotted anywhere near the Caribbean, you are to get outta Dodge."

"Roger." Simon had a bad feeling. He glanced at Janna for acknowledgment of the orders, but her gnawed lower lip meant she was deep in thought. More worried about the involvement of her damned ex, he bet. "What about the computer files Janna hacked into?"

"These files are a gold mine," the contact officer said, his deep voice crackling over the airwaves. "Tech Officer Harris is a damned fine hacker."

Simon gave Janna a thumbs-up sign, and she responded with a brief curve of her lips.

"She's right here. She knows. Did you track the uranium?"

Static zinged the transmission, but then Thorne replied. "We know the courier's route and schedule. Officers have been dispatched to intercept."

Janna saw Simon roll his eyes at the operative's jargon. A former U.S. marshal, Jack Thorne was a crack officer, but his superserious single-mindedness put some people off.

"Lighten up, Thorne," muttered Simon as the voice detailed more data about the uranium package.

Janna frowned. The breakthrough on the uranium wasn't all she wanted to know. "Simon, ask about Gabe. Please."

Without looking her way, he nodded. After Thorne finished, he said, "Did you find any files on Gabe Harris?"

The pause after Simon's query made the muscles in Janna's chest tighten painfully. What did Thorne's geeks find? Had Gabe been party to the stolen uranium sale? Had he sold government secrets? Dread made her forget to breathe.

"Affirmative," Thorne finally replied. "There were a couple of entries in a daily-planner file. One under the name of Gabriel Horne and another under his real name. Was Harris undercover or something?"

Or something. Simon angled his head and raised his eyebrows in question. He watched Janna's reaction. How deep did her feelings still go?

Her expressive eyes widened. They broadcast a flurry of emotions—anxiety, alarm and a desperate need to know the awful truth. And in their gray depths, did he see hatred or love for the abusive bastard?

And did he even want to know?

He couldn't leave the contact hanging. Undercover. If that was the first conclusion Thorne drew from finding Harris's dealings with Roszca, he'd let him believe that. If the dead operative had committed treason, the truth would come out later.

For the moment, Simon saw no reason not to play along.

Apparently, Janna agreed. She bit her lip and nodded.

"Yeah, deep undercover," Simon said over the secure connection. "I have to report to the AD how much Roszca knew. If he made Harris. What can you tell me?"

Again, a pause.

Simon saw Janna press a hand to her chest as if to hold in her fears.

He took her other hand and squeezed gently.

She worked up a limp smile, but her forehead pleated with worry.

"I copy," Thorne said. "Raines said to keep you and Tech Officer Harris in the loop."

At her nod, Simon said, "Let's hear it."

There was a rustling of papers. Then, "I have the printout right here. It looks like Harris as Horne made some arms deals with our boy, but then Roszca had him followed. Roszca didn't get where he is by trusting blindly."

"So Harris was made," Simon prompted. He glanced at Janna, pale and rigid in her chair. She gripped the lifeline of his hand as if she'd drown without it.

"Affirmative. After that, Roszca pressured Harris to hand over what ATSA had on his arms-dealing network. Farther down the planner, there's a reference to sending a package to Harris. Code for a contract on his life. At that point, whatever ATSA had been trying to accomplish with Harris undercover was aborted. He was extracted and put on the New Dawn Warriors case. He was killed, but not by Roszca's doing. Ironic."

Janna wrenched her hand from Simon's grip and grabbed the handset. "Thorne, why the contract? Why did Roszca want to kill Gabe?"

"I thought that was clear. Harris gave him nada. Not even fake reports."

Simon scooped up the phone as Janna clasped her hands together and shot to her feet.

"Oh, thank God," she whispered. Tears flowing, she rushed to the companionway and up on deck.

Simon finished the call and waited at the console. He'd give Janna a few more minutes to deal with whatever the hell she was dealing with.

He spun out of the swivel chair and made his way up on deck. There she was, leaning on the port rail, her beautiful face turned up to the sliver of moon.

The soft gold glow from the companionway—the only light on deck—mixed with the shadows to highlight the sweep of her long legs, the angle of her cheek, the streaky wheat and gold of her hair. And he couldn't get enough of looking at her, fool that he was.

She must've scrubbed as hard in the shower as he did. Her smooth skin glowed pink, inviting, especially there on the graceful arch of her neck. Her budded nipples thrust against the thin cotton of her tank top. No bra. Lust shot through him at the same time that a deep longing welled up within him— sharp and sweet sensations that stopped him in his tracks.

He should've refused this op, should've switched duty with Jack Thorne. Something. Then he wouldn't be caught in a maelstrom. The tender glow scared the hell out of him. Lust he understood. And anger.

They'd made love—sizzling sex in nature's hot tub, an experience permanently branded on his DNA. She'd taunted him and teased him after a rare honorable impulse—and his guilty conscience, to be truthful-had interfered.

How could she come on to him and still have feelings for a dead man who abused her? That's what steamed him.

The more he thought about it, the hotter he got. The sultry night had nothing on the heat waves rising from him. Stalking toward her, he scraped a hand through his damp hair.

Janna turned toward him. She smiled, a sweet curve of lips

that made his heart skip a beat in spite of his temper. "Oh, Simon, you have no idea how relieved I am that Gabe didn't give Roszca classified information."

He stopped an inch away from grabbing her and shaking some sense into her. Close enough to inhale her almond-scented shampoo. Too close. He backed up a step.

"No, I reckon I don't have any idea. Let me see if I got this straight. Your husband beat you and abused you. He sold stolen arms to terrorists. But since he didn't betray his country's secrets, you'll forgive him?"

She flinched, eyes wide, as if he'd slapped her. "Forgive him?" Frowning, she shook her head.

"How twisted did his abuse make you? How can you still love the bastard after the way he treated you?"

Her witchy eyes bored into him for a long minute. Then her taut mouth relaxed. "Simon, I don't love Gabe. He killed any love I felt for him along with any chance at a real marriage. Toward the end, I hated him."

At her admission, every muscle in his body tensed. His eyes burned, trying to scorch through the tangle to the truth. He'd misinterpreted her reactions, but how? "But you're so obsessed with proving him innocent. And a few minutes ago, when Thorne told us he didn't sell out to Roszca, you reacted like Gabe had come back from the dead. I don't get it."

"I'm relieved, yes. Aren't you?"

"Yeah, I reckon." He jammed his hands into his rear pockets, so he wouldn't give in to temptation. "Relieved we don't have ten more loose ends to tie up, loose ends that would turn out to be tails of venomous snakes. Relieved ATSA doesn't have a treason case. Relieved it ends here."

"Precisely." She sighed and lifted her shoulders in an slow shrug. "It ends here. If Gabe had betrayed his country to Roszca and his terrorist clients, ATSA would've conducted an investigation, including the sordid story of my marriage. This way, the investigation of his arms dealing can be contained. I can close the door on Gabe and get on with my life."

Simon considered her words as he stared up at the moon soaring high with the stars. The waning moon shed little light, but Janna was deliberately blotting out all light. "*Close the door?* More like slamming it shut."

He stalked forward and fisted the rail on either side of her, bracketing her in place.

"Simon, what do you mean? What are you so angry about?" She challenged him, eyes aflame with mercury fire.

"I'm glad to see you're not scared of me anymore. That's a step, but you have a long way to go."

"Let me pass, please. I don't have to listen to this." Cheeks flushed, she went from wary to ice-princess frost.

He didn't touch her, but he didn't move out of the way. She needed to hear this. "Your Dr. Mary was right—"

"Dr. Marah. Marah French." Apparently seeing he wasn't budging, she spun on her bare heel and showed him her back. The telltale burn scars blazed above the low-cut tank top like neon reminders of her husband's cruelty.

Anger. Tenderness. Anguish. The emotions wrenched his heart until he thought it might twist apart.

"Dr. Marah French, then," he said, clenching his jaw for control. "Whatever. She was right. You haven't dealt with the abuse. Not down deep. You're still seeing it as *your* shame, not his."

She jerked erect, her back straight as the deck boards, hands clamped on the rail beside his. "How dare you! You can't possibly understand."

"I can because I know you, Janna. Besides, you told me yourself. You saw the abuse as an intellectual problem to be solved. But it was *his* problem, *his* fault, not yours. There are some human defects—glitches, in geekspeak—you can't fix with tinkering or research or—"

"Logic." Shoulders lowered, she turned around, fixing him

with a tear-filled gaze. "Simon, I know that. I learned it the hard way."

"But it didn't free you. These new rules you repeat like a mantra are just a new kind of trap. A cage you've built around yourself. You hide what he did. You hide from the world." He could see the hurt in her eyes, but he wouldn't back down. She needed to hear the truth from someone who lo—someone who cared.

"That's not true. I'm not hiding the truth. I just don't want anyone's pity or scorn."

"I don't buy it. You hide the truth the way you hide the scars on your back."

"They're ugly." She crossed her arms over her breasts and hugged herself, trembling.

"The *truth* is ugly. What Gabe did to you was ugly. If I could get my hands on him, I'd do worse to him." Acid churned like poison in his gut, and fury drummed along his nerves. He longed to punch something, but he didn't want to frighten her, so he gripped the rail until his knuckles hurt.

"I—I couldn't stop him. I couldn't…" Her voice trailed off in a sob.

"You couldn't fix it, so you're afraid people will see his cruelty as your fault because *you* still do. Who have you told? Your mom? Dad? Your friend Deena?"

She winced at the truth in his words. "I told *you*."

He made a face and lifted his arms in a gesture of frustration. "Nice try. I dragged it out of you. After I saw the scars. Who else knows?"

"No one. Only Dr. French."

"Not Yelena, when you asked about her bruises?"

Janna shook her head. Tiny diamonds glittering in the light, tears beaded her lashes. "I…there wasn't time."

"Uh-huh. And if Roszca had allowed the picnic, what would you have told her then?"

She bit her lower lip and looked toward the island. "I…don't know. One of the bodyguards might have accompanied us." Her face crumpled and she covered her eyes.

"Excuses—you got 'em." Simon ached with her pain.

He couldn't berate her anymore. Like a fractious mare who'd jumped one fence but shied at the next, she needed reassurance now. He smoothed his hands down her arms and pulled her into his embrace.

She fit against him like she belonged there, her firm breasts pillowed against his chest, her thighs warm against his, their bare toes touching. Inhaling her female scent, he wished the reason for this closeness was different.

"Sweetheart, you're right about a treason investigation. It would've dug out the abuse. Maybe spread it across the *Washington Post.* More pain than you should have to bear. More than I bet even Dr. French meant you needed for healing. You don't have to announce what he did to the world."

She wept on his shoulder, her tears cleansing for both their souls. After a few last hiccups, she said, "Dr. French said I should tell my family. My friends. You."

When she raised her tear-stained face, he brushed his knuckles across her silken cheek, smoothed damp hair off her flushed skin. "Me, huh?"

She nodded and her arms came around his waist.

"Now you've told me. Maybe the next time will be easier."

"I'll try."

A bird somewhere on the island chirped his sleepy approval. The gentle rocking of the boat kept time with the rhythm of their hearts.

Janna felt the breeze flutter her hair, saw it ruffle his. Standing there in his cutoffs and nothing else but his earring and perpetually shadowed jaw, he was so indelibly male. Rugged and tough, yet so tender.

He'd forced her to face her weakness and her fears, and then he'd comforted her. But comfort was no longer what she needed. Or what she saw in his eyes.

Desire drew his skin taut across his jaw, hardened his features. His honey-brown eyes beckoned her to fall in. She could see her image in his darkened pupils, feel the heat in their depths. Feel the power of his desire against her belly.

"Janna, I said sex was a bad idea for us. I've never been too wise about bad ideas. I want you more than I've ever wanted any woman." His roughened voice shivered over her flesh like a caress.

She couldn't deny him. And she couldn't deny her need for him. Currents of desire streaked through her. Remembering the incredible pleasure of their lovemaking in the water made her breath hitch, her knees weak. She wanted those raw sensations again, waves of pure feeling she experienced only with him.

To feel, to celebrate life.

When he trailed a finger across her lower lip, heat spiraled from the base of her stomach. She clenched her trembling thighs together.

Before she could speak, he lowered his mouth to hers, and she reveled in his taste as if for the first time. Sea salt and male musk and heat. He was sparks of fire in the dark of night. He was strong and sexy and gentle.

She pulled him closer, clutching at his shirt. But he held her gingerly, as if expecting her to panic.

No fear.

No panic.

In his arms, she felt her soul expand and soar.

She sighed a soft moan and sank against him, urging his arms tighter around her. Their tongues met, darted and tangled with the same urgency coursing through her body.

A need deep within her flared up, hot and molten. A need only one night wouldn't satisfy. More tears clogged her throat, but she fought them down.

"Simon, wise or not, I want you. I need you." She twisted up the hem of her top, lifted it off over her head and dropped it at her feet.

"You are so beautiful." His mouth descended on hers. He cupped one breast and caressed the nipple with the tough pad of his thumb.

Heat zinged from her tingling nipple straight to her womb. Her thigh muscles quivered and she could barely stand. She fumbled at his cutoffs and began undoing the snap.

"Whoa. Slow down, sweetheart," Simon murmured, stopping her hand and bringing it to his mouth, "or this'll end much too soon."

Still gripping her hand, he used his free hand to yank the white chaise longue cushion onto the deck. Then he tugged her hand to pull her with him onto the makeshift mattress.

He tucked her close, so they lay side by side. "You won't be sorry, Janna. I'll make it good for you." Desire burned with golden fire in the depths of his eyes.

Almost moaning with the effort of control, he lifted her hand to kiss each finger. Her eyelashes drifted lower as he kissed his way up her arm until he nuzzled the tender spot inside her elbow.

She nearly jerked off the cushion. "Oh, Simon, I had no idea my elbows were so sensitive."

"Ah, but I think your breasts are even more sensitive."

"You're a breast connoisseur?"

He traced a finger of fire down her breastbone and across each eager nipple. "Breast connoisseur, belly connoisseur." His lips followed the wake of his finger. "Any part you have with this soft skin. Your breasts are perfect. Your nipples are the same pink of those flowers on the island."

"Hibiscus," she murmured, as he bent to her left breast, then the right, brushing his mouth over the peaked nipples. The abrasion of his whiskers on the sensitive skin flowed arousal through her, lapping higher and higher each time.

"Of course. You researched it. You know their Latin name?" A wicked gleam lit his eyes.

His nonsensical question hovered in her passion-fogged brain. She blinked to focus. "Oh, um, yes, I know it."

He grinned. "In a minute, you won't." He flicked her left nipple with his hot tongue, swirling, then laving and lapping as though at an ice-cream cone. When he opened his mouth and suckled her, she arched upward with the pleasure that spiked a tingling pulse between her thighs.

"Sex in the saltwater was fantastic," he murmured, lifting his head from her needy breasts, "but tonight, I want to see you. All of you."

Chapter 15

As Janna shimmied out of her shorts and panties, dizziness pulsed in Simon's head, in his loins. In his heart. His need for her overwhelmed him.

He loved how she looked, all hot and bothered, on the white cushion with her streaky hair a silken halo around her head and her lips pink and swollen from his kisses. The reddened skin—beard burn—on her jaw gave him a guilty twinge, but she seemed oblivious.

The yacht's light gilded her moistened breasts, her flat belly, her long legs. Her runner's legs, strong, shapely legs. His gaze riveted on the curls at their apex. A darker honey-gold, they hinted at the passion inside her.

That she trusted him enough to bare herself to him touched him more deeply than her desire for him. He was used to women wanting him, but trust had never been an issue. Janna had journeyed from distrust of all men to reliance on him to free her from her fears. In spite of the hurdles she had yet to overcome, she opened herself to him.

It humbled him.

Trembling with hunger for her, he tossed away his shorts so fast that she laughed. He craved her with an ache as powerful as a fever.

At last, they were skin to skin, her kissing him with feverish hunger that matched his. She twisted to give him access as he sampled her shoulder, her breasts, her hips and thighs. He inhaled her unique feminine scent, the hot musk of her skin. He stroked her as they moved together, exploring each other.

She smiled softly, pleasure shining molten in her eyes. She traced the contours of his chest with her soft, clever fingers, tickled his sensitive aureoles and plucked his nipples until he ground his teeth. She ran her palms down his back to his butt and scraped her nails over the base of his spine until he nearly levitated.

At the wildfire streaking over his flesh, he groaned and strained to give her time to enjoy. Dammit, he would hold out long enough for her. He would.

He massaged the wet silken folds between her legs, first in gentle circles, then slipped a finger, and another inside. "You're so ready for me, Janna."

Moaning, she reached for him, explored and measured, cupped and stroked. "Yes, Simon. Now."

Arms around her, he rolled onto his back, bringing her on top of him. "You're in control. I won't hurt you, Janna."

"Oh, Simon, I know." Rising above him like a goddess, she straddled his pelvis. Sighing, she bent to kiss his chest.

He palmed her beautiful breasts, eliciting a renewed leap of desire in her eyes.

Shimmying against the hard-to-bursting ridge beneath her female flesh, she said, "No riding or jockey jokes, Simon?"

"See what you do to me? Have your wicked way with me, woman. But no spurs."

Chuckling, she pressed her knees against his hipbones and lifted herself onto his straining body. As she shimmied onto his length, he groaned at the exquisite sensation. She was slick and small and tight.

Unable to stand the slow torment, he pushed himself deeper into her, luxuriating in the velvety heat enveloping him. The wonder of their joining, the joy of the soul-deep oneness he felt with her stilled him.

Stunned him.

Awed him.

She locked her legs tight against him as they moved together. Ancient rhythms rocked them, and they kissed endlessly with a growing, pulsing wave that promised greater pleasure. His climax clawed at him, but he would not rush her.

She gasped against his mouth, her eyelashes fluttering, lush mouth slack with the churning sensations.

The inevitable coiling tension built in his loins. He stiffened, fire surging in his blood, poised on the edge of the rising wave, straining to hold back until she joined him. "Let go, sweetheart. Let it take you."

And then she cried out, her strong legs gripping him at the onset of her release. Her body rippled against him, radiating her pleasure into him.

Her internal spasms squeezed him, sent him over the tidal wave's curl to join her in a flood of ecstasy.

Janna didn't know what awakened her, but she resisted full consciousness, preferring to luxuriate in the remnants of a rare good night's sleep. In the comfort of the bed.

She burrowed into her pillow and backed toward the heat source. When she hit an unyielding wall of bare skin, her eyes flew open.

Her heart clattered, and a stony ache compressed her lungs.

Oh, God, don't wake him. What would he do? Would he punish her because it was too early? Or too late?

Seeing the half light of early morning through the porthole spun her out of her nightmare and into reality. She peered at the man beside her. Close enough to touch. Unruly brown hair, not groomed blond. The glint of a stud earring.

Simon. Not Gabe.

Relief rushed through her as she exhaled slowly. She pressed a hand to her roiling stomach. How could she have made such a blunder?

Simon lay on his side, his back to her. His even breathing reassured her that he slept peacefully. He'd climbed into bed last night wearing nothing but a satisfied male grin. An expanse of tanned, muscle-toned skin invited snuggling.

The wall stirred. She froze, mesmerized by the slide of muscles as he turned. She held her breath. Would he waken? What would they say to each other this morning?

They'd made love two more times during the night in the master cabin's queen-size bed, Simon's bed. The sheets smelled of sex and salt air and Simon. She'd lain beneath him in passion and felt only pleasure, not one second of panic.

Well, maybe a few seconds of panic, but not from fear. Panic because, in spite of her rules, in spite of her intentions to the contrary, she was desperately in love with him. Every moment of intimacy meant loving Simon more. Loving him meant setting herself up for more pain.

She'd survived Gabe. She could survive a broken heart. The important thing now was to hide her true feelings from Simon, to keep the mood light, the time together temporary.

During her marriage, she'd learned how to maintain a calm, cool facade with pain and rage steaming inside her.

She could do it again.

Maybe she should get up, get on with her day as though

nothing had happened. Better to face him clothed rather than in nothing, even if clothed meant only a bikini.

She started to peel back the sheet.

Simon rotated to face her. Eyes closed, inky lashes fanned across his cheeks, he slept on. He threw one leg across hers and one arm over her torso. Emitting little grunts of pleasure, he tucked her head beneath his chin.

Janna exhaled gingerly. How could she get up now?

To tell the truth, she didn't want to.

Cuddling in the curve of Simon's hard body was heaven in spite of the sun's rays beating through the porthole. Maybe she could extricate herself before he awoke, but for now, she burrowed into his clean male scent and lean strength. She allowed herself to pillow her head on his chest and to lay one hand on his firm belly.

The dark hair that arrowed down from his chest felt soft and silky beneath her questing fingers. The even rise and fall of his breathing lulled her to relax again.

A moment later, she felt tension in his muscles and a hard length against her thigh. Her pulse kicked up and unwanted heat surged in her belly.

She should've slipped away when she had the chance.

"Mmm," said a sleepy, smiling voice against her hair, "my second favorite way to wake up."

Okay. Light and affectionate, here we go.

Janna kissed his chest. "Good morning, sleepyhead. I was about to get up, but didn't want to wake you."

"Back to business, Q? Hitting the computer already? Wham, bam, thank you, sir?"

He called her Q. Knowing he was already distancing himself from her pierced her heart. "I wouldn't put it that way, but yes, we had our night. Our wonderful night. But it's time to focus on the mission."

A muscle in Simon's jaw jumped. He propped himself up

on an elbow. "You're right. The mission ends tonight—success or failure. And us? What we've had?"

"Simon, we agreed. Our time on this yacht is all we can have." She hoped he didn't detect the quiver in her voice.

His mouth quirked in his cocky pirate grin. "*You* agreed. I didn't. We have a good thing going. Why end it?"

"You may think my rules are a cage, but I need them. What about your rules, Mr. No-Strings?" Leaving the bed naked with no clothing in sight didn't afford her much dignity. Chin high, she slid out, clutching the sheet in front of her.

He tossed aside what little cover she'd left him and rolled off the other side, putting the bed between them. More at ease with his nakedness than she was, he yawned and stretched.

Since it would be the last time, she feasted her eyes on his hard body—on one hard part, in particular. Pulse leaping, she jerked her gaze upward before he could notice.

A look as hot as the sun baking the morning glazed over his grin. His dark eyes skated over her as he stalked around the bed toward her. "I've had my rules, true. But being with you makes me see that it's no kind of life if *no-strings* means being alone. The thing about self-made rules is you can break them, even throw them out. I want to see where this—us—leads."

She backed up a step, but came up against the wall. "Not me. No relationships. No traps. I'm in control of my life. Those are my rules." *And I'm sticking to them.* But the words shattered in the air.

He cupped her face in his hand and burned her with a smoldering look. "Rules are—"

"Made to be broken," she gasped out, barely able to breathe. "I know. But not this time."

"You afraid I'll beat you? Isolate you? Run your life?" He stepped aside so she could escape.

Escape? All she wanted was the return of his touch. "No, Simon, I know you won't do any of that. But—"

"Can you deny that you care for me? That you crave my… *hard drive?*"

She slugged him in the biceps. *"Simon!"* How could she deny this man who made her laugh even when her pulse tripped over itself with anxiety and desire at the same time?

He grinned as he drew a finger down her cheek. "Come on, sweetheart, stretch your rule. Think of it as adding more RAM. We'll take it slow. Easy. You can get out anytime you want."

Or you can. She ought to say no. She ought to run. Her pulse jittered with trepidation, but at the passionate promise in his eyes, her insides melted.

She turned and kissed his finger. "You're the biggest con artist in the Caribbean, but okay. I'll take a chance on us."

All the blood rushed from her head as he kissed her. His firm lips held hers for a long, breath-stealing moment.

Then his smile nearly blinded her. "You won't be sorry. I'd like to take you to my mountain cabin. The stable where I board Rebel has a gentle mare you could ride. You do ride?"

"I ride, and I don't even need gentle."

"Hoo, baby! Now you're talking!"

She felt a blush heat her cheeks. "You're impossible."

After a glance at his watch, he plucked clothing from the drawer beneath the bed. He stepped into silk briefs and linen shorts. "My last meeting with our damned elusive target is in one hour. I'll go make coffee."

She was taking a big chance. A dangerous chance. But she loved him so much she couldn't bear to end it so soon.

But would he? Would he start to fear that she'd leave him?

Tears stung Janna's eyes and emotion tightened her chest.

Simon spent the late morning in conference with Viktor Roszca. He named an obscene seven-figure sum as his final offer, supposedly authorized by Colonel Wharton.

Then, Roszca's lips curving in the self-satisfied smile of a jackal that had beat other scavengers to a fat, juicy carcass, he expounded on his favorite subject—himself and his business acumen.

Frustration drilled into Simon's temples later as he returned to the dock.

Luring Roszca into leaving his island had proved tougher than he'd thought. The competition of a yacht race hadn't tempted him. Kidnapping the man's mistress tonight was the last chance. Simon had most of the plan nailed, including a farewell note he'd have Yelena write.

The main hitch was the tunnel door. Janna had a one-liner from her lock guru saying he'd get back to her. Simon crossed mental fingers that Houdini would produce a way to crack that door without explosives—and soon.

His escort tag team left him at the land end of the long dock. He lifted one hand in a mock salute. "It's been a blast, guys. Don't be strangers."

Neither Cleatian bodyguard reacted. As one, they executed a military about-face and marched back to the compound.

Simon climbed into the dinghy with the mooring line in his hand. Turning the key, he caught a flash of pink bikini bra at the *Horizon*'s companionway.

Damn. There was a second hitch. Janna.

He'd said nothing to her about using Yelena as bait for Roszca. Janna was so focused on rescuing the woman that she didn't seem to see the possibility. If springing the captive mistress served a dual purpose, why should it matter? Why should he feel guilt finger-walking up his spine about not mentioning that part of his plan?

He shouldn't.

Because it might not work anyway.

His edginess stemmed from a different burr under his saddle. Janna again.

Their lovemaking hadn't been just sex. Not for him anyway. With her, not only did the climaxes blow him away, but he felt this eerie connection with her down to the deepest part of him.

It scared him.

He wasn't used to chemistry morphing into…hell, into what, he wasn't sure. But whatever it was, ending it now was not an option. So his libido and his jumbled emotions had opened his big mouth. He'd talked her—and himself—into trying a real relationship.

She agreed but for how long? The thought of losing her jolted fear through his gut like a blowtorch.

Ending it made more sense. They came from different universes. She had baggage. He had baggage. But his rules against involvement were traps as much as hers. When you were locked between fear and trust, taking a chance on each other was as daring or crazy as riding a zebra in the Preakness Stakes.

All the odds were against them, but dammit, the emotions filling his chest outraced logic and odds. Admiration for her strength and her mind. Fierce protectiveness roused by her vulnerability and compassion. And need more intense than he'd known was possible, need that fisted into him with a violent rush that shocked him. Need that would send her running for the hills if he didn't rein himself in.

He slapped the boat's steering wheel as he guided the small craft away from the dock.

Later in the day, Simon and Janna sat on the white leather wraparound settee in the salon. They'd spent the afternoon finalizing plans to spring Roszca's mistress. The plans of the Isla Alta compound covered the cocktail table.

The FBI expert hadn't yet responded to Janna's plea for a fast answer. If he didn't come through with access through the tunnel door, Simon's plans were toast.

He tapped the builder's drawing with his index finger.

Yelena's rooms were at the end of the front wing. The mistress didn't share Roszca's bedroom full-time. "I think he has her confined to her quarters—at least, when I'm there. I saw Ivan taking in a tray."

Janna's soft lips clamped into a thin line, and her chin trembled. "Or else he's hurt her again, injured her."

His heart squeezed at the softness of hers. He threaded his fingers through hers and brought her hand to his lips. He wanted to rescue Yelena for Janna. He ought to tell her the rest, but not now. "Janna, if I can get that woman out of there, I will. But we need access through that damned tunnel."

It was his last chance to lure Roszca out to sea.

Savoring her silken skin, he realized he'd had enough plotting and planning. Enough acting professional with this woman who set him on fire with a look, who made him so hard he could barely breathe.

She gave him a wobbly smile and gently withdrew her hand. "I've been working on a contingency plan in case Houdini can't help us." She pointed to the garden area beyond the guest cottages. "I think the tunnel exits somewhere around here. There are outbuildings—garden and toolsheds—and the hillside rises steeply from there."

He slid closer and rested his hand on her bare knee. He'd like to put his lips there, too. "Makes sense that that's where it'd be. Right direction, too." Nodding, he pondered the possibilities. "Not far from Yelena's end of the house."

"Maybe she knows where the tunnel opening is." She bit her lower lip and scrutinized him.

How did that help? Simon narrowed his eyes, suspicion edging out seduction. "What are you getting at?"

She scooted to the edge of the seat. Her bare thigh sliding against his blitzed his concentration again.

Her eyes glowed silver with fervor as she again pointed to the drawing. "Here, Simon. Beside the path to the gate is all heavy, wild growth. Ferns and low palms covered with climbers. Sansevieria and succulents. Good cover."

"I suppose. Why—?"

"We could open the front gate with my electronic lockpick, get in the house and scoop up Yelena. Then we could escape through the tunnel. From that side of the steel door, the lock should be no problem."

He felt his jaw start to go slack, but he controlled it. One word branded his brain and froze his hands beneath the ever-present layer of sweat.

We.

"We? *We?*" He leaped to his feet and stalked across the room. "Janna, this is a one-man op. No way *you're* going in with me."

She shot to her feet and glared at him, hands on hips. "If you can't use the tunnel, you can't succeed without me and my electronics."

He deduced the answer, but he had to ask. "Explain."

"The cameras. Security cameras sweep the gate and surrounding area. I have a disrupting device that would zap them with static or shut them down."

The way she looked at him, all fiery-eyed and eager, stirred his protective urges. He knew she'd had self-defense training—weapons, hand-to-hand combat and all that—but it made no difference in how he felt. His gut twisted into a granny knot at the thought of her slinking through the dark.

"You could give me the gizmo."

Desperation etched around her mouth, she clenched and unclenched her fists. "There's no time to teach you how to use everything. I can do it, Simon."

She would accuse him of trying to control her. Damn right. He had to try to stop her with *her* weapon—logic.

"Dammit, Janna. Our original plan will work without jeopardizing the mission and showing ATSA's hand. Going in the way you want is too dangerous. We could be caught. Killed."

She marched around the cocktail table and got in his face. "Yelena doesn't speak much English. You might need me to translate. She needs our help."

She was grasping at straws because she ached to save the woman. He shook his head. "She speaks enough. Besides I need you to bring the *Horizon* around to the tunnel exit to pick us up. No telling what shape Yelena's in if she could even swim here. We'd have no time to waste."

He could almost see her brilliant mind making the leaps. "So first, we pretend to motor away and stop past that point, just out of sight. Any more excuses?"

He combed a hand through his hair and inhaled a lungful of air. The actions didn't calm him or give him enough time to get creative, except in his language. Filling the salon with colorful expletives he'd learned on Baltimore streets, he paced back and forth.

When he stopped and gripped her shoulders, Janna startled and blinked, but stood her ground.

"Dammit, woman, the thought of the muscle twins jumping you fries every nerve ending in my body to a crisp."

Her lush mouth compressed. "Preventing a fellow officer from doing her job goes against ATSA regs."

How the hell could he feel this whirlpool of emotions, terrified for her and proud of her and wanting to kiss her to oblivion at the same time?

"I'd be following regs if I reminded you exactly *what* your job is. As your superior officer, I could *order* you to stay on board to monitor movements in the house."

Her creamy cheeks flushed crimson. He could tell she wanted to argue, but his reminder of orders slammed the door.

Her shoulders slumped slightly. "So that's it? You're ordering me to stay on the yacht?"

When he realized he felt her delicate bones beneath his hands, he loosened his grip. He massaged gentle circles on her shoulders. "No. I could, but I won't. I trust you and your electronics. Your idea might work."

Her gray eyes lit up like Independence Day sparklers. "You mean it?"

"I mean it. On one condition."

"Anything."

He slid one hand up to lift her chin. After capturing her delicious lips for a slow kiss, he said, "Be careful what you promise, sweetheart."

"What condition, Simon?"

"I won't jeopardize the entire mission. If things get hairy—we can't get through the gate fast or there are extra guards or something—we abort. No questions."

She paused, a hint of challenge flickering in her eyes, and then she nodded. "Agreed."

Pulling her close, he tucked her hair behind one ear and nibbled at her earlobe. Man, that was soft and silky. Her skin carried the flavors of soap and salt and her own sweet energy.

His body swelled and hardened in a raw flash of sensation. He wanted her. Now.

Speech demanded extreme effort. "Meanwhile, we have time to kill."

Her eyelids drifted shut and she let her head relax. "Mmm. What did you have in mind?"

He gathered her up into his arms and kissed a trail down her elegant neck. "We can add on a few hours to our one night. What do you say?"

Chapter 16

Janna's skin tingled wherever Simon's lips tasted. Her body thrummed at every pulse point. She was no dainty doll, but she felt feminine and light when he picked her up and carried her effortlessly to the master cabin.

Setting her on her feet, he backed her up to the wall and plastered himself against her. Kissing, stroking and kneading her flesh, he murmured hot words, sex words that hypnotized and made her light-headed with want.

She clung to him, rocking her mouth over his with a wild desperation approaching madness. She wrenched his T-shirt over his head as he tore at hers. The remainder of their clothing vanished as if burned away by their spontaneous combustion.

She wanted him with every molecule in her being. To imprint him on her flesh, in her heart, on her soul.

As he tumbled her onto the big bed beneath him, she fell into a vortex of impressions—racing heartbeats and bumping pulses, hard muscle and soft flesh, sweat-slippery skin and slick arousal. Bottomless kisses filled her senses with his salty male scent, with his dark gaze, with the raspy brush of his whiskered jaw.

"I want to make it good for you, Janna, but I can't hold back a second longer." His voice was a harsh croak, taut control making his words barely intelligible.

"Don't hold back, Simon," she murmured, arching upward to meet his thrust. A strangled moan tore from her as he buried himself to the hilt.

There was no gentleness to this mating, and she wanted it that way.

He took her body and she took his.

Urging him to move inside her, she curled her fingers into his tight buttocks and rocked her hips, frantic for him. Their movements became molten undulations, him thundering into her, her shimmying her hips with him, squeezing him with her inner muscles to wring every last sensation from the release.

Telltale twinges shimmered through her veins, cascading into liquid spasms that spiraled her into a thousand pieces of glittering, white-hot light. A hoarse groan exploded from him as his climax slammed into him, seizing him deeper into her, propelling her beyond aftershocks into liquid fireworks.

An aeon later, he collapsed atop her with an incoherent murmur.

As the last torrid sparks ebbed, she held him tight against her, cradled him inside her. Her nerve endings were scorched, her heartbeat shaken and stirred. "What was *that?*"

Simon's lips curved against the side of her neck. His voice rumbled through her as he said, "If you don't know, sweetheart, we did something wrong."

"I think we did everything right."

Chuckling, he rolled to his side and out of her. He cradled her against him. "You're okay then?"

"More than." She nuzzled him and caught his mouth for a satisfying kiss.

"Whoa, babe. Give me a few minutes to recover, and we can try it sweet and slow."

Still in a sensual haze, she had no objection.

When Simon awoke, night cloaked the cabin and stars salted the inky sky.

They'd made love again, as he'd promised, long and slow, learning each other's sensitive spots, exploring each other's bodies. And then they'd slept in each other's arms.

Somehow, holding Janna as she slept brought what had been plaguing him into sharp clarity. He remembered what he wanted to ask her.

She stirred and edged closer to him.

He smoothed her hair and waited until her breathing evened. He'd let her rest awhile longer. It'd be her last chance for the night.

She'd come a long distance from fear to sleeping trust. The frantic way she'd held him and cried her need for him told him she didn't want to end this intimacy, either. Not really. She was just afraid to break her damn rules.

Once they were safely away from this island and Viktor Roszca, she'd see they could stay together. For a while.

No commitments, though. Nothing permanent. No strings. No setting themselves up for a fall. Just see where their feelings took them. They'd end it by mutual agreement. Yeah.

But not anytime soon.

Just the thought of losing her cramped his heart into a hard knot.

"You should be smug and smiling, not frowning dark enough to start a thunderstorm." Janna sat up and leaned over to kiss his forehead.

He shoved away his stormy thoughts and grinned. "Just thinking about later. Making sure I don't forget something."

"I need to put a few more things in our wet packs. Oh, and

check for a message from Houdini." Hair tousled and skin flushed from their lovemaking, she looked so beautiful he wanted to make love to her all over again.

She started to rise, but he pulled her down. "I want to ask you about something you said. And I have something to tell you." Better she knew his plans for Yelena now than in the middle of the op.

She sat cross-legged beside him, naked and open, finally at ease with her body in front of him. "Ask away."

"What did you mean when you said we could heal each other?"

"Intimacy with you has helped me free myself of the fear of being touched. I can live a normal life without jumping or turning to fight whenever someone touches me casually. I can move on, knowing that sex can be freeing and beautiful, not merely a means of domination."

"I got that part. The part about healing you." Oh, great, he'd helped rid her of fear so she could have sex. The thought of her coming apart in any other man's arms blasted a fireball through him. "Have I created a monster? I thought we had an agreement. Are you gonna be Janna the boat bunny now and hop from bed to bed?"

"Whoa! What gave you that idea?" She hugged herself, covering her breasts with her arms. "But why not? Isn't it what men do? What *you* do, Simon?"

"Dammit, you turned the tables on me. That's what I get for debating with a brainiac." Sure, one-night stands were what he did—correction, what he *used* to do. "Not while we're together. And I don't share."

"Don't worry," she said, smiling. "We do have an agreement. I don't plan to make any wild lifestyle changes."

More relieved than he could admit to her, he scrubbed his knuckles across his rough jaw. "But me? I don't need healing."

"Not the same way, no. I hoped our time together would release you from your guilt. You can't blame yourself for not saving me from Gabe's abuse."

"I should've helped you before he hurt you. When he told me to back off, I should've been suspicious."

"Gabe warned you off?"

"When you got engaged. Warning bells should've rung in my head. I was blind and deaf. I abandoned you. I failed you."

"Simon, neither of us suspected what he was really like. You couldn't have known. No one knew. And then I denied it for too long. I wouldn't have admitted it to you or anyone. But I'm fine now. Really."

"Not yet. But you will be. Once you tell your family."

She nodded. "I'll try."

He cleared his throat and propped himself on an elbow. "I have to tell you something about Yelena."

Looking stricken, she clutched his arm. "Oh, God, something's happened to her!"

He patted her hand. "No, nothing like that. Our plans to rescue her. You must see how she's the perfect bait." Damn. That was about as smooth as the jagged cliffs on the island.

"To lure Roszca to follow us, you mean." She grasped it immediately, but he could see the shock in her eyes. As brilliant as she was with electronics, she hadn't seen this possibility as a strategy.

"Exactly. Once I get into her room, I'll have her write a note. We'll leave her door open as we leave. A guard is bound to see it. We want Roszca to know she's missing soon enough to chase us."

Janna pulled her hand away from his arm and rolled off the bed. Avoiding his eyes, she yanked on her panties, shorts and tank top. "You planned this all along. That's why you weren't too worried about Roszca not going for the yacht race. You're using her."

He sat up, facing her. He could do nothing about her anger except hope she'd see it his way. Eventually. "Janna, it's no big deal. The end result is the same. She gets free of an abusive situation. And we reap a bonus. We get our man."

"Why didn't you tell me before?" Her gray eyes were hard granite stones, giving no hint of the heat in them earlier.

"I'm telling you now." He lifted his shoulders in a shrug of chagrin. How could he tell her it was the only chance they had to get Roszca?

Crackling static emanated from the radio at the helm.

"There's our favorite international criminal," Simon said, stepping into his shorts. "He must've decided to come clean and turn over the uranium."

Janna watched Simon walk away before hurrying into her cabin. She stripped and washed up in the adjacent head.

She mouthed silent congratulations to herself in the mirror. She hadn't reacted emotionally when Simon told her he planned to use Yelena as bait. She hadn't even felt that his secrecy was an act of betrayal. He was the senior officer. Plans were his responsibility.

He wasn't trying to control or manipulate her. He trusted her alternate plan, didn't he? What hurt was that he didn't trust her enough to share his plans until he had to. A pang of guilt reminded her that she hadn't trusted him enough to point out his lack of trust.

Janna felt more barricaded than the mysterious metal door in the tunnel. Hadn't she learned the hard way to protect herself? Love couldn't protect her.

Love without trust couldn't last—for either of them—even if Simon loved her, for which logic told her she had no reason to suspect or hope.

So in spite of agreeing to try a relationship, she had to end their affair. It was the only choice.

But if following her self-imposed rules of no involvement was supposed to immunize her against more hurt, why did she feel as though she were dying inside?

She tugged on her tank-style suit and slipped on a T-shirt over it. Might as well be ready for the evening's festivities.

"Janna," Simon called through the closed door. "Roszca's inviting us for a farewell drink. Says Yelena wants to say good-bye."

When she opened the door, the sight of him lounging there gave her pulse a little kick. His hair a spiky forest, his jaw darkened with stubble and wearing only his ragged cutoffs, he tempted her to drag him down on her bed.

Straightening her shoulders, she said, "I'd like to go, if only to see with my own eyes if Yelena's all right."

"No telling how long this farewell might take. A few drinks under his belt set Roszca off on one of his verbal marathons. Are you all ready for later? All the gizmos and gadgets in your bag of tricks?"

She considered, ticking off the equipment in her head. "I need to regulate the electronic disrupter. The lockpick might need adjusting to work at optimum speed. And—"

"Reckon you're not ready after all. Neither rescue plan leaves room for error or delay."

She wondered if the relief that flashed in his eyes had the same reason as hers. Doubtful. He just wanted to keep her out of the volatile situation as much as possible.

"Then it's better if I stay here," she said. True for more reasons than organizing. She needed time away from Simon, time to stiffen her resolve.

"Agreed. I'll make your excuses. He sure made them for her about the picnic." His mouth tilting in a self-deprecating grin, he indicated his old cutoffs. "I'd better go change into classier duds."

Fifteen minutes later, dressed in black linen shorts and Henley, Simon buzzed away in the tender. Janna saw the bodyguard named Ivan waiting for him on the dock.

She went to the computer to check e-mail. At last, there was a message from the new FBI lab at Quantico. "Please, Houdini, work your magic for me."

Hoping for the easy solution she doubted even existed, Janna

clicked open Houdini's e-mail. She skimmed his opening ban-
ter until she saw what she needed—his solution to breaching
that metal door.

I got three methods for you, kid.
1. Best choice is an electronic lockpick...

Janna gave a thumbs-up sign. That she had, a state-of-the-
art little number with digital decoder capabilities. All you had
to do was plug— Uh-oh. She kept reading.

But only if you can plug into the base.

Damn. The electronic lockpick wouldn't work from the
smooth back of the door. She'd been afraid of that.
What else?

2. A burglar's drill with a diamond bit.

She was fresh out of those. Neither the yacht's stores nor her
pared-down high-tech gear possessed such a device.

3. C-4. Blow the sucker.

Janna rolled her eyes. Out of the question. A blast would
bring all of Roszca's guards down on them.
Without a way through the tunnel, they had to go with plan
B—*her* plan.
She sent Houdini a thank-you message and then set to work
preparing her equipment. Since this plan was riskier, she'd
pack for all contingencies.
She checked the surveillance monitors. Simon's GPS button signal flashed his location strong and clear. On the video
monitor, she saw him and Roszca seated on rattan chairs with

their drinks among the potted palms in the courtyard. No guards. No threats. No problems.

She returned to collecting equipment.

As she was about to seal her waterproof pack, she heard the sound of a boat approaching to the island's dock. Was one of Roszca's bidders arriving early? No added complications, please. Oh, please.

She dashed to the companionway binoculars.

One man climbed from the open outboard into the spot of a dock light. He sketched a military salute to the boat's driver, who sped away.

Janna stared in fascination at the newcomer. His hair was longer. His chin bore salt-and-pepper stubble. He wore a rumpled polo shirt instead of a white dress shirt. He looked thinner, less muscular, but she recognized him.

Leo Wharton.

Her chest grated as though soot filled her lungs instead of air. She could barely draw a breath.

The renegade colonel had escaped custody only yesterday. Somehow, he'd made his way unobserved to Isla Alta.

She had to warn Simon.

Wharton turned away from his vanishing transportation and headed toward the house.

Janna calculated that she had five minutes, tops.

She ran to the helm.

"I am sorry Janna could not join us," Roszca's mistress said, clutching her sherry glass in both hands.

Yelena had just joined the men in the courtyard. Simon scanned her features, but could detect no new bruises or injuries. She looked pretty without stage makeup to camouflage and without a swollen lip.

Apparently, keeping her prisoner in her suite of rooms suited Roszca nearly as well as physical domination.

Tamping down his growing disgust for his host, he said, "She regrets not being able to come say good-bye to you. Since we're leaving later, she had preparations to make." He shrugged and sent Roszca a smug just-between-us-males grin. "Female stuff. Who knows?"

"You will please give her my good wishes," Yelena said.

"I will. And she sends you hers," he responded. *You can tell her in person in a few hours. One way or another.*

At a barely perceptible nod from the master, she lowered her gaze to her lap. Simon reckoned that was the end of her participation in the conversation.

"Allow me to refresh your drink, Simon," Roszca said, rising from his fan-style chair. He crossed over to the drink cart.

"No more rum for me, Viktor," Simon said, setting down his glass. "I'll need a steady hand on the helm when the *Horizon* sets out later."

"I understand," his host said, pouring himself a double shot of Russian vodka, his preference over the native drink. "A night run across the sea. That reminds me of the time…"

Damn. Roszca was off on another of his rambling tales. Simon surreptitiously glanced at his watch. Ten o'clock. At this rate, the household wouldn't settle down until well after midnight.

A commotion in the foyer brought him back to attention. Male voices, one angry and insistent, the others protesting but less strident. A mix of English and Cleatian.

Viktor Roszca scowled at the interruption.

Yelena's eyes widened. One hand flew to her throat.

Roszca set down his glass and stood. "You will excuse me, please. I must go see what is happening."

"Simon," Janna's urgent voice said in his ear, "Leo Wharton's on his way in. I called Thorne. Get out of there fast." Then a click and silence.

Wharton. Here. The implications raced through his mind.

His heart smashed against his rib cage, knocked hard and dropped to his toes.

Janna! A monstrous fear for her gripped him in its jaws. He wanted to order her to get away. To race the *Horizon* to a safe distance at light speed.

But she wasn't there anymore. She'd broken transmission.

Adrenaline drummed his pulse and rushed white noise in his ears. Training kicked in and shoved panic into a back stall. The masquerade was over. Wharton would out him. He had no chance of escape.

Simon rose to his feet, ready.

Before Roszca could walk to the foyer, Simon saw Wharton shove past the confused guards. He swaggered into the courtyard like a conqueror.

Roszca halted in mid-stride. *"Glot nesmit!"* He blurted out his surprise in his native tongue, but recovered and held out a hand in greeting. "Leo, I am so pleased you could join us. Your man Simon negotiated quite fiercely on your behalf."

Wharton turned to his phony lieutenant.

Simon assessed his chances. The colonel had lost weight, but it made him look harder, more dangerous. His six-foot-three topped Simon by four inches. Ivan and the brawny twins, along with three other guards, hovered in the doorway, awaiting orders. All of them carried weapons.

There was no escape for Simon. He could only stall for time. Give Janna a chance. Maybe she was leaving already. His ears strained for the sound of a motor, but he heard nothing.

Wharton stood unsmiling, his remote, guarded expression yielding nothing. "We meet again. I trust you've enjoyed the amenities on my yacht because your piracy is at an end."

"Colonel." Simon met the man's burning-coal gaze. His peripheral vision caught Roszca's puzzled expression. "The *Horizon*'s a sweet craft. The galley needs a few items, though. I have some suggestions for—"

"Silence!" Wharton's barked order had the authority of a military man who was used to instant obedience.

"What is going on?" Roszca came to stand between the two antagonists.

"You want to tell him, Wharton, or shall I?" Simon knew his smart-ass 'tude could crash and burn him, but he couldn't seem to help himself.

Simon's needling succeeded in cracking the colonel's military bearing. His dark eyes radiant with rage, he drew his brows together into a slash of impatience.

"Tell me what?" Roszca snapped fingers at his guards, who filed into the courtyard to encircle the others.

"I have no further interest in anything this man has to say," Wharton said in clipped tones to his curious host. "He is no agent of mine. Simon Byrne is an officer of the American Anti-Terrorism Security Agency."

Simon saw Roszca's mouth thin to white as Wharton's revelation sank in. He heard Yelena's sharp intake of breath.

Roszca gave orders in guttural Cleatian, fury at betrayal tightening his voice. Sergiy and Stepan grabbed Simon's arms and yanked him closer to their employer.

Ivan escorted a tearful Yelena from the courtyard. Simon caught a glimpse of her ashen face as she was hustled away to be locked in her room.

No escape for her, either. Regret stung his throat.

"Is this true?" Roszca jabbed him in the chest with an index finger as the clean-head twins held him in their steel grasp. "ATSA has sent you here undercover? You have abused my hospitality to spy on me?"

"Ah, Viktor, my friend, *spy* is such an ugly word," Simon began. "I prefer—"

Roszca's fist ripped sickening pain into his belly. The force bent him double. Gasping for breath, Simon struggled to stand erect. Hatred burned in his chest.

"You're done…Roszca," he bit out. "Operatives intercepted the uranium. We have evidence that'll hang you."

A nod from the arms broker sent Sergiy's fist slamming into Simon's chin. Color exploded behind his eyelids. He crumpled to his knees, the guards' manacle-like grips his only support.

Pain radiated through his head. The taste of blood, hot and thick, welled in his mouth. Crimson oozed down his chin and dripped onto the tiles.

"Take him away. Make sure he is secured until we can…dispose of him," Roszca ordered the guards.

Black spots swam before Simon's eyes as the two men jerked him to his feet. Pain seared his belly and his chin. His legs wobbled as he was dragged from the courtyard.

Behind him, Roszca's voice rang in his ears. "The woman!"

"What woman?" Wharton asked.

"His companion. She is still on board." His next words were in Cleatian, orders shouted to his men.

Simon knew what those orders were.

"Leave her alone!" His voice a frog's croak, Simon wrenched around in his captors' grasp. "She's not part of this. She knows nothing."

The guard slugged him in the back with his gun butt. Simon sagged again as they hoisted him along.

The taste of blood, coppery and sharp, focused his mind.

Did he buy Janna enough time to escape?

And pain focused his heart.

He'd wasted so much time fearing love, but it sneaked up on him anyway. Now it might be too late to tell her.

His captors drag-walked him outside and past the guest cottages. Simon guessed where they were taking him. He still had a chance. He would get to Janna. If she hadn't made it. If the slimy arms dealers had her…

His gut ached. His jaw and lip throbbed. Anger burst within

him like pyrotechnics and blasted away the pain. Terror for her was agony, a torment of fury and fear and love.

He had to break free. He had to reach her.

Simon turned to look at one of the twins in time to see a gun butt crashing down on him. Pain exploded at the base of his head.

Then everything went black.

Chapter 17

Janna crouched in the dark beneath a broad-leafed plant. Strands of a spider web feathered against her cheek. Hoping the spider had fled, she pushed her wet hair off her face. She tied her sneakers and hooked the swim fins to her pack.

She scooted farther back amid a thicket of ferns beneath a palm. A green parrot flapped away from the intruder. The scents of decayed leaves and wild orchids traced through the air. She knelt there to await the inevitable reaction to Wharton's arrival.

The grasses beneath her were soft and cool on her wet, bare legs. The only sounds were the chorus of insects and frogs, the occasional skitter of a chameleon in the ground cover and the clatter of her frantic heart.

Her skin began to prickle from the drying salt water. Mosquitoes and no-see-'ums discovered new blood and whined in for a feast. Fearful of drawing attention to herself, Janna clenched her jaw and tried not to swat at them as she watched.

And waited for what seemed like aeons.

So far, the gate remained firmly closed.

Why didn't they rush out to drag her from Wharton's yacht?

She'd have heard a shot, so Simon must still be alive. If she knew him, he was using attitude and wisecracks as delay tactics.

To give her time.

Which she'd used to her and Simon's advantage. She hoped.

After warning Simon, she'd contacted the ATSA boat on the satellite phone. Thorne reported that they were at least an hour away because they'd returned to Gitmo for fuel. He ordered her to get out, to head toward them.

She calculated that Thorne and company couldn't arrive in time to save Simon. Roszca or Wharton or one of the guards would surely kill him before abandoning Isla Alta.

She could no more have left Simon there to die than she could've flown to the moon on her laptop.

So she tossed a few additional items in her wet pack and went overboard. After arranging a surprise for the intruders, she swam to the island and hid at the end of the dock.

The tropical nights were cooler than the days, but moisture that wasn't saltwater trickled down her temples and between her breasts anyway.

To make her promotion to tech officer, she'd gone through training at The FBI Academy. At Quantico, she'd learned about tactics and hazardous materials, self-defense and weapons. She was actually a pretty fair shot with her compact Sig.

The loaded Sig sat in its holster at her waist, just in case.

But the only test of her skills and knowledge had been with fellow officers, not in the field with real bad guys.

Bottom line—she was a technical expert, an electronics specialist, a geek, but not a field officer.

What if she failed Simon? What if her strategies didn't work? What if she couldn't bring herself to follow through?

An image of the cook's broken body at the bottom of the tunnel pit morphed into an image of Simon. The thought twisted through her, piercing her chest, her stomach.

No. She swallowed down the incipient panic and willed away tears. She could do this. She would get Simon out. Yelena, too.

Seeing no one outside the compound walls, she risked clicking on her headlamp. She fished the handheld GPS from her pack. The screen flickered to green. The signal blinked.

Simon was on the move. Out the back wing and toward the gardens. At the location of one of the garden sheds, he stopped. That was it. No more movement.

Was he locked up in the shed? Or was it the entrance to the tunnel? What had they done to him? She shut off her lamp and stowed the GPS. Janna's stomach tightened.

Now they would come after her.

She remembered that the tactics instructor had said, "Impatience kills operations. Learn to wait."

She prayed for patience. She also prayed to be invisible.

As though she'd conjured them, the four guards whose names she didn't know jogged through the gate. All wore shoulder holsters with handguns. Heckler & Koch 9mm semiautomatics, she thought. They passed by her without a look into the shadows and continued onto the dock. A moment later, Sergiy and Stepan followed at a lumbering pace.

Roszca's yacht, the *Prowler,* sat on the dock's left side and the four smaller craft on the right. The guards jumped into the two inflatable tenders to the yacht, two in each. The twins remained on the dock as the boats took off toward the *Horizon.*

Before swimming away from the yacht, she'd attached a clump of C-4 explosives to the gas tank, along with a remote-activated detonator. Her preparations should succeed as long as no one used a cellphone that would interfere with her signal.

Tears tightened Janna's throat at the thought of what she must do. Raw anguish burned in her chest, up her throat and into her throbbing temples. She hissed in a breath. She saw no other choice.

She gripped the remote control device with both hands to stop the trembling.

Patience. Wait for the opportune moment.

The boats tied up on either side of the stern. Guns drawn, three of the guards climbed onto the swim platform.

Janna pushed the remote control button.

She visualized the electronic signal zinging toward the detonator.

One. Two. Three.

A sharp bang split the night. Smoke rose from the yacht's stern by the fuel tank. Through her binoculars, she saw the three men on board and the fourth in the inflatable wave their arms and move their mouths. Janna heard only the blood roaring in her ears.

In the next moment, a fireball erupted from the deck. A thunderous blast reverberated through the cove. The yacht blew apart. Bodies flew through the air. Shards of fiberglass and wood fell like hailstones.

Janna could no longer see the guards or their speedboats. Their grisly deaths were too hideous for anyone, no matter what crimes those men had committed. Horror was white-hot pain in her lungs. Her heart was a lead weight in her chest.

She forced herself to breathe, to block out the shock. She couldn't fall apart. Simon needed her help.

At the sound of the blast and the roaring fire, more people streamed from the house. Roszca and Wharton ran to the dock.

Janna counted. The four nameless guards—now dead. She squeezed her eyes shut and inhaled. She wouldn't think about that. The twins. Roszca and Wharton.

Missing were Yelena and Simon.

And one other. The last guard and yacht captain, Ivan.

Where could Ivan be? At the computer, calling for help? Doubtful. Guarding Yelena? Or Simon?

Janna's brain raced through the possibilities. She had no time to waste. She had to move.

Crouching low, she edged through the trees and climbers toward the gate. It closed automatically behind the last to exit.

In case Ivan was monitoring the cameras, she turned on her palm-sized video disrupter. Electricity on these islands was irregular, so interference happened often. For the moment or two needed to access the gate code, a watcher shouldn't be suspicious. The cameras' rotation stopped.

Yes! The disrupter shut them down.

Then she extracted her digital lockpick and attached the keypad decoder wire to the gate lock.

Come on. Come on!

A moment later, the five-digit code slid into place on the readout, and the gate swung open.

She tucked the lockpick away and hurried into the compound. The gate closed behind her. Once against the house and out of camera range, she shut off the disrupter.

She could hear shouts and the roars of flames and motors from outside. Good. Her diversion still occupied them.

Off to the right was Simon. The front door stood wide open. Yelena was inside. Closer. Who would Ivan be guarding?

She had to know.

Gripping her Sig, Janna crept along the wall toward the shed where Simon was being held.

Simon's limbs felt too heavy to move. Pressure like a steel band clamped his neck, his shoulders. A boom and then a roaring sound like fire came from far away. He must be dreaming. Darkness like a thick, black morass pressed him down, but he hadn't lost consciousness. He'd turned in time to receive only a glancing blow. No concussion. But—

Janna.

Would he ever see her again? She was brave and beautiful

and too brainy for the likes of him, but being with her made him a better man. She was such an adorable geek and too earnest. Who else would laugh at his awful jokes? Would he die without telling her that he loved her?

Yeah, oh, yeah—love. She was the yin to his yang, the only woman who made alone seem lonely. Hell of a time to figure all that out. A heady tenderness swept through him as his brain affirmed what his heart had known all along.

He opened his eyes. Even his eyelids hurt.

Use the pain to focus. Get free. Find her.

He tried to roll over, but he couldn't lift his arms, his feet. He realized that his hands and feet were tied behind him with rope, heavy sisal judging from the rough texture. Made sense.

The good-time boys had stashed him in a garden shed.

And in a garden shed, there must be tools. Sharp tools.

Thin rays of light—from the security lighting around the garden, he reckoned—threaded in through cracks in the boards. As his aching eyes became accustomed to the dark, he saw that he'd called it right.

On the wall to the left of the plank door hung rakes and shovels. Aha, and hedge clippers. A light beam winked on the blades. *Come to Papa.*

Since the damn things wouldn't follow orders, Papa would have to slink over there. Scooting and sliding on the dirt floor, Simon inched toward the dangling clippers.

The exertion winded him. Dizziness swirled in his head. He inhaled deeply to banish the black spots. His belly cramped where Roszca had connected. Simon hoped to hell the bastard had broken a finger or two.

One more push and he made it to the wall. If he could sit up, he could knock the clippers to the floor.

A cough outside stopped his breath.

A guard. The clippers crashing to the ground would bring the guard inside.

Simon slumped on the floor. Twisting his legs around so he could push partially erect, he had a better vantage point. He surveyed the shed for another idea.

And saw a second door. A steel door with an array of Christmas lights beside the handle.

Janna kept an eye on the corridor as she listened at the wooden door.

From inside the room came soft sobs and sniffles.

Yelena.

The door was locked. No key in sight. Another barrier. Janna sighed as she lifted her stainless steel, tubular lockpick from her pack. She preferred the electronic kind, but low tech was necessary for your basic offset lock. Setting the tension, she inserted. She rotated until the cylinder turned.

The handle clicked. *Ta-dah.*

At first, she didn't see the weeping woman. The mournful sounds guided her across the Persian rug, around the lace-covered four-poster bed. Yelena sat on the floor, backed into a corner, head on her updrawn knees.

Janna fought away tears of empathy. No time for that. "Yelena, I've come to free you," she said in Cleatian.

The other woman looked up with a soggy gasp. "*Winzc?* What? You cannot be here. Janna?"

"Yes, come with me. I'm taking you away from here," she said, elated. She was relieved to see that Yelena had suffered no more injuries. Her eyes were red from weeping, but no bruises or swelling marred her delicate features.

"*Nich,* you can't. You speak my language. Who are you? What is happening?" Wide-eyed with fear and amazement, she stared at Janna.

"It's a long story," Janna said with a lopsided grin. Kneeling before Yelena, she explained the bare bones. She stood and held out a hand to the frightened woman.

After a moment, Yelena took Janna's hand and got to her feet. "U.S. agents? You can do nothing on Isla Alta."

"If nothing else, we can get away. Don't you want to be free of this cruel man who beats you?"

Yelena gripped the dressing table beside her and turned away from Janna's gaze with shame coloring her cheeks. "I don't know. I don't know. If he finds me, he will…punish me." Fresh tears spilled from her eyes, and she picked up a rosary from a lace doily.

Coming to stand behind her, Janna put her hands on the woman's trembling shoulders. She swallowed down her remembered denial and fear, just like Yelena's, and stared at her in the mirror, willing her to believe.

"He won't find you, I promise. If you stay, first he will kill your spirit. Then he will kill *you*. Come with me."

"How do you know how it is?"

Janna gazed into the mirror—at one woman cowering in uncertainty and shame and another who had been there, but who now stood erect and intense with purpose.

She inhaled a shuddery breath. "I suffered as you have. I—I had a husband who beat me. Who controlled my every hour. Who convinced me it was my fault. Believe me. Getting away is the only answer." She heard uneasiness in her voice as she began, but her tone was firm by the time she finished.

The sincerity of Janna's last words or the ferocity in her eyes must've struck a chord because, after a moment, Yelena nodded. "*Dak.* I'll go with you."

Janna gave her a quick hug. She directed Yelena to change from her silk skirt and slingback heels into comfortable shorts and sturdy walking shoes.

When she noticed the woman's gaze scanning the room, she said, "I'm sorry you can't take any of your belongings."

Yelena's dark eyes flashed and she spat on the floor. Her chin came up. "I want nothing of his, nothing from this house. I am ready."

"Let's go. Your first step in taking control of your life will be helping me free Simon. There's a little matter of Ivan the Terrible." Janna grinned at the startled reaction.

Simon's nerves crawled like the mosquitoes partying on his arms and legs. In the distance, he heard shouting and a low roar. The air bore the acrid smell of smoke.

What the hell was going on?

At first, his arms ached at being bound behind him, but they were going numb. He could hardly feel his fingers, but he could move his legs. His head hurt like the devil's steel-drum combo was jamming inside, but the dizziness had abated.

Where was Janna? Had she made it to the ATSA contact boat? Or did Wharton and Roszca have her?

His blood froze at the thought.

And why had nobody come back to interrogate him?

Or kill him?

He heard a female voice calling something in Cleatian. Ivan answered, sounding confused, hesitant.

Simon rolled to his side and snaked closer to the plank door. Leaning against it, he peered through a crack.

Two legs in khaki trousers. H&K 9mm at his waist. Ivan.

But he couldn't see the female. Yelena? Approaching, she continued speaking. He detected an edge of fear in her light voice—and something else. *Flirtation?*

There was a loud thump, the familiar sound of a hard object connecting with bone and flesh.

Ivan groaned and his knees buckled. He toppled to the ground. Then somebody dragged him away by his feet.

Heart pounding a deafening tattoo, Simon strained to get closer to his peephole. He heard movement, rustling and whispers, but could see nobody. He strained at his bonds, but there was no give, only abrading against his flesh.

Moments later, a thump sounded at the plank door. It swung outward.

"Simon! You're alive! Thank God!"

He'd never heard such a beautiful sound in his life. Or seen such a welcome sight. Euphoria bloomed in his soul and banished his aches and pains.

At the waist of Janna's black tank suit, she wore a gun belt equipped with her Sig and a knife sheath. Her streaky hair hung wet about her face as she stood over him like an Amazon. She blew him away. Except…

Fear returned in a rush. "Janna, what the hell are you doing here? You should've gotten away. They could come at any minute."

She knelt beside him. "I couldn't leave you."

"How did you do this? What about Roszca and his men?"

As she explained, she slit away his bonds with her knife. "I created a…diversion so I could get on the island unnoticed. I started to get you first, but when I saw Ivan, I went back for my partner here. Yelena distracted Ivan with a poor-little-me act so I could sneak up and whack him with a rock. He's tied up in the other shed."

She chafed his arms to help restore circulation.

His head spinning again but not from pain, Simon dragged his hungry gaze from Janna to Roszca's mistress—correction, former mistress.

Yelena sent him a shy smile. "I go with you."

He grinned. *"Dak, glot."* He'd learned that *glot* meant "good."

"Are you all right?" Janna's eyes crinkled with concern as she helped him stand.

He shrugged off her coddling. "Dazed for a few minutes. That's all. I look like hell, but you look gorgeous. Lara Croft and Wonder Woman all in one." He nodded toward the electronic lock and wished he hadn't when his head rang like a gong. "Get us outta here, Q."

"Roger!" Janna dug out her electronic lockpick and handed Simon his headlamp. She connected her keypad decoder wire to the digital lock and pushed some buttons. In seconds, the numbers clicked into place and the lock popped open.

Simon guided Yelena into the tunnel, cautioning her to keep to the left. As they edged by the deep pit, he peered over the edge, but couldn't see if the body was still there.

He called back to Janna, "You bring any C-4? Roszca's goons could follow us through the tunnel as soon as they discover that Yelena and I are missing."

Janna clicked on her headlamp as the steel door locked behind her. "No need. I changed the code. Without one of these babies—" she held up the electronic lockpick before tucking it into her pack "—they can't open it."

He started to shake his head in amazement, but thought better of it. "Sweetheart, you rock. When we get back, I'm buying that T-shirt that says Geeks Rule."

At his side, Yelena said, "What is *geeks?*"

They both laughed.

"I'll explain later," Simon said. "Let's get out of here first."

The trek through the ocean-carved tunnel was faster and easier this time. No horde of bats descended on them, and they knew their way. In about ten minutes, they arrived at the mouth of the cavern.

Shivering, they emerged into the heated blanket of tropical air. The sliver of moon hung in the midnight sky. Only a few stars were visible. Darkness crowded the thickets of ferns and palms along the shore. Shadows formed black holes among the rocks.

The three of them sat on the ledge, hidden under the overhang. Janna handed Simon his swim fins and donned hers.

"Damn, you thought of everything," Simon said.

"Not quite." Mouth tight, she pointed toward the dock.

Simon saw two men smoking cigarettes at the end of the dock. Wharton and Roszca.

Roszca's yacht partially blocked his view of the rest of the dock. The water in the cove stood empty of all but some floating debris. Odd.

"I can't see any guards. And where's the *Horizon?*"

"That was…my diversion," Janna said, faltering. "I set a C-4 charge before swimming to shore. The guards headed out to the *Horizon* to get me. There were so many of them and…"

"You blew up the boat. Roszca's thugs, too." And the violence was eating her up. Wishing he could shoulder the burden, he wrapped an arm around her. "Sweetheart, you bought us time and shaved the odds. They would've killed us without a qualm. You did the only thing you *could* do."

"Except now, we don't have a boat."

"Sure we do. I wanted to try my captaining skills with a larger craft. Here's my chance."

"You mean the *Prowler,* Roszca's yacht?"

"A hundred feet of muscle? Oh, yeah. Ivan keeps it spit-shined every day. She should be ready to go."

Janna shifted in his embrace, but didn't pull away. "I hate to burst your bubble, but a megayacht like that needs a crew of at least three to man the engine room. And she's no speedster. Either one of the other boats could outrun her."

"Stepan and Sergiy are strictly bodyguards. You saw the other guards with Ivan on board. They were the crew. With them wiped out—"

"Roszca can't use the *Prowler* to chase us," Janna concluded. She straightened, looking more confident. "His choices are as limited as ours. The two inflatables were destroyed in the blast. That leaves Roszca's other boats—the fishing boat and the speedboat."

The *Prowler* blocked their view of the remaining boats, but Simon stared hard in that direction, considering the possibilities. The speedboat boasted an aerodynamic V-hull and closed bow for racing. She was white with custom graphics of blue flames along the sides. The fishing boat was longer and more stable, but heavier and wider. Even with her more powerful 480s, the fishing boat wouldn't be able to catch the sleek speed-boat.

"Hot damn!" Simon grinned and gave Janna's shoulders a squeeze. "We're about to limit his choice to one, the fishing boat. The speedboat is the runaway favorite to get us out of here. Roszca bragged about her dual 350 MerCruiser engines."

"She ought to do 35 at least."

"Perfect for a chess rematch. We just have to wait for our buddies to leave the dock."

As if on cue, a shout from the compound turned both men's heads around like hounds catching a scent. Throwing their smokes in the water, they hotfooted it toward the house.

"They find my room empty," Yelena said. The fear returned to her voice, but she didn't move.

Janna patted her hand. "Or the twins found Ivan."

"Let's go." Simon slid off the rock into the water.

With Yelena, who had no swim fins, between them, they swam the short distance. Simon released the lines holding the speedboat to the dock as the two women climbed aboard.

"Yelena says that Roszca keeps a key hidden on board," Janna told him when he joined them in the leather-upholstered cockpit.

On hands and knees, Yelena was searching beneath the bucket seats and in the map compartment. "No key here." She looked up mournfully.

"Then you'd better hope this monster's not too different from a Chevy Nova. Hot-wiring is our only option."

Janna pulled Yelena aside as Simon scooted beneath the console. He heard the smile in her voice as she handed him a headlamp. "Don't tell me how you learned to steal cars."

"Baltimore streets were an education, no lie." He flicked the light over the tangle of colored wires. Hoo boy. He hoped to hell he remembered how to do this. "I need your blade."

"I watch house." Yelena took up a post on the rear bench seat where she could see the dock and the compound.

"Hurry, Simon." Janna passed him the knife. "We need power fast. They're bound to notice we're drifting away from the dock. If we have to hit the water, we could hide in the tunnel and wait for Thorne."

"I'll have this in a minute. We pull away, the bastard's bound to come after us. But stay low." He gave Janna a wink and a thumbs-up, then continued stripping wires.

Still after his man, Janna thought. If they sailed away on the arms broker's speedboat, he'd pursue them in the fishing boat. Just what Simon had in mind.

She smiled, crouching to sit on the floor of the cockpit. Simon, the never-say-die guy, cocky and stalwart to the end.

He'd expected her to follow orders and leave him for the wolves. How tragic that he assumed he'd be abandoned. His next reaction had been concern for her safety. His faith in her technical skills and praise at how she'd saved Yelena and him flooded her with pride.

How could she *not* love this man? But following her heart meant too much risk. Didn't it? She shoved away her thoughts before the wave of longing from deep inside overcame her.

A couple of whirrs from beneath the speedboat's stern and one diesel roared to life.

Then nothing.

"*Dammit.* I had it."

"They see us!" Yelena whispered, her voice choked with tears. "Viktor will take me back."

Angry shouts came from the island.

Janna looked back to see Wharton and Roszca racing toward the dock. Not far behind came the three remaining guards.

Her heart stumbled when she saw the long, dark objects that Ivan and Wharton were carrying.

"Hurry, Simon! They have assault rifles!"

Chapter 18

"Almost got it," Simon said from beneath the console. His voice was taut with concentration.

Footsteps pounded down the dock.

Another whirr and one of the massive MerCruiser engines growled to life. Then the second.

Janna let out the breath she didn't know she was holding.

"Pity to get saltwater on this fine upholstery." Simon had to yell to be heard over the roar of the engines. He slid up and into the captain's chair. The speedboat had drifted away from the dock and into the moonless night on the outgoing tide, but progress was too slow.

Hands on the wheel, he cocked his head. "You want to take the wheel? You're the boat expert."

Janna's nerves screamed with tension. She shook her head. "You can handle it. Finish your chess game."

She switched on the navigation, GPS and depth sounder. "No running lights. We want them to think we're trying to lose them."

Roszca, Wharton and Ivan were climbing into the fishing boat, leaving Stepan and Sergiy on the dock to guard the compound.

Bullets whizzed by and splashed in the water beside them as loud pops exploded in rapid succession from the fishing boat. The former Marine colonel hadn't lost his touch.

Yelena screamed.

Janna bit down on her knuckles to keep from crying out.

Engines rumbled behind them as the fishing boat started up. Janna saw Roszca at the helm. She couldn't see his face, but almost felt the heat of his fury.

"Keep down," Simon warned. "They can't see us, but that new AK-74 has a long range. We don't want them to get lucky."

She pulled Yelena forward and urged her below through the companionway between the two bucket seats. "Why would he shoot at Yelena? Doesn't he want her back?"

Simon's dark glance told her the naïveté of her optimism. Events had gone way beyond Roszca retrieving his mistress. He couldn't let them escape. *None of them.*

Simon shifted into forward and pushed the brass-knobbed throttles ahead. "Here goes my first move."

"Hit it, Simon! Leave 'em in our wake," yelled Janna.

He did.

With a roar like thunder, the speedboat zoomed out of the Isla Alta cove and into open waters. An eerie phosphorescent wake spread out behind them. Around the sickle moon like a cocked eyebrow, a few stars winked. The midnight-blue Caribbean rolled away into velvety blackness.

"The phosphorescence is our bread crumb trail. We want them to keep up with us, but not too close." Simon turned the wheel to start a zigzag course. "Come on, you bastard. Counter this opening."

The running lights of the fishing boat veered with them.

"Now we just have to find Thorne's boat," Simon said.

Janna dug through her pack for the satellite phone. "Here you go."

Simon sent her a slow wink. "You call him, Q."

She understood as soon as she raised Thorne. His response blasted her ears more than the growl of the speedboat's engine. "Where the devil have you been? I've looked all over the damned Caribbean for the *Horizon.*"

"You're looking for the wrong boat." She explained briefly and requested their location.

When she disconnected, she directed Simon to continue zig-zagging as though trying to lose their pursuers, but basically to stick to the heading Thorne had given her.

North toward a small uninhabited island.

"They're on our tail," Janna said in Simon's ear as she kept an eye on the bulkier craft. "He must know they can't catch us, but they show no sign of quitting." Thank goodness. Help with manpower and arms was still too far away.

They sped north in seamless darkness for the next hour. Janna could see from Simon's sideways glances that he wanted to talk to her, but the engine noise rendered conversation impossible. Just as well. Contemplating the inevitable split hurt too much on top of everything else.

As a denser shadow loomed into view, Simon said, "I'll slow just enough to lure them into the trap. My next and final move in this game, I hope." He eased the throttle back.

The fishing boat sailed closer and more bullets zinged at them. The shots went wild because Simon was motoring in free-form zigzag.

Crack. Crack. Crack. Bullets slammed into the transom.

"They figured out my trajectory. Pray they don't hit the gas tank. Where the hell is Thorne?" Simon jerked the steering wheel to starboard, spraying a wide arc of saltwater with their turn.

From around the island's back side raced two U.S. Coast Guard cutters. Blinding spotlights homed in on Roszca's boat.

Simon steered away, giving the authorities right of way as they flanked the fishing boat. In short order, the fishing boat was out-maneuvered and surrounded.

"Check," Simon said as Roszca and the others were taken into custody by uniformed men and women.

Everyone gathered on the afterdeck of one of the Coast Guard cutters as dawn spilled its first orange-and-pink rays across the turquoise waters.

Simon was just finishing briefing Thorne on their narrow escape from Isla Alta. "Roszca's other two thugs are stranded. I bet they'll radio for help before long. You'll be able to pick them up, too."

Thorne made a note of it on his PDA. "Don't imagine Wharton's too happy with you, trashing his yacht like that."

Simon glanced over at the former colonel, handcuffed and surrounded by burly Coast Guard sailors. Others guarded Roszca and Ivan. "Janna gets the credit. She made one hell of a diversion."

In a few minutes, he joined Janna and Yelena at the starboard rail. Her swimsuit now dry and her hair a bright halo, Janna had never looked more beautiful to him.

In spite of the tropical temperatures, the Cleatian woman hugged herself as though cold. Pale and with a pinched mouth, she avoided her former lover's furious looks. Simon thought how lucky she was to have Janna for an ally.

He said, "The other cutter'll hang around Isla Alta waiting for Sergiy and Stepan to leave the island. This one'll head back to Gitmo with the prisoners."

As he spoke, the second cutter began a slow turn.

"And Yelena?" Janna asked.

"Thorne was vague. He said to hold on about that."

Janna staggered as the departing boat's wake rocked them, and Simon caught her.

"Feels good having you in my arms again," he murmured in her ear. As soon as he said the words, a hotter image of the two of them rose in his mind.

They'd take time for each other once the danger was past. He had a lot to tell her. And a lot to show her.

"Thanks. I'm okay now." She gave him a thin smile and eased out of his arms.

Bad timing. He hoped that was the reason. She was too tense, too uptight. "Think I could buy that speedboat cheap once the government's done with it?"

She looked relieved at his change of topic. Not a good sign. "You abandoning your precious horses for boating?"

He laughed. "Just adding to my stable. New experiences are broadening, enriching." His heart thumped as his words' serious implications registered. "Enlightening. They make a man see what's really important. Janna—"

"You have no right to hold me!" Roszca's imperious tones cut Simon off. Red-faced and bulldog-belligerent, he was haranguing a poker-faced Thorne. "The United States has no authority over me. I demand you release me and my assistant. I am a Cleatian citizen. This is an outrage."

"We have jurisdiction, don't we?" Janna asked.

"Yeah. I don't know why Thorne's letting Roszca rant."

"No," Yelena murmured, as if she feared Roszca's release.

"As you know, Mr. Roszca," Thorne cut in, "my government can charge you with a long list of crimes. But we are not the first. As for our authority, that will not be a problem."

As he finished speaking, a man stepped on deck with the cutter's captain. Tall, silver-haired and distinguished, he wore a gray-and-red military uniform emblazoned with three stars. A general.

Simon heard Yelena gasp. Breaking away from the rail, she ran toward the newcomer.

"Papa!" she exclaimed as he drew her into his arms.

"Mr. Roszca, I believe you know General Nikolai Azov. Your capture has been a joint mission of our two governments." A tiny smile lifted one corner of Thorne's mouth.

The international arms broker's complexion had blanched to the color of putty.

"Check and mate," Simon said.

Assistant Director Raines tapped the file folder on his desk. "At his request, Thorne has joined the team intercepting Roszca's uranium courier. I hope that ends as well as your op. Excellent work. My congratulations."

ATSA had stopped two of the uranium bidders, but only temporarily since they had no evidence. Stepan and Sergiy had joined their boss, Wharton, and Ivan as guests of the U.S. government. Confiscating the weapons-grade uranium had not gone as well. The courier had vanished.

"Thanks." Simon said. "No sweat with the uranium. You can count on Thorne."

Janna chanced a glance at him from the other guest chair. She hadn't seen Simon since Roszca's capture two weeks earlier. She and Thorne had returned to D.C. while Simon remained at Guantanamo Bay to interrogate their prize. The only evidence of his injured lip was a small scab, and he was back in form in old jeans and his pirate T-shirt. Except he had shaved. His jaw was smooth. An anomaly.

She dreaded the coming confrontation with him, yet she needed his moral support for what she planned to say to Raines. Her stomach churned, and she inhaled slowly to subdue her anxiety.

Raines held up the memo beside the file. "I do have one question. What is this message from the quartermaster at Guantanamo Bay about damage to the pier?"

Simon slouched lower in his chair. "I brought the speedboat in a tad too fast. It's just a few splinters. Sir."

In spite of her riotous nerves, a smile skated across Janna's mouth. Simon had underestimated the power of the speedboat and rammed the pier. A few splinters? More like a few pilings would need replacement.

Her amusement disappeared when Raines turned to her.

"We're all lucky that Gabriel Harris passed no secrets on to Viktor Roszca. Thorne's assumption that he was undercover simplifies the cleanup. You understand that the agency will confirm that story, Tech Officer Harris?"

"Thank you, sir. I'm more grateful than you can know that it's over." Trembling inside, she lifted a white cardboard box from her lap and placed it on his desk. "The agency should have these."

Raines removed the lid and unfolded the tissue paper. "But…those are the medals awarded posthumously to your husband. You should keep these to remember him by."

Janna stood, shoulders straight, chin up. "Do whatever you want with them. I want nothing of Gabriel Harris's. I have scars to remember him by. He beat me and made marriage a prison. At last, I'm free of him."

She turned and walked out of the room.

Simon found Janna staring out the window in an empty office. All his muscles had clenched with dread that she'd disappear before he could find her. She wore a blue jacket from one of her nun suits, but over a short skirt. Still professional, but sexy. At least, a man could see some leg.

Crossing to her, he wrapped his arms around her stiff shoulders. "I was never more proud of you, Janna. That was the bravest thing I've ever seen."

"Not really, but thanks," she said as she leaned into him. "You were right. Telling someone the truth has lifted giant boulders off my chest. I told Yelena first. That's why she agreed to leave the island with me. I'll discuss it with Dr. French as soon as I finish with the agency shrink."

"How're you doing with that? Living with the deaths of those men?" He kissed the top of her head, just where a streak of buttery hair met caramel, and basked in her familiar scent.

Her shoulders lifted on a sigh. "It's tough, but I know I had no choice. Getting you out of there was driving me."

"I do appreciate it, sweetheart. I'd have ended up like the cook in that pit." Holding her restored his sanity, but something about the stiff way she held herself sent worry skittering across his nape. He needed her, but he might not have time to figure out how to tell her.

"You need to get away," he said, "chill out and adjust. I talked Raines into a few days off for the both of us. We can go to my cabin and relax, do some riding. If you want."

She turned in his arms to look at him with solemn eyes rimmed with violet shadows. She wasn't sleeping. Back to her old fears and doubts.

"I don't think so." She shook her head. "Simon, I know I said I'd try a relationship, but it won't work. I'm sorry."

"Hell, this is about my using Yelena as bait. I didn't tell you sooner because I wasn't sure it would work." He knew he'd blown it then, but his mouth had run away unbridled. As it might now if he wasn't careful.

"You didn't trust me?" She backed away from him. Her chin trembled, her confrontational tone only bravado.

He scrubbed a hand across his nape. "I trust you more than I trust myself. My first plan was a bust. I didn't want to go two for two. Hell, sweetheart, what man wants to look like a failure to the woman he loves?"

Her witchy eyes rounded like gray moons. "Loves?"

"I couldn't put the word to how I felt until those muscle-bound Cleatians pounded it into me." He'd done some soul-searching in that shed while he'd frantically searched for a way to get to her. "Hell, I'm not saying it right."

An encouraging smile curved her lips. "I think you're saying it just right. Go on."

His heart would burst if he didn't get this out. "When I thought I'd never see you again, when I thought I'd die or you would, I realized what's important. I love you, and I think—I hope—you love me. You're the missing pieces of me."

"Are you sure?" Her brow knit. "What makes you think I won't leave you like your mom or Doc or Summer?"

Warmth infused his chest at her insight. "You gave me the reason by breaking rules to rescue me. I ordered you to leave. Thorne ordered you to leave. But you didn't leave me. Instead, you stormed in like an avenging angel. I'll cherish the time we have together and count myself luckier than most."

He'd taken the leap from fear to trust. But would she? He had to force himself to breathe over renewed fear.

"Simon, I do love you. I think I've always loved you. That's why I can't do a slow see-where-it-leads affair. It's tearing me apart. I was never so scared sticking to my rules."

"Me, too, sweetheart." He lifted her trembling chin with one finger and willed her to absorb his faith and trust. "Your rules and mine kept us safe, but safe for what? A life with you, no matter how short or how long, is way better than an empty life. I'll make mistakes, but I won't ever hurt you or try to control you."

"I trust you, Simon. When I came close to losing you, my heart knew to trust you. I knew you were risking injury—" she touched his jaw with the tips of her fingers "—even your life to buy me time. But without my rules, what happens?"

"We make it up as we go along. I can't do a slow relationship, either. What is it you geeks say? 'When the going gets tough—'"

"'Upgrade.' But what—" She shook her head in puzzlement.

"Yeah, upgrade. I want to upgrade. I know I'm facing long

odds. My brain wonders what a diplomat's brainy daughte
would see in a streetwise nothing. But my heart tells me to rur
for the roses. I want marriage."

"Marriage?"

Before Janna could register his meaning, his mout
locked onto hers. All her circuits blew. Her temperature
soared to a tropical level. A long, deep thrill slid through her
and she clung to him as he devoured and demanded all tha
she was.

When the fog cleared, she knew her answer. And new anc
different details came into focus. The light scent of an after
shave. Smoothness where there'd been stubble. She laid a palm
on his jaw. "Simon, why did you shave?"

He grinned. "Can't have a wife with perpetual beard burn
But your parents might disapprove, clean-shaven or not."

"Their judgment doesn't count. They thought Gabe was the
perfect husband. You, on the other hand, are streetwise, but for
get *nothing*. You're honorable and kind. You don't need to dom
inate others or grandstand to be a man. You respect me and
admire my intelligence."

He grinned. "I depend on that sexy brain."

"See what I mean?" In so many ways, he showed her tha
he'd be her partner, not her lord and master.

"So what d'you say, Janna? I'm dyin' here." His brown eyes
puppy-dog soulful and irresistible, pleaded his case.

All her fears evaporated—dumped, deleted and wiped clean
Her heart swelled, the wounded places healed and filled with
love. "Simon, you've taught me that sometimes rules are pris
ons, that sometimes you have to break the rules. A life with you
is worth tossing out all my rules."

"So maybe you'll come with me to the cabin after all? I need
your geek wizardry."

The devil in his con man's eyes warned her, but she had to
ask. "Okay, I'll bite. What for?"

"So you can turn my software into hardware."

"Ooh, I should've seen that groaner coming. I'm afraid you'll need extensive attention to your circuits."

His kiss turned her groan into a sigh of pleasure. Her heart soared, free of its bondage of rules, free to love, free to live. She gave herself up to the joy of loving and being loved.

1106/18a

SILHOUETTE®
Sensation™

FEELS LIKE HOME
by Maggie Shayne

When Chicago cop Jimmy Corona returned to his small hometown, all he wanted was to find a mother to care for his son while he did his job. Shy, kind-hearted, Kara Brand was the obvious choice. But danger soon followed Jimmy, and only Kara stood between his son and certain death...

THE SHERIFF OF HEARTBREAK COUNTY
by Kathleen Creighton

A congressman's son is murdered and everything points to Mary Owen, the newcomer to Hartsville... but Sheriff Roan Harley can't quite make the pieces fit. At first his interest in Mary is purely because of the investigation. But where will his loyalties lie when he realises he's in love?

WARRIOR WITHOUT RULES
by Nancy Gideon

Bodyguard Zach Russell was charged with protecting risk-taking heiress Antonia Catillo, but his weakness for the beauty was getting in the way. Threats on Antonia's life were growing serious as their long-suppressed attraction rose to the surface. Could Zach crack the case before it was too late?

On sale from 17th November 2006

Available at WHSmith, Tesco, ASDA, Borders, Eason, Sainsbury's and most bookshops

www.silhouette.co.uk

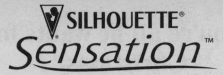

SILHOUETTE®
Sensation™

1106/18b

EXCLUSIVE by Katherine Garbera
Bombshell – Athena Force

Investigative reporting was Tory Patton's calling, and when her fellow Athena Academy graduate was taken hostage, nothing would stop her from taking the assignment to save her friend. But the kidnappers weren't who they seemed… and suddenly this crisis came much closer to the academy than anyone could ever guess.

THE BEAST WITHIN by Suzanne McMinn
PAX

The thing Keiran Holt feared most lived inside him—and possibly could cause harm to the woman he'd married. But Paige wasn't the only one who had spent two years looking for her missing husband. Would he be captured before they could save their once passionate marriage…and tame the beast within?

MODEL SPY by Natalie Dunbar
Bombshell –The IT Girls

A former supermodel from a wealthy family, Vanessa Dawson was perfect for the Gotham Roses' latest mission: Two top models were dead and it seemed a drug-ring was operating from the highest level of the fashion industry. Vanessa went undercover to get to the truth, but soon shoot-outs replaced fashion shoots as the order of the day…

On sale from 17th November 2006

Available at WHSmith, Tesco, ASDA, Borders, Eason, Sainsbury's and most bookshops

www.silhouette.co.uk

1106/067/MB057

You're all he wants for Christmas…

*The greatest Christmas gift, wrapped
with the warmth of desire.*

*These sensational heroes are all destined
to find true love this Christmas…*

On sale 20th October 2006

www.millsandboon.co.uk

M&B

M033/TH

LOCK THE DOORS, DRAW THE CURTAINS, PULL UP THE COVERS AND BE PREPARED FOR

THRILLER *STORIES TO KEEP YOU UP ALL NIGHT*

"*Thriller* will be a classic. This first-ever collection of thriller stories, from the best in the business, has it all. The quality blew me away."
—*Greg Iles*

"The best of the best storytellers in the business. *Thriller* has no equal."
—*Clive Cussler*

Hardback £16.99

On sale 20th October 2006

MIRA

FREE

4 BOOKS AND A SURPRISE GIFT!

We would like to take this opportunity to thank you for reading this Silhouette® book by offering you the chance to take FOUR more specially selected titles from the Sensation™ series absolutely FREE! We're also making this offer to introduce you to the benefits of the Mills & Boon® Reader Service™—

> ★ **FREE home delivery**
> ★ **FREE gifts and competitions**
> ★ **FREE monthly Newsletter**
> ★ **Books available before they're in the shops**
> ★ **Exclusive Reader Service offers**

Accepting these FREE books and gift places you under no obligation to buy; you may cancel at any time, even after receiving your free shipment. Simply complete your details below and return the entire page to the address below. You don't even need a stamp!

YES! Please send me 4 free Sensation books and a surprise gift. I understand that unless you hear from me, I will receive 6 superb new titles every month for just £3.10 each, postage and packing free. I am under no obligation to purchase any books and may cancel my subscription at any time. The free books and gift will be mine to keep in any case.

S6ZEE

Ms/Mrs/Miss/Mr..Initials ....

BLOCK CAPITALS PLEASE

Surname ....

Address ....

....

....Postcode ....

Send this whole page to:

The Reader Service, FREEPOST CN81, Croydon, CR9 3WZ

Offer valid in UK only and is not available to current Mills & Boon® Reader Service™subscribers to this series. Overseas and Eire please write for details. We reserve the right to refuse an application and applicants must be aged 18 years or over. Only one application per household. Terms and prices subject to change without notice. Offer expires 31st January 2007. As a result of this application, you may receive offers from Harlequin Mills & Boon and other carefully selected companies. If you would prefer not to share in this opportunity please write to The Data Manager at PO Box 676, Richmond, TW9 1WU.

Silhouette® is a registered trademark and is used under licence.
Sensation™ is being used as a trademark. The Mills & Boon® Reader Service™ is being used as a trademark.